Twisted 50
Volume 1

www.Twisted50.com

Thanks and Acknowledgments

Create50 is powered by people who want to help create something extraordinary. Aside from the writers whose work is included in this volume, we must also thank everyone involved.

Cristina and Elinor, thank you for working so hard in putting this book together. Lucy, Emma, Judy, Lucia, Vicky, Hattie, Julian and the whole team, thank you for pulling it out of the bag. To the Create50 community, the writers, the readers, the proof readers, far too many to list, thank you. And Danny for building and maintaining the site, thank you.

Chris Jones
Founder of Create50
http://www.Create50.com
Follow me on Twitter @LivingSpiritPix

Twisted50 was first published in Great Britain by Create50 Limited.

Copyright © 2016 Create50 Ltd and respective authors.

This book is copyrighted under the Berne Convention. No reproduction without permission. All rights reserved.

ISBN 978-0-9956538-0-1

Twisted 50
Volume 1

Written by

Stephanie Wessell, Troll Dahl, Susan Bodnar, Marie Gethins, Kendall Castor-Perry, Kim Rickcord, Caroline Slocock, Karen Sheard, Lucy V Hay, Stephen Deas, Diana Read, Scott Merrow, Steven Quantick, Dylan Keeling, Steve Pool, Jacqui Canham, Nick Twyford, John Ashbrook, Gordon Slack, Richard Craven, Adam Millard, Penegrin Shaw, Geoff Bagwell, Steven Stockford, Andrew Williamson, Alex Thompson, Joshua Saltzman, Rachael Howard, Christopher Patrick, Charles Maciejewski, Hillier Townsend, Bartholomew Cryan, Jonah Jones, Duncan Eastwood, Shirley Day, Richie Brown, Gareth Eynon, Nick Yates, Maggie Innes, Elizabeth Hughes, Kristopher Rickards, Jeanette Hewitt, SV Macdonald, Jessica Brown, Leo X Robertson, Chris Jeal, Sasha Black, Thomas Cranham, Neil Bebber and John Read

Edited by Elinor Perry Smith
Produced by Cristina Palmer-Romero
Create50 Team Leader: Chris Jones

Twisted50 is the first book to arise from the Create50 community and initiative. Can you write a short story? If you can, join our growing community of supportive writers at Create50. It's free to join at www.Create50.com

Join the writing community www.Create50.com
Check out the book series website www.Twisted50.com
Follow Create50 on Twitter @MyCreate50
Join the Facebook page for updates
https://www.facebook.com/MyCreate50

Introduction
By Cristina Palmer-Romero

The darkness fascinates me. Our fears drifting through the dark provokes a multitude of reactions.

To be given the opportunity to ask writers to share their most Twisted musings was an opportunity not to be missed. We all have different notions of scary and twisted, whether we write gory matter or deliver delicate blows, horror writers dare to venture into these spaces. Not because they are weird or insane, but because they have the courage to peel back the layers from the ordinary, as they ponder what life might look like in an alternate reality.

Producing this project went beyond my expectations. I never would have thought that such a supportive and cohesive community could have been achieved online, with writers from all over the world. The level of commitment that each and every writer demonstrated in perfecting their craft and encouraging other writers to hone their skills, was extraordinary.

As the project gathered momentum I saw a great leveller in the writing community. Placing new writers alongside accomplished writers, young and old, new horror writers & horror aficionados, meant that this jamboree of writers facilitated a platform for creativity to thrive. Imaginations were stretched. Creative boundaries were pushed. Every. Single. Day.

I am immensely proud of this project and 'my' writers.

My top tips for cracking horror:

Great horror asks troubling questions – write as though no one will ever read it, and answer those terrifying 'what ifs'.

Don't censor yourself.

Write from your gut and with integrity.

Feel the fear of your characters and double it on the page.

Make your characters do what you really wish they wouldn't do.

Listen to your instinct, write from there, not what you think readers/agents/publishers want.

Experiment.

Be wild and courageous.

Learn your craft.

And read every day!

Cristina Palmer-Romero
Project Leader and Producer // Twisted50
www.Create50.com
Follow me on Twitter @CristinaPR73

Table of Contents

Bite by Kendall Castor-Perry 1
Witches by SV Macdonald 5
Shenanigans by Chris Jeal 9
Aftermath by Geoff Bagwell 13
Summer Sky by John Read 16
The Lizard King by Stephen Deas 17
Beyond the Flesh by Diana Read 22
The Audition Altar by Leo X Robertson 27
The Beholder by Stephanie Wessell 33
doG lived by Troll Dahl 38
True Fear by G P Eynon 43
Five Days by Susan Mayer 48
A Change Too Far by Adam Millard 54
The Sugarloaf and the Red Shoes by Marie Gethins 55
Paper Cuts by Kim Rickcord 61
Insects by Caroline Slocock 67
Itch by Karen Heard 70
The Retribution of Elsie Buckle by Lucy V Hay 75
SPELLINGS by K.J.B. Rickards 80
Full of Surprises by Scott Merrow 82
Food Bank by Dylan Keeling 86
Silver Load by Steve Pool 91
Trying on Tobias by Jacqui Canham 96
Sodor & Gomorrah by N W Twyford 101
The Spider Taketh Hold by John Ashbrook 107
Flat Hunting by Gordon Slack 112
Lolitasaurus by Richard Craven 116

Keeping A Head by Jonah Jones 121
Project Approved by Andrew Williamson 122
Meat by Neil Bebber 126
The Ballad of Liam and Chantelle by Steven Stockford 132
Do Blastocysts Dream of Foetal Sheep? By Alex Thompson 142
A Curious Boy by Josh Saltzman 149
The Beating of My Heart by Rachael Howard 155
Deadlands by Christopher Patrick 159
Feedback by Charles Maciejewski 164
Us by Hillier Townsend 167
Flight 404 by Bartholomew Cryan 172
Our Tormentor by Duncan Eastwood 178
The Biggest Fear by Shirley Day 182
The Cyclist by Richie Brown 187
Killer Heels by Sasha Black 191
What's Yours Is Mine by Nick Yates 197
Second Chance by Maggie Innes 202
Sum of My Memories by Elizabeth J Hughes 207
Fingers by J.M Hewitt 211
Gooseberry Pie by Jessica Brown 216
Helper by Steven Quantick 219
The Left is Sinister by Thomas Cranham 225
Bloated by Penegrin Shaw 228

Bite
by Kendall Castor-Perry

'Use by December 2010.' Seriously? Well I'm sorry, but I didn't get bitten back in 2010, did I, itch cream that reduces irritation and swelling, I got bitten this morning. You'll just have to ooze out of retirement and do your job, won't you.

It's not like it's painful, the bite. But it's been getting pinker all day. And it does... aaaah... itch, that's better. They always go for the thin, smooth skin, don't they? Bugs, I mean. Like that soft patch of skin on the top of your foot. Or like mine, in front of the elbow, just where the nurse stabs you with that sharp little sucky tube when you go give a blood sample.

And that bug this morning, it didn't bite me just once. No, five times, count 'em, the little blood-red dots there in a perfect pentagonal formation. Or maybe the son-of-a-bitch had five mouths. But that would just be freaky, right. I mean, Mother Nature doesn't do things in fives, does she?

Hang on... avoid alcohol when using this medicine? That's going too far. See that bottle of Jack there? I'm just about to get real friendly with it. Your girlfriend didn't just leave you out of the blue. Mine did. Yep, Lynsey, the girlfriend whose idea it was to bike the river trail this morning.

"The weather is optimal," she said, "and some physical exertion is good for the health of the human body". I know, weird, right? But she really did say it like that. Softening me up for the big good-bye, I suppose. She didn't get bitten, she rode through that swarm of bugs like they weren't there, but one of them sure found me.

I flipped out when it bit me, my arm twitched and I nearly went over. Huh. The way she looked at me. Like she wanted to grind me right into the ground under her heel, like a bug.

And it was all going so well, our relationship. Fate's way of saying that I'm better off without her, I guess. So, farewell, sweet, itch-reducing, out-of-date unguent. And hello, Jack.

*

Fuck. Jack. What did you do? Feels like someone dragged a chainsaw through my head. You were supposed to help. To be my friend in my time of need. Thank God it's still dark outside. Wh... Shit. Who put that fucking golf ball in my arm? And what the fuck is that pink caterpillar thing doing inside it? It's kind of... ewwww, squirming. Squirming inside the huge blister that's managed to grow around those five bites in just a few hours. Jeez, the thing's even got red lit-up eyes, five of 'em. Bloody pentagons everywhere today. Must have been a carnivorous glowworm or something. I have got to get that thing out of me. Right now, hangover or not. Fucking wildlife. Get them before they get us, that's what I say.

*

OK. Antiseptic, check. Wads of absorbent cotton, check. Box cutter with the new, well, new-ish, blade, check. Worked a treat on that big splinter last year. Ouch, yes. Still sharp. If I sit in the big chair here, I can brace my elbow against its back and cut into my arm more precisely. Why waste money on the ER, right? And anyway, what would they know about squirmy little bugs you meet when you're out riding with your girlfriend? Ex-girlfriend.

I do like this chair, though, it's so comfortable. Maybe I'll wait for morning, when the light is better and I can see what I'm doing. Don't want to slice an artery open or anything. Yes, that's what I'll do. Sleep on it. Thank you after all, Jack.

*

I'm standing by the river. Smells crisp. Earthy. No-one about, which is weird, because usually everyone is powering down this trail on their bikes when the summer weekend weather is so nice. And there's the swarm of those damned bugs. Sort of copper-coloured, with five lights at the front, eyes I guess, like those LED tail-lamps you get on a trailer. They have a nest, like a metal soccer ball hidden in the weeds by the path. That's where they are all flying out from.

And then they're gone, like they have a mission or something, and it's quiet. Something bumps me from behind.

Bite

So I turn around, slow-mo, like you do in a fever dream, because that's what this is, right? The Jack, the out-of-date itch cream, the bite, who knows.

And there's the copper-coloured caterpillar thing, like in my arm, except now it's tall as me. Looks a bit like the big beetle larva I found in a rotting log once, a wrinkled sausage burnt at one end. It's... beautiful, and I think... yes, friendly. Definitely friendly. It bows towards me like an attendant in a Japanese department store, bowing down, down, down. Five red eyes on the top, lit up, the eyes look right at me, shining with love, and then the top opens up like a beautiful, beautiful five-petaled flower or a mouth and then it jumps at my head –

*

It's morning. My head doesn't ache any more, amazing considering the bottle of Jack, and I feel really warm, and ever so comfortable. I told you this was a good chair. The sunlight looks deep blood-pink through my eyelids, like when you're not quite ready to believe it's time to get up and open your eyes, and you're just in that waiting-room state until the better part of you finally makes you get your shit together and crack those eyes open. The dream was weird, sure, but I feel OK. Yuh, OK.

That better part of me does its trick, and the new day floods in like someone sliced my eyelids right open. Huh. Cloudy. Well, looks like cloud anyway, a big, fluffy cloud, through the goop that's coating my eyes. Blood-pink goop. Actually, that cloud looks more like a wad of absorbent cotton as it gets closer. Why would a cloud get so close? It wafts past my eyes, clearing the bloody crustiness away as it passes.

Wow. I really need a shave. I can see each and every day-old bristle thrusting out of my hung-over face, like I have super high-def vision.

My... hang on, why am I looking up at my own face? My gigantic sleep-deprived face, with the five perfectly-arranged little red lights on each eye's iris. And at my gigantic finger and thumb, charging towards me. Huh?

This doesn't feel like a dream. Come to think of it, it doesn't feel like anything. Not even when my gigantic finger and thumb pinch me around my waist, well, around where my waist would normally be, but um, hang on, I don't think I have a waist –

And Christ, that was fast, and now I'm in mid-air. Held in my own finger and thumb. I can see it's a nice day, just a few copper-coloured bugs circling outside the window, and I'm looking right into my eyes, the eyes with the five red lights, my gigantic face looking right back at me. But that's not me behind those two eyes. I'm behind these eyes. These five eyes –

And there, that's Lynsey, a giant Lynsey, she has the five lights in her eyes too, and she's naked, and she's rubbing my dick, the dick on the naked, gigantic me with the eyes that I'm no longer behind, and now I know for sure that it's not me, it's the bug, the bug that bit me, that's inside the me with the dick, the growing dick, and that Lynsey was bitten too, and now I know what they are going to do because there's a bit of the bug left behind that showed me what happened. They are going to fuck and make a baby but it won't be a human baby, it will be a special bug baby with five of everything, and they've been waiting so long to get here and humans are the ideal hosts and Lynsey and I are the first but we won't be the only ones –

And I'm falling. I hit the floor but it doesn't hurt. I look up and I see my hard dick, the dick on the me that I'm not in, I see it enter Lynsey and it's the end of the human race and the beginning of the bugs' next phase, and I look at Lynsey's foot, straining against the floor as she pushes against my dick, and I can see the bloody hole in her own skin, that soft skin on the top of her foot where she must have ripped out her own bug, the bug holding the human Lynsey, and the fucking-bug Lynsey looks down at me with those perfect five-light eyes, raises her foot-

Witches
by SV Macdonald

Thrills of excitement run through his body, leaving him weak and trembling. Tonight. Tonight the moon will be dark. Tonight they will come.

Darkness falls and he waits at his open window. Bats swoop in and out of the square of light. The night is silent and forbidding, like the start of a nightmare. Not even the screech of an owl to make it real. But somewhere in the woods they are gathering. He is sure of it.

Midnight strikes. And with the last stroke (he knows because he counted) comes a high, keening shriek that pierces his skull with lancing pain. Blackness flows through his brain and he flounders, collapsing vacant and empty on the bed.

Morning. Sunlight pouring through his window. His head aches. He stumbles upright, not quite sure how he managed to fall asleep in his clothes. The low morning sun beckons him outside.

Suddenly he remembers – the dark of the moon! Draining a mug of strong coffee, he grabs his coat and his camera and runs outside. Into the woods.

Shaking with anticipation and caffeine he follows the track through the uneven growth of birch and sycamore that fills this abandoned quarry complex. The path is uneven, littered with strange growths of rusty metal and piles of odd-coloured shale or rock. Fallen leaves cover holes deep enough to snap an ankle, and every now and then a length of hidden cable reaches for the sky, as if someone has sent power lines directly from the centre of the earth.

It takes no more than half an hour to reach his destination. The sun is still low enough to send hazy beams through the trees and this only accentuates how dim the light actually is. The sunbeams fall on a growth of young birch trees that create a natural circle. The centre of the circle is clear of undergrowth – or any growth at all, in fact – and beaten flat as if many feet have stood there.

And on each tree is painted a symbol.

He is so excited he could hug himself with delight. Automatically he lifts his camera and fires off a few shots of the circle as a whole, and then some of the individual trees. The dark red symbols glow in the sunbeams as if they are burnished with gold. He steps forward into the centre of the trees. The day suddenly becomes darker and a new breeze sends chilly fingers down the back of his neck. He gasps. In the centre of the circle, directly in front of his feet, are the remains of a fire. White ash and charcoaled wood. And one yellowed and blackened bone.

He takes a step back. Each compass point of the circle is marked by a little heaped mound of earth, each large enough to conceal a shallow grave. He counts them, and counts again. There is one more than there was yesterday.

He is sure of it. But the circle is not yet complete. He glances around the clearing. There are other changes. A scrap of stained cloth caught on the ragged bark of a tree. Something that might have been a handprint pressed into the earth near the fire. A little bundle of feathers tucked under a rock. And the inside of the circle is perfectly clean, apart from the dead fire. Not even a stray crisp packet or fallen leaf.

He knew it. They came.

The circle this morning is like the pictures he took last month and the month before. He *knows* it isn't just bored kids or someone sleeping rough. He *knows* it is witches.

He takes a step towards the edge of the circle. The air there is heavy and dense, as if rain is coming. His first thought is that he might see a rainbow. His second is that he is going to get wet.

Huge, heavy drops of rain begin to fall through the trees. Each drop snaps on the dry leaves like a footstep. Spooked at first, he turns at every sound. But soon there are too many to follow and he feels a bit stupid. Who could it be, anyway? Just some old duffer walking a dog.

But deep inside his instinct knows better. And that instinct is telling him to run.

The raindrops are closer together now, and they hit the earth with a crack, crack, crack like a whip. Bravado straightens his shoulders. Time to go home. He tries to move casually, as if someone is watching him. But the rain has made the earth slippery and he is wary of falling, out here in the woods. If he broke a leg someone would eventually find him. But it just might not be today. Safer surely to stay in the circle until the rain stops.

Witches

The leaves rustle like laughter behind him. He spins again. Nothing. No-one. Just being stupid.

The raindrops are getting heavier. Each strike takes on a life of its own. It seems to his overwrought mind that they are surrounding him, holding him there in the circle with the bloody red symbols and the mound of fresh-turned earth.

He closes his eyes. Takes deep breaths. It's just the rain. Just the rain. Just the –

His eyes fly open. A drop of rain so large he can follow its trajectory from the sky. It splashes at his feet. It glows with a fierce grey light and swells and grows and then she is there, an image straight from the pages of his books at home. Cloaked and gowned in grey. Beautiful. Glowing. No, *blazing* with fierce, pale fire.

And cold fear runs down his back. Pools in a sick knot in his stomach. He forces himself to turn away. To begin to run.

More huge drops strike the earth, one for almost every tree in the circle and each blossoms into a cloaked grey figure as terrible as the first.

Male and female both. Surrounding him.

Laughing.

The earth exhales a fine, soft mist. The camera falls unheeded from his hand. It strikes the damp earth without a sound. Words form like numbing whispers in his head, '*Who dares... who dares... who dares...?*'

The desire to *know* is plucked from his mind and suddenly he sees it all, replayed like a film in the haze. The yellow blaze that lit the harsh faces of the witches. The chanting. The stately dance they wove through the trees. The shadows that moved in the blackness around them. The bound and bleeding child with shattered eyes. The Initiate, with her pale and resolute face kneeling before the dark Priestess, her hand reaching out to make her choice. The flashing knives. The blood painted on their faces and on the trees. The chittering, swirling shades that licked the scarlet drops from their gory feet.

The chanting that rose to a crescendo as the Initiate sank into the ground and then rose again, cloaked in grey, her mortal remains buried in the earth below. The final keening scream as the dying child was tossed onto the fire. And then the choking acrid smell of burning flesh and bone.

Sickened, he gags on bitter, coffee-flavoured bile. His legs want to fail, to let him sink to the earth and into insensibility. But he is gripped by the vision before him and now she says, '*Choose...*'

In one hand she holds a grey cloak, and in the other a knife. The blade is blackened and sour with the blood of the sacrificed child. The coven draws suffocatingly close, tightening the circle around him. Grey cloaks merge with the soft mist into a barrier he cannot breach. And the chant fills his head like white noise.

"*Choose, choose, choose...*"

His breath comes short and fast. The sudden knowledge that they will decide if he does not, as the knife twitches impatiently towards his heart. An agonisingly long moment of wishing with all his heart that he had stayed in bed. And then he watches his hand creep out and his fingers touch the cloak.

*

The rain stops. The earth is wet. The wood breathes out a fine mist that covers the soft, turned dirt of the new mound in the circle. The one that makes it complete. It is just a bunch of trees now, with some blurry paint on the bark and a pile of rags near the centre. Left by kids, maybe. Or someone sleeping rough. And a camera soaked through and ruined by the rain.

Shenanigans
by Chris Jeal

I get into my car and sink into the plush leather of the driver's seat. Placing my mobile phone on the dash, I take a deep breath and enjoy that new car smell. It's great to finally be able to have the things I've always wanted – even if it has cost me a lot more than just money.

The phone's screen lights up and a jaunty voice calls, "Hey John, you slow-poke. You now only have three hours left to complete Shenanigan: *Bloody Heartbreaker*." This is the Host, the voice of The App and possibly that of the Devil himself, or maybe someone much, much worse... I jam the keys into the ignition, fire up the engine and drive away into the night.

Thirteen months, that's how long The App has been around and five of those months was all it took for society to break down and take a shit on itself. The App changed everything. No one knows who created it, or where it originated from, but on Tuesday 22nd June 2016 it appeared on everyone's phone, tablet and laptop. Every network, every town, every country got The App. At first people thought it was a scam, *one weird trick to make you rich*, but when they realized it was legit and they saw what it offered, people went crazy for it... literally.

The App offers cash prizes to perform dares, or *Shenanigans* as the Host calls them. Pick a Shenanigan from the list, film it, upload the footage and the money is transferred to your account – simple as that. The dares started pretty tame, with things like *Eat Worms!* which paid £50 or *Slap a Friend!* for £80. Once people got into the swing of it and the money started pouring in, things escalated rapidly. *Eat Worms!* changed to *Eat Glass! Slap a Friend!* turned to *Mutilate a Friend!*

I steer onto the common and pass through what was once a thriving neighbourhood; now everything looks like it's been chewed up and spat out. The police can't stop it, and those that still patrol the streets are more likely to commit Shenanigans than prevent them. If you did get arrested, it's doubtful you'd make it back to the station.

Headlights pick out movement in the road up ahead. I stamp the brakes and crunch gravel, grinding to a halt in front of two scabby women dragging a barely conscious blood-covered man across the road. One of them points a fleshy stump where her arm should be at me. *Probably did that to herself.* Mutilation and self-mutilation Shenanigans equal big payouts – a year's wage to hack off a limb is a reasonable proposition for those who are desperate.

I grab my phone and check the Shenanigans list to see if I can make some cash by flattening these fucks into the gravel – I quickly change my mind as I consider the mess it'll make of the new car. I palm the horn, "Get the fuck outta the way." They scurry off into the darkness with their prize, no doubt taking him somewhere to indulge in some slice 'n' dice.

I drive on.

Things have gotten even more interesting since the new app-upgrade: The App 2.0. Now Shenanigans are streamed live as the Host offers bonuses and cash multipliers to encourage you to get even more creative and twisted.

The first time I witnessed 2.0, I was in the supermarket. I turned into the frozen goods aisle and walked into a Shenanigan in progress, a man beating a screaming blonde woman to the floor. When he'd knocked the fight out of her and she was choking on her own teeth, he started tearing at her clothes; it was then the Host called out from the man's phone, "Make it multiplayer! 10X the cash if you make it a party! Have fun with it. Share with friends!"

People who had been watching didn't take much persuading to wade in on her, too – everyone has a price – and it wasn't long before it was a game with twelve players. When they'd finished with her, blondie's limp body was dumped in with the frozen potato waffles.

Sure, someone could have intervened, tried to save her. But who'd pass up that kind of cash? And those that didn't get involved? They were too busy with their heads down, checking The App for an 'easier' Shenanigan – these people are in denial, thinking they'll just take on the tame stuff. But it doesn't take long for your moral compass to fracture and you're doing the real nasty shit.

I pull up at Pennington flats, kill the engine and once more take in that new car smell. I tap The App, and speak into my phone, "This is John Glenn, going live with Shenanigan: *Bloody Heartbreaker.*"

"Make this your best Shenanigan yet, tiger," chirps the Host. "Remember to use your official App gear for bonuses and multipliers!" I open the glove box and pull out my official App

Shenanigans

Shenani-cam retina recorders™. These are awesome, contact lenses that record everything. Some people still use head cams. Amateurs. I slip the retina recorders over my eyes and check my other gear, all bought from in-app pop-ups and advertising. I have my 'App *scream for me slice-'n'- dice* knife™', my official 'App *I can't feel my legs!* restraints™' and my 'App *Deepest itch* internal flayer™' Using all these official items brings bigger bonuses and multipliers. I simply refuse to use any other brand.

I pocket my phone, bag my gear and bail from the car. I make my way to the tower block entrance and key in the door code, all the while keeping an eye out for anyone who might be looking to Shenanigan me.

Inside, I take the lift.

A *ping* announces my arrival at the top floor and the doors clatter open. I step out and make my way towards a reinforced door protected by security bars.

"Let's get messy, mah boy!" the Host shouts from my mobile. "Don't puss out!" he adds. *No way. Not me.* I knock on the door, and after a moment a voice calls from the other side, "Who is it?"

"It's me." Locks slide and chains clang. The door opens. Tanya stands there looking delicious in a stunning evening dress. "Well, look at you," I grin. I enter, kissing her as I pass, looking at the bandaged stump where her arm used to be. She's been such a good girlfriend; that arm paid for my first house.

I rock down the hallway towards the kitchen. The taste of Tanya fizzes on my lips and for a second I wonder how much of a multiplier I could rack-up if I fried and ate a bit of her.

Inside the kitchen, candlelight hugs flutes filled with champagne and casts shadows on a table laid with a beautiful spread – I love date night. I place my bag down and wonder whether to start with some genital mutilation to get things rolling. I'm thinking I can earn at least fou– *A sharp pain in my lower back.*

For a second I feel like I've shit myself, as my trousers flood with hot liquid. I look at my feet, blood pools around them. *Oh shit,* I stumble back, crashing to the floor. Tanya looms over me, clutching a knife, wearing a small camera strapped to her head. It's nowhere near as cool as my *Shenani-cam retina recorders™* and I snort at how stupid she looks.

"How did I know that you were coming to torture me and be a

Bloody Heartbreaker, John? You're really behind with your tech." She pulls her phone from her pocket and holds it up for me to see. "The new App 3.0 alerts me when anyone in my contacts list accepts a Shenanigan."

3.0?!? How could I have missed this?
Tanya taps the phone's screen and holds it to her mouth, "This is Tanya Morrison, high-jacking *Bloody Heartbreaker* from John Glenn."

"Well this is an exciting turn, Tanya! Make that no good scallywag scream!" Tanya stalks toward me with the knife. "Whoa! Bonus Alert! Thirty thousand if you cut off his winky and feed it to him."

Tanya smiles, "Accepted." She eyes my crotch, "Grilled or fried, John?"

I look at the blade of the knife as it grins by the candle light. "Wait!" I shout. Tanya pauses, unimpressed. I continue, "That isn't an official App knife... use the knife in my bag... it'll up your multiplier." A warm smile spreads across Tanya's face.

"You are always so sweet, John. Doing this is gonna break my bloody heart."

Aftermath
by Geoff Bagwell

Smith eased the door closed behind him, careful not to wake Elizabeth and the baby. After another bad night they were finally asleep, and the longer they stayed that way the better. These days, sleep was the only refuge from the nightmare.

Outside on the pavement he stopped. The street was deserted. Over his shoulder hung the rifle he'd found last year, next to the body of a dead soldier. The empty street, together with the rifle, made him feel... well, maybe not safe, but saf*er*.

Feeling safe was a luxury of another age, like the assumption that the flashpoints of the world's bloodiest conflict would only ever be seen on a television screen. These things were gone forever, since the brief respite between the Cold War's end and the Holy War's beginning had turned out to be just that – a respite.

But the winter had been long and many had died. Of the survivors, most were sick and weak. And in the land of the frail, Smith thought, even a 30-year-old accountant can survive.

And he had to. They had a baby.

He scanned the row of Victorian terraced houses. He thought he saw a movement in a window and frowned. He stared, concentrating on the laced net curtains, assessing the risk. His finger crept towards the trigger of the rifle and rested there.

Nothing. Just his imagination. Slowly, he took his finger from the trigger guard and allowed the tension to ease from his shoulders. He began to walk.

A casual glance and the street appeared as it had when they moved in – typical London terraced housing a mile south of the Thames, built for the poor of the nineteenth century, inhabited by the wealthy of the twenty-first.

Except it wasn't the same. According to Smith's watch (analogue, of course, now semiconductor- and quartz-based devices no longer worked) it was ten past eleven in the morning. Yet a dusty grey haze hung in the air, the twilight which now passed for daylight. And in another two hours, darkness would begin closing in, until a starless night smothered everything by two o'clock in the afternoon.

Smith walked on. Past front gardens where shrivelled flowers had fought to root then failed to bloom; past trees either diseased, dead, or dying; and past animals, skulking in shadows. Most of these were pets – or their mutant offspring; cats and dogs who were nowadays more likely to be food than fed. Left to fight for survival amongst the rats and other vermin, they stood little chance, their hunting genes lost to domestication.

Smith reached Costcutter. After a quick glance over his shoulder, he went inside.

Sanjeev had been sitting on a stool behind the counter. Now he stood, his right hand instinctively resting on the AK-47 hanging across his body.

"Brian, my friend. How's it going?" Apart from Elizabeth, Sanjeev was the only person who spoke to him like this. Civility and manners were a waste of energy, better conserved for the effort of staying alive. "How are Elizabeth and the baby?"

"They're fine."

Sanjeev kept smiling, but his eyes held only pity. These were not the days to start a family. "So what do you need?"

Smith glanced around. The store was small, little more than a newsagent, but it had once sold all the essential groceries. Now its shelves were hopelessly barren. He turned back to Sanjeev. "What have you got?"

The smile faded and died, "Wait."

Sanjeev went through a door behind the counter. When he returned he held a cardboard box. He placed it on the counter and picked items from it, one at a time. "Nappies, one pack; wipes, two packs; baby food, four jars."

"That's it?" Smith said.

Sanjeev shrugged apologetically. "That's it."

Smith thrust his hand in his jacket and pulled out a fistful of currency: Elizabeth's wedding ring, a gold chain which had belonged to her mother, a pair of gold earrings, other stuff he hadn't even wanted to look at. "Is it enough?" he asked.

Sanjeev nodded. "I'm sorry," he said as he took them.

"Yeah," Smith said. "We all are."

Aftermath

*

The house was quiet when he got back; Elizabeth and the baby were still asleep. He trod softly along the hall, then slowly climbed the stairs. In the bedroom, he stood beside the bed.

Thin, grey light crept in around the curtains. Mother and baby lay face to face, and even in sleep Smith saw the anxious lines creasing Elizabeth's forehead. Then he shifted his gaze to the daughter he himself had delivered three months ago.

Lying on her side, her profile was one of delicate perfection: the graceful upturned nose, the tiny ear like exquisitely carved mother-of-pearl, the kiss of lips, the gentle swell of her cheek. Something hard knotted in Smith's throat and, though agnostic in belief, he suddenly understood how many could only attribute such beauty to a benign creator.

Then she moved. Slowly she settled onto her back.

And now Smith saw the other head. It sprouted from the crook of her neck, puffy and bulbous, with empty eye sockets and twisted features. Its skin was translucent like an over-inflated balloon, and just below the surface a network of veins throbbed and pulsed, mocking Smith's hope that it would shrivel up and die.

He turned away. He swallowed before the lump in his throat could become the sob he felt rising up from his guts.

Don't wake them. Sleep is the only escape.

And then the other thought came, as it so often did.

The nuclear winter was bad; but it will be nothing as to the nuclear spring.

Summer Sky
by John Read

It seemed strange that I could admire the beautiful, deep blue sky at such a time.

I was surprised that on the most dreadful morning of my short, troubled life, I would even notice, never mind enjoy, the simple splendour of a gorgeous summer sky.

And yet, as my jelly legs climbed the creaking wooden steps, Mother Nature's pretty distraction gave me an unexpected strength for my imminent meeting with the fearful Madame.

What I'd been dreading for so long didn't seem quite so bad after all. The world was still beautiful and life would go on.

For some.

As I reached the platform, the sweet aroma of roses filled my head with blissful memories of summers past. The joy was as fleeting as the blink of an eye. Chased away by sudden, thudding, overwhelming sadness.

I remembered the merciful advice of a few minutes earlier. "Don't hesitate or all is lost."

I walked swiftly towards the motionless figure of Madame. She was all I had expected and more. Unyielding and merciless.

I kneeled at her feet and said a small prayer, then placed my neck in the half circle. Instantly, with false bravery, I held out my arms in readiness.

A bead of liquid dropped onto the sawdust, inches below my face. Perspiration, or a tear? I knew not. Nor cared. I just longed to see the blue summer sky one last time.

I heard a swoosh and the roar of a crowd. Then silence.

Madame Guillotine had done her job well. My prayer was granted. Once again I admired the summer sky, as my head settled in the basket.

The Lizard King
by Stephen Deas

Howard has his spot at the end of the platform. All the seats are long gone before the trains come as far as Leicester Square but it gets him close to the exit at Edgware. So he stands in his spot, tunes out the jostling, the background buzz of conversation, the Tannoy announcements that might as well be in Martian, and stares down at the shining rails and at the little black mice that live down there.

He watches one dart under the remains of a dirty plastic bag; it emerges in triumph a moment later, clutching the discarded end of a French fry. It skips along, heading for darkness.

Something shoots out from the heaving tide of business suits and briefcases, fast as a striking viper, long and sinuous like a rope. A blink and gone again.

So is the mouse.

Howard risks a glance down the line of shoes, up trousers and jackets and into faces. Dangerous territory this, eye contact with a fellow sardine. Maybe he's imagined it, but he's sure, over the clicking heels and rustling newspaper, that he heard a crack like a whip with a silencer. Maybe someone else heard it too. Their eyes will meet and they'll both know they weren't imagining things, that something odd really happened.

And then quietly forget about it.

It's a bit worse than that though. The man on the platform a few feet along from Howard is a lizard. Suit, striped accountant shirt, long dark blue coat, gloves, briefcase, the same uniform as all the people crowding beside him, but definitely a lizard. Hairless green scaled skin, eyes yellow and slitted, mouth far too wide.

Howard looks away. Staring is rude. Long days, too much stress, too much caffeine, that must be it.

A second glance. Still a lizard.

Around him, people fidget their feet and mutter about the time or the weather. No one seems to notice the alien in their midst.

Another mouse scuttles between the tracks. The lizard glances at his watch and then his eyes snap to the mouse. His jaw splits open, gaping wide. A snake-like tongue flashes out. With a crack of air it snaps back, mouse and all. The lizard man tilts back his head and swallows.

Shuffling of feet, the drone of idle chatter. A train comes. No one seems to notice when it stops in the tunnels between Warren Street and Euston, or when the doors open into a dirty brick wall. The lizard man picks up his briefcase and walks out. The doors close, the train moves off. The faces around Howard are blank. Nothing out of the ordinary has happened.

The lizard man is there again the next day. Same time, same place, same people standing around him. He looks like a regular, the way he stakes out his place on the platform near the edge. His snake-whip tongue cracks now and then, snatching passing mice from their myopic lives.

Howard stands behind him this time, careful to keep a few people between them. He doesn't want to get close, but the crowd doesn't like it, jostling to remind him he isn't where he's supposed to be. The commuter rush is a living thing. The rule of the waiting herd is simple: no eye contact. It resents how Howard pays attention now, as though it knows that one of its parts isn't playing the game but doesn't quite know who or where or how.

Howard knows them. The same faces, day after day. The rumpled, folded one, too much skin and not enough skull who always has a seat somehow, barricaded behind his Evening Standard. The young suits, sharp dressers, slicked back hair, striped shirts, three or four, not always the same but always the same place and the same presence, loud and expansive. The painted secretaries and the unpainted ones, the quiet woman who sits in the corner bunched into herself behind a book. The young man, stubble-faced, jeans and T-shirt, who stands as close to her as he can and sneaks glances into her cleavage when he thinks no one is looking. The older man with the thinning hair and the dark, almost latino skin, who watches the young man doing it and scowls because in his mind he wishes he could do the same.

And the lizard man.

Newspapers rustle, book pages turn, braying laughs don't stop. Pressed together the crowd has no secrets and so, by unspoken consensus, it sees nothing.

At the weekend the lizard man is a no-show. On Monday morning, Howard must explain why he's an hour late into the office, something

The Lizard King

other than the truth, riding the train back and forth looking for the lizard man to board. In the evening he travels home with a friend, Rogie. The lizard man is obvious, blatant, but Rogie doesn't see it

The train comes. They all board the same carriage.

"OK," says Rogie, "Where is he?"

Howard points him out with quiet words, though if Rogie was ever going to see yellow eyes and a green lizard head then he'd have seen without needing direction.

"You mean the Asian guy?"

"What Asian guy?"

"The one standing just behind the redhead and in front of the black dude."

There is no Asian guy. There is a man with a lizard head.

Rogie thinks Howard is going crazy. Stress maybe. Too much caffeine.

Another stop goes by. Warren Street. Howard grabs hold of Rogie's arm.

"We're going to stop!"

Tubes stop in the tunnels all the time. Happens every day. Probably a slow train ahead. Rogie shakes his head. "You need help, man."

"He's going to get off."

"We're in the tunnels, Howard. He can't get off."

The train grinds to a halt. The doors open.

"See! The doors!"

Rogie can't hide the worry in his face. "The doors are closed," he says.

The lizard man pauses to sniff the air and then steps calmly into the black outside. The doors close. The train begins to move again.

Rogie is frowning. He gives a strange look and pushes to where the lizard man was standing. The crowd hates him and vows vengeance, but by the time the train stops at Euston, Rogie has inspected every face and made no secret of it either. On the platform he watches the train recede. He stares after it long after it's gone.

"You're fucking with me," he says.

They argue. It has to be a joke. A trick. No one can vanish between stations. The doors were closed. In the end, Rogie storms away. He's seen something he can't resolve. It scares him. He is angry and

19

humiliated. Howard thinks he should try seeing a man with a lizard head and see how he feels then.

The next evening, Rogie is already there, waiting. He waves a phone. The lizard man is also there, same place, same time, right on cue. Howard nudges Rogie.
"Standing in front of the tall black guy."
"Same guy I saw yesterday. Asian."
Bold as brass, Rogie points his phone at the lizard man. Takes half a second of video. On the screen the lizard man is no longer a lizard. Howard doesn't quite know how this ought to make him feel. It's one madness swapped for another. Maybe he should get some rest. Take a few days off. Maybe he's been working too hard. People have nervous breakdowns from working too hard. Maybe he should see a doctor. Or maybe it's too late. Maybe the next stage it to wander around naked, digging holes in the back of his garden in the middle of the night.
"I don't have a garden," Howard says.
"You can see he doesn't have a lizard for a head now, right? I think you need to see a shrink."
They board the train. Three stops as always and then it slides to a halt between stations. Rogie pulls the phone out again. The doors open. The lizard man gets off. The doors close. The train moves away. Rogie pushes his way through the carriage, inspecting faces. The crowd hates him again. The faces don't expect to be noticed. It's not the way of things.
At Euston, Rogie and Howard look at Rogie's video. They see the doors open. The Asian guy is there, still with a human head. He steps off the train. Clear. Plain as the sun in the sky. Rogie plays it over and over, staring like he's seen his own death. "No way," he says. "That didn't happen." Then they get drunk together, throwing the strange lizard man into an oblivion of wine.
Howard sleeps badly that night. Tossing and turning, strange dreams. He sees men in suits peel back their faces and show the lizard beneath. Lizards, snakes, yellow eyes, narrow slit pupils. They carry him down a night-lit street as though a coffin. He sees a couple necking in an alley, a drunk, a police car. The drunk stares and rubs his eyes in disbelief, then turns to relieve himself behind a green plastic dustbin. The others see nothing.

The Lizard King

When he wakes, he phones in sick. A gulp of water and then a rush to the bathroom to vomit up the night before, clutching his toilet-bowl like a lover. He stumbles to the basin, scooping handfuls of water to wash away the grime of sleep and the taste of bile. He looks at himself in the mirror.

A head of dull green scales stares back, yellow eyes with narrow black slits, the flicker of a long forked tongue.

Howard screams. The mirror slides to the floor with the roar of an onrushing train. The ceiling spins to take its place. He crashes and lies still.

He wakes in the middle of the afternoon, to the throb and lethargy of a hangover's end. The lizard is still there in the mirror. But that's okay. He doesn't feel human now. Not remotely. He feels hungry.

He goes outside. The sun is bright and its warmth is heaven. Birds sing. He drools, watching them in the trees, joyful at the heat of summer. Children walking their way home from school glance at this strange man beating his chest at the sun and then glance away, back to their idle conversations of football teams and trading cards and X-Box and YouTube. They don't see what he is.

Something moves in the bushes. Without thought Howard's mouth yawns. A rope-like tongue snaps and lashes and snatches a flutter of wings. Howard swallows it whole. The feathers tickle.

He dresses. Too late for work but not too late for the rush. He rides the tube to Warren Street and sits on the platform and waits. The crowd grows as afternoon sinks to evening, the pulse of it as the trains come and go like the rhythm of a slow-beating heart. No one sees him while he sits, only when he stands. Then they embrace him, warmer than before.

He spies Rogie.

"Hello Rogie," he says.

Rogie looks at him. Not the blank unseeing gaze of just another part of the crowd, but with eyes that stare and see. Really, truly see.

His mouth droops.

He screams.

Turns.

Runs.

Beyond the Flesh
by Diana Read

The horizon shrunk away into darkness. Rubber soles squeaked on the shining tiles, each step drowning Simon's nasal passages in disinfectant. He always liked the perfect symmetry of the endless door-lined hallways. Simon counted the steel doors just as he counted the wooden ones in his old secondary school. The flow of numbers helped calm the people anxiety. He loved numbers, 12 especially. Door 12 belonged to Mr Harrison and that was where his talent was first recognised.

"I know your heartbeat, sir," Simon replied on that gloomy September day, to an unwelcomed question about his home life. Mr Harrison had looked at the 12-year-old boy before him and laughed.

"Do you really? That would be quite a trick to see."

Simon hunched over in his seat like a vulture, head tilted to observe a potential carcass. "155 beats per minute."

Mr Harrison snorted, putting two fingers to his wrist and, humouring the boy, looked up to the clock.

60 seconds passed. "My God." The teacher looked down at the lanky, dark-haired child. "That is exactly spot on. But how..." he trailed off, feeling disconcerted by the unblinking stare of those cold, brown eyes.

"158 beats per minute."

Mr Harrison's brow furrowed. "It's a good trick but I'd appreciate if you stopped it now. We need to discuss why you've been late – "

"162 beats per minute."

"Stop it now. Please."

"167 beats per minute. Are you scared of me, sir? I showed this to a girl I met and her heartbeat frequency increased too. I asked why and she said she was scared. She called me a freak and ran off. Do you think I'm a freak, sir?"

The man heaved a deep breath. "No," he exhaled, "no, I don't think you're a freak, Simon. But I would like to know how you're doing that."

22

Beyond the Flesh

"I don't know, sir. I look at the neck and I can see the vein pulsing. I look at the chest and I can feel the heart's rhythm. I can always see it. I can always see people's insides."

"Well," large hands clapped together, "if you're that good at analysing people's bodies, then I guess you should be a doctor."

Simon's tongue skimmed his dry lips. "Will that let me play with people's insides, sir?"

"You'll certainly be able to go inside and fix the problems people have. Think of the fun you can have healing them."

"Yes, sir."

12 became Simon's lucky number, but he still liked counting the others. They were the second most loved thing in his life. 221, 222, 223, his feet turned down another infinite corridor.

224, 225, 226, a mournful wail echoed in the empty hallways, amplified by the drab concrete exposed underneath cracked plaster.

227, 228. Simon stopped, facing a steel door. This one was different to the rest. This one was his. Even without the counting, the small peg from which hung a white lab coat definitely showed this door to be his.

Scarred fingers ran over the coarse material, its colour off-white. Simon had it washed recently but he supposed it was too old to ever get back the brilliant shine. Just like his lab coats at university. They were always stained, his more so than others. But the tutors never shouted at him. Instead they called him 'genius' and 'unrivalled', but he didn't care for those words.

And so it didn't bother Simon when those same lecturers called him 'strange' and 'disturbed'. Those words came when he started to explore his interest by cutting up the practice organs they were told to repair.

Simon couldn't help it. He liked the way he could grope the soft, fatty tissue, compressing it between gloved fingers. Or the way the slippery muscle felt even more delectable than handling uncooked animal liver. Or the way the body part would wriggle, and twist through his hands. Or the way he could pluck at the sinews like fleshy guitar strings. Or the way his finger would slip into the organ, encompassing his digit with bloody, moist pressure.

Simon couldn't help it. Just like he couldn't help going through the metal door into a small, white room. One wall sported a window.

Within was only space enough for a locker, a file cabinet and a cart trolley overflowing with gleaming instruments.

From the trolley, Simon lifted a scalpel with the delicacy of a mother handling a newborn. It was just as precious, kept meticulously cleaned and polished. A standard he maintained from his core surgical training within the NHS.

One month into his blossoming career, Simon helped operate on a patient for the first time. The operation had been messy and required much assistance, but they pulled through and the patient was stabilized. Everyone involved, and some who weren't, went to celebrate after a hard day's work. But not Simon.

Simon stayed behind, looking at the crimson liquid dripping from the plastic wrapping around his fingers. Drip, drip, drip. His tongue darted across dry lips.

In the partial darkness of the hospital, he snuck into the patient's private recovery room, scalpel in hand. The man didn't even wake up when the metal slowly sliced open the sewed seams of his skin.

Only when the blood started dripping onto the hospital floor did Simon become aware of a nurse's banshee scream behind him. Drip, drip, drip, he worked at squeezing the thin blade between muscle tissue. Each new twist jetted out more blood like a partially clogged fountain. Thunderous footsteps came behind him. Rough hands threw him away from his craft.

Simon didn't understand, as the night duty doctors came to shout in terror and the security guard's hold cut the circulation in his arm, what the fuss was about. He put the patient together, he picked the patient apart. Both required a scalpel and only one Simon found truly enjoyable.

Yet others didn't seem to share in his enjoyment. So with his unrestricted hand, Simon pulled out a spare scalpel from his coat. It stabbed into the guard holding him. The man reared back in pain and Simon ran. He ran and ran and ran, only stopping when his lungs screamed for death and his legs burned for oxygen.

172 beats per minute thundered through his skull. He breathed. He calmed. He walked into the dark alleyway plagued with rubbish and rats.

Mind coming back to the white room, Simon looked through the long window. On the other side was a much larger space, shadows sneaking around its corners, forced there by the blindingly bright beam shining down on a half-clothed patient.

Simon opened the narrow door by the window and pulled the cart trolley after him with its little wheels squeaking. His gaze focused on the female fastened securely to the chair for her own protection. He liked this patient. She was lucky.

Little whimpers came from the patient who Simon swore to help, the pathetic noises muffled by the duct tape. Those simpering sounds were just like the ones Simon made when he hunched in the grimy streets, hiding away from the flashing blue and red lights.

But then Boss found him, recognising the notorious face in every recent news report. Boss approached him, saving him. Just like Simon approached the struggling patient now, scalpel held ready. Boss had turned Simon's life around in that dingy backstreet. Simon supposed it was good manners that he showed the same kindness to the strapped-down female before him.

The scalpel slashed across the patient's chest. Blood spilled down the precise incision. There could be no better way of turning a life around than turning it into death.

Simon went to take another implement from the trolley behind him. Looking into the shadow-infested darkness, Simon regarded the sealed bags hanging from every part of the wall, the preserved organs within ready to be taken away by Boss's men.

With scalpel in one hand and orthopaedic saw in the other, Simon turned to the patient, still struggling weakly. He didn't understand why they did that. Couldn't they see why they were here? Didn't they know their donation would help a lot of people? Then again, Simon only loved human anatomy. Why they did things remained a mystery.

The scalpel split the skin further. Simon pried it apart to a cacophony of moist squelching. The orthopaedic saw whirled noisily, cutting straight down and through the breastbone. Grasping the smooth, hard ribs, he pulled them back. Crack, crack, crack. The breaking noise lashed the silence. Supple bones rotated on the spine's hinges. Flesh tore open.

Her chest gaped, innards exposed. The archways of ribs welcomed the intrusion of Simon's scalpel and its severing of the tendons and valves.

Out of the blood-soaked cavern, Simon's hands emerged, grasping the precious heart.

It was small. A fluttering butterfly beating its wings at 180 furious beats per minute. Between his fingers, the tiny heart would continue its fibrillation for another three minutes. From this gaping female he needed the scrupulously clean liver and kidneys. Sadly, the heart couldn't be kept alive and useful for more than an hour. Even then, it would require complex machinery not in Simon's possession. As such, Boss was kind enough to let Simon explore his true passion.

From underneath the heart, his right hand came up to his lips. His tongue skirted across them, tasting the splash of metallic blood. The tongue extended. Coarse flesh licked his red-stained finger in one long, sensuous stroke. His left hand brought the heart to his face. Stained lips against it. Clammy warmth throbbed through them.

Simon popped the bulging, undulating muscle between his teeth and bit down. It was tender, rupturing easily in his mouth. He was so lucky to experience the divine explosion bursting past his lips. But that was to be expected. The child patient was his lucky number, twelve years old, after all.

The Audition Altar
by Leo X Robertson

"So what brings you here today, Geoff?"

Geoff Harkness sat opposite Zoe Trope. She leaned forwards over a cheap plywood desk. He stared into the flashing red light of the camera behind her, answers to her question cycling through his head. From the wall hangers stared winking bug-eyed cartoon demons, the type idiots get tattooed on their ankle for their eighteenth birthdays: 'Jimmy Crowley Presents: Sexy Sofa' the demons proclaimed. He went for, "Well, as you know, the economy isn't so…"

The economy! Jesus…

She flicked a hand back and forth and closed her eyes smugly. "Just relax, Geoff. I'm not trying to grill you. I just want to get a sense of who you are, and if we're a good fit for you."

What a joke! They're offering a job, right? Fit complete!

"Right," Geoff said, sighing. Feeling an oncoming slouch, he became rigid, and wondered what the hell to do with his hands, especially without looking at them. Even the lovely new suit his parents had bought him for graduation began to cause anxiety, showing wear after a few years of interviews alone.

"What I mean is," she continued, peering over her square glasses at the CV he'd handed her when he came in, "are you interested in the kind of work we do here?"

"If I'm honest, I'm not sure."

I should get out of here. There's surely another job vacancy.

She laughed through her nose. "Granted, many find it difficult with the camera on. Not to be intrusive, but", she snorted, "you're a man: I assume you've engaged in similar activity off-camera?"

"No! I never… I would never… not at all to say I disapprove, or I wouldn't be here either… I mean, I'd love to be considered. Here. Today."

"I get it, Geoff."

"You'll see there," he said, looking in the reflection of her glasses to gauge where she was reading, "that I have a great number of references who would attest to my professionalism. If that's a concern of yours. Before we get started. Well, you'll decide when we start, but, you know…"

Interrupt me, please! Interrupt me!

"You're impressively overqualified for the job. Although saying that, you have a woeful number of Twitter followers! Anyway, as you can imagine, the kind of people who come in here don't normally present their CVs."

She laughed, and he laughed with her, stopping just after she did. She was younger than him, wasn't she? Something about her attitude, but she didn't look it. He with his blonde locks and smooth skin; her with her general look of dehydration and fatigue. She was dressed well enough, but wore professionalism like a costume: ill-fitting pinstripe suit, extreme scrape-back of ponytail, dots of white powder in violently plucked eyebrows.

"I'm sorry about that," he said.

"No, don't apologise. I only read your CV since you brought it in. But really, the ones who succeed in this industry are able to act natural, you know, relax, be themselves…" She swung her shoulders about.

"Uh-huh." He scratched his neck and looked around. His heart sped up as his eyes locked on the famous black leather sofa behind him, lit in unsexy fluorescent light.

"Mmhm," she said, and nodded. "I just had an idea!"

"Please. I'm happy to be fully flexible to your needs."

"Could we conduct the interview during your… evaluation?"

That sounded like extra pressure. But in just one hour it could be over, either way.

"Yes! Absolutely," he replied.

Too enthusiastic!

There was a difference between emphatically pretending you're a team player versus bigging up the interviewer's every simple suggestion. Zoe looked like a woman who could tell when a man was faking it, or at least liked to think she could, as demonstrated by the return of her smug smile.

"Great!" she said. "Over by the couch. Geoff? You're still in that suit."

"Oh."

The Audition Altar

As expected, he had to strip. If he got the job, hopefully he'd get more comfortable taking his clothes off, enjoy it, even - though from what he'd already seen of the market, he'd just be chuffed if the pay was indeed competitive, as their advert had boasted. He removed his jacket and hung it on the back of the plastic chair, took off his trousers and folded them on its seat.

She motioned for him to face the camera, but not to look into it. She herself stripped down to a PVC bra and pants and put on a pair of matching fingerless gloves, to which she looked much more accustomed than the suit.

When he was almost finished, she said, "Just down to your pants is fine, Geoff. Unlike other companies I won't name, we like to leave some illusion."

He smiled with relief, but his face fell again as she removed a long leather belt from the drawer. She slapped it in one palm and said:

"Highest education level?"

"Bachelors with First Class Honours. Finance. Top of my year."

"Only a Bachelors' degree?"

In one fluid motion, Zoe lassoed the belt around his neck from across the desk. She made her way round to him and flipped a perfectly manicured foot up against the buckle, effortlessly choking him.

It hurt. It was real. Real! But surely what happened next wasn't real? The acting in the audition tapes he'd seen, the shoddy special effects - it always looked so fake. It had to be.

"Tell me about your final thesis. What attracted you to your chosen – " His tongue protruded thick and purple, and she couldn't help but laugh. Dropping her leg with Olympic grace, she slipped the belt's tab into the hole that gave him a finger's worth of space away from asphyxiation, and dragged him to the couch with the remaining strip of leather, pressing his red hot face into the couch, which he luckily found to smell only of hand sanitiser.

She straddled him from behind and angled his face to the camera, sitting on his back and reaching beneath the couch, sliding a tray along the carpet. A number of metal objects jangled together.

"So, Geoff," she said, reaching down for an object from the floor, "tell me about your work experience."

"Well..." he said, swallowing to stop from coughing, "you probably saw from my CV that in my undergrad I performed an internship each summer with three of the world's leading – "

He felt the rake of a sharp knife down the flesh of his back. Once, twice. Zoe performed this with a professional deftness but caught the knife a few times as it staggered down, tearing centimetre-deep flaps from his skin. He tried screaming to release the lancinating throb that followed, but quickly came the slap of a PVC glove on his cheek.

She leaned in: "If you're going to scream, make sure they can see your face. You're doing just fine."

"Leading management consultancy firms," he continued, "where I was fortunate enough to work with – "

She connected two of the large cuts with a horizontal slice and worked her fingertips into the bloody opening, tugging the skin downward like the red plastic strip on a polythene package, which felt like a hangnail of this magnitude ripped back instantly.

"'Fffffff – " He gritted his teeth and she tightened the belt, which choked off his next scream. "FIVE OF THE TOP TWENTY FORTUNE 500 COMPANIES!"

"Oh yeah!" she said, riding him and using his skin and the belt as reins. "Me likey!" She licked her lips. She'd make sure that when he could see the extent of the damage, it would be too late to escape. "Name them for me, you slut."

Blood soaked into the white cotton of his boxers and dripped down the couch. Whispering with the least movement of her lips possible, she said, "You've got them right where you want them. Don't fade now."

She released the belt and flipped him over, tugging his hair to keep him awake. Geoff's vision was smattered with black dots. Through them, he saw her smiling at him against the tube lamp's glare. He smiled weakly back, then his attention turned to the large bloody hook clutched in her left hand – *all of this is just for show, right?* – and gradually his vision picked up smaller details: the safety blades sticking out her bra; the slender knife shining cleanly in her other hand; the Hydra-like shadow of three long wavering necks that took over a third of the ceiling.

"They're here," she whispered, holding back tears of excitement to keep her make-up intact.

The Audition Altar

"Exxon," he said. Her smile broadened. His suffering bloomed into a dull warmth. A smell, like a rubbish bag of rotting teeth, filled the room.

"'Hewlett – " He gasped as the blade flew across his face and sliced his cheek open at one side. "P-packard!" With the "p", he spat out stinging fresh blood. He tongued his cheek's new flap: she'd really cut him!

"Yeah," she said.

"General... Electric." Now she tugged at his hair and drew the blade across his forehead. He protested with a weary shake of the head, a weak flailing of his arms, as she peeled back his flesh. Was all his blood loss some anaesthetic? To Geoff, the scalp-peeling just gave a vague tugging sensation.

From the floor was the sound of sticky foul creatures emerging from a primordial pool. The warmth of blood running across his forehead was unmistakeable. He closed his eyes, fading mercifully into fevered dreams.

The plasterboard of the wall erupted and more slick-sounding slops spilled into the room.

He heard her soothing voice: "Okay, Geoff. It's okay. Just give me one more. Just one more."

He gave a tired laugh. "You'll... like this one..."

"Give it to me, Geoff."

"A...aaa..."

"Could it be? Say it, bitch. Say it. Oh God! In all the time I've done this, I've never seen them come so fast!"

"Ppppp..."

"The whole thing. It's just one word. Tell me it's true and this is all over, I swear."

Scalp from his hairline was now tugged back to the crown. Around both their legs squirmed cold creatures.

"...Apple."

"APPLE!" she screamed, leaping into the mass on the floor and digging the knife into Geoff's belly, wrenching it back with full force to reveal ruby red bowels, which began to spill off the couch and into the carpet like bloody vomit from a newly carved mouth. The lights glowed blindingly bright and bulbs exploded, showering the room with a snow of glass and phosphor dust.

He made no sound.

She backed away into the darkness. "I never thought we'd get this deep."

"Zoe…" It was a voice from the room's growing mass, speaking in a thousand dead tongues.

She waded back to the couch and sat beside Geoff, steadying herself against the slip of his blood. She took off a glove and with this hand stroked his bleeding face. She placed a hand inside him and felt his organs pulse with the staggered movement of his diaphragm.

"I'm so sorry," she said. "I was just amazed by how much he took, how he barely even resisted! I know I wasn't supposed to… 'enjoy myself' this much, but I never thought he'd be the one you want!"

The cold pool was up to her knees.

"See how much you still had to learn at entry level, impatient girl? For your disobedience…"

A squelch echoed through the room's remaining space, sharply followed by Zoe's screams and the crackling of a hundred of her bones breaking at once.

Geoff felt her rag doll corpse flop on top of him. Soon came the slithering ribbed tongues all over him, lapping up his blood, running along the rips in his flesh, thus restoring them, like Prometheus' liver, to be torn out again and again in their home dimension of pure pain.

In their many mouths with putrid breath, the tongues said: "Geoff?"

"…"

"You got the job."

The Beholder
by Stephanie Wessell

You know that feeling when someone's watching you, but you don't actually see them? It's like a physical touch, making you raise your hand to the back of your head, or turn around to see who's there. I googled it. It's called *scopaesthesia*. And I've got it.

I want to be an etymologist when I'm older so I investigated the word to test its truth. It has Greek roots: *scop* comes from *to look* and *aesthesia* means *sensation*. That figures: this is a real, physical thing that makes my skin sort of jiggle. I've had it on and off since Year Nine last year, but it's perpetual now. That means *without intermission or interruption*.

I can be alone in my bedroom – a stupid baby pink because Mum went before she could do her promised re-paint – and feel eyes studying me. There's a heat to this scrutiny: it drills into me, like one of Dad's power screwdrivers that makes smoke rise from the friction. The gaze is usually behind me, but I turn my head and it seems no one's there.

It feels like a man. Someone adult. I call him The Beholder, which comes from the old English *behalden*, meaning *to keep*. I think he does keep me. I'm like his pet. That's not why I chose the name though, I chose it because of the phrase *beauty is in the eye of the beholder*. He seems to like my body. I want to think that his intentions are good, but I haven't always been sure that they are. It's confusing.

The Beholder is elusive, meaning *difficult to catch*, even when I'm feeling brave. Sometimes I feel like he wants to linger, looking at my chest, but can't because if he were in front of me I'd see him. So I actually purposefully close my eyes and let my arms fall to my sides. I put my shoulders back – correct posture makes you look and feel better, Mum drummed that into me – and I can feel his intense assessment. It's scary and exposing but somehow exciting, until the heat gets too much and I flick open my eyes, crossing my arms. I expect to see him, leering right in front of my face, but he instantly jumps behind me. It's playful and sick, all at the same time.

He used to scare me but I suppose he's kind of helpful, because knowing he's there makes me think about how I look. I try hard with my make-up, count the calories, and save my pocket money for what the magazines call *the five key accessories that make an outfit*. I wear a padded bra. When you're constantly on show, you have to be aware of your appearance. That's what Mum used to say. "Make sure you're presentable, Hannah, you never know who's looking." It worked for her; she said she "turned heads" when she was about my age. Possibly she had scopaesthesia too.

Even now, Dad says I should slow down. He says many things. Mostly: "You're not dressing like that on my watch." He looks at me in funny ways too, but I *see* him do that, as well as feel it. He wants to still treat me like a baby, so I certainly don't want to be *his* pet anymore.

Mum was still here when the Beholder first came. I was doing my homework when she came into my room and placed some Veet strips on the desk beside me. I'd never really noticed the hairs on my legs before, but she said that I was growing up and it was time for me to "start maintenance."

Now, looking back, this was a funny word for her to use, because it means *the process of preserving a condition*. Was *maintenance* going to keep me like a little kid? No - the pain of pulling those wax strips off convinced me of that. "Your new beauty regime, get used to it," Mum said.

Afterwards, as she made me parade my smooth legs in front of Dad, the complicated look in his eyes proved that I might really be becoming a woman. He said quietly, "She's too young," and left to test the Wi-Fi access in the shed.

I was kind of embarrassed so I went back upstairs to get on with my homework. On the way I stopped to look in the full-length mirror on the landing. My legs looked like a model's: long and elegant, especially when I stood on tiptoe, as if I was wearing heels. I liked them.

Weirdly though, as I admired them, I started to feel as if someone else were admiring them too. It was kind of imperceptible, which sounds like a contradiction because that means *so slight as to not be perceived*, but gradually the feeling grew until it was very real, and rather scary. I rushed into my room and put trousers on.

That was then: this is now. Now I think I'd leave the trousers.

So, anyway, there's a *little* part of me that thinks Dad might have been right, but mostly I reckon he was talking bollocks. Mum was

The Beholder

helping me make the best of myself. Maybe she somehow knew she was going, so felt she had to start early on the whole life advice thing. Maybe she'd always had the Beholder herself, but felt him slipping away and towards me, as she got older.

That kind of makes sense, actually. Later on that Veet day, I heard her arguing with Dad about how he didn't find her attractive anymore. It was sad to hear, because I think she was right. He kept telling her that looks weren't important. But she called him out on that, saying he should be glad she hadn't "let herself go" like other women her age.

Well, she certainly went. The Beholder was there when it happened.

It's horrible remembering it but here goes. We were in town. Crossing the road, coming out of House of Fraser. Mum had taken us to have our make-up done at the M.A.C counter. It was what she called "our little treat", and I suppose you could have called it that, but I think Mum wanted it more than I did – at first. The foundation they put on her face gave her more colour than it'd had for ages. She was glowing. But then the make-up lady said it was because of the fantastic new anti-ageing blemish concealer she'd just applied, and Mum's glow dimmed a little.

We were crossing the road. I could feel eyes looking at me... The make-up lady had said that the best products enhance your features, they don't change them, and that I didn't need concealer like my mum so she was just going to do a few light touches to emphasize my beauty. *Beauty*. Meaning *a quality that gives aesthetic pleasure*. I was embarrassed but, looking in the mirror, I allowed myself to wonder if she could be right and – bam – instantly the Beholder was there. His scrutiny, penetrating and constant, touched me from somewhere amid the shoppers passing through Cosmetics on their way to Linens. But I couldn't see him

I digress. That means I'm *leaving the subject temporarily*. It's an interesting word, from the Latin *digredior* meaning *depart*. Kind of apt. Departing childhood. Dearly departed.

Like I say, we were crossing the road. The Beholder was with us. He kept making me turn around, looking for him looking at me. I felt good I think, all kind of grown-up, but Mum had her head down ever since the make-up lady said those things. I wondered if Mum knew I was the only one looking at her: she certainly wasn't looking around as much as I was, no scopaesthesia for her.

We were crossing the road. I've said that, I know. I'm sorry, it's just... I'm just going to say it quickly.

We were crossing the road...

We were crossing the road as The Beholder's gaze got suddenly so strong that I turned to my right, sure this time that I would see him but of course he moved and instead there was the dusty bonnet of a big blue van and I could see the driver who was bald look at me but very briefly and not in a Beholder type way so I knew it wasn't him but in his panicked eyes I instinctively knew to get out of the way and I fell back but Mum didn't fall with me and suddenly I was on the tarmac and the Beholder wasn't looking at me because all eyes including his were on my Mum.

One last, full-on stare. Did she feel it before she – ?

I think he saved me instead of her.

A counsellor came to see me after it happened. She still comes, but says she may not have to for much longer. Gill-with-a-G isn't too attractive, and has dangly earrings that jingle when she nods her head earnestly. As a word, *earnestly* is pre-eleventh century, from the old English. It means *with serious intention*, which is funny because I don't feel the same hotness in her stares as in the Beholder's or Dad's.

I have to rate how I feel about the same list of things every time she comes. It's boring. The Beholder watches me as I reel off the numbers and she ticks the boxes. I try not to look around, because I don't want to arouse her suspicion, but I make sure I sit up straight so she – he – sees me at my best.

I've never told her about The Beholder. Somehow he feels like a secret, and if I shared him, it would spoil my connection with Mum, you know? Because now I'm certain that Mum knew about his presence. I think Dad senses something too – sometimes he looks at me as he used to look at Mum, as if he knows she's there, in me, but can't reach her. Or maybe he thinks the Beholder is stealing me from him.

I asked Dad if he'd paint my room the other day. Like Mum said she would. Get rid of the pink that makes me look like I'm into all that princess, baby shit. I even looked up the meaning of colours to persuade him: I found that pink symbolizes immaturity. It also symbolizes unconditional love and nurturing, but I didn't tell him that

The Beholder

bit. It seemed he knew that already, because he looked kind of agonized and refused to do it.

So Gill the counsellor said why didn't I do it myself. "A step towards being an adult," she said. She reckoned that if I did it well and responsibly, Dad might see how over-protective he was being and I could move on. She'd feel she could leave us alone.

Alone means *having no one else present.* Shows how much she knows.

So here I am, stretching up to the far corners of my room, slapping the roller up and down while Dad's grumbling downstairs. So far it's looking good. I used to think I'd want it green but since looking into colour symbolism I've decided on red. *Incarnadine,* it's called: a word derived from Latin, which developed into the Italian word *incarnatino,* meaning *flesh.* I like that.

I'm enjoying being slapdash. I like the paint splattering onto me – I reckon the drops highlight the smoothness of my thighs and the curves of my boobs, just visible within these loose dungarees. The Beholder watches with interest. I think he likes me being more open with my body than Mum was. And even though I can't see him I sense his smile, as the glistening red emulsion drips down, down deep, into the places I know I'll show him soon.

doG lived
by Troll Dahl

It was coming! Lili's piercing scream echoed through the 10th floor apartment, rattling the blinds and shaking the ornaments; or was it just the underground train that barged unapologetically beneath the building's foundations a million times a day, never letting up even during the night? Perhaps the booming thunderstorm outside her apartment windows which had been brewing all afternoon like some dark portent, finally unleashing itself on this grimy evening? It felt like she was doing it and by God she could have.

The pain was stabbing quicker than ever. Severing, ripping, beyond anything she had ever imagined. She couldn't have made it to the hospital even if she'd had enough notice. She had only just had enough strength to get to the bedside phone and dial before the tearing agony had felled her. Her body couldn't take this. How was this natural? No way.

What had the operator said? Forty minutes? Forty God damn fucking minutes? There are delays on the roads, she'd said. A storm drain had burst and the main highway had flooded within a couple of hours of this monstrous downpour. She could hear the cascading rain threatening to drown her now, somewhere in the background. A cacophonic orchestra played, composed of thunder, lashing rain and female screams of agony, punctuated by loud electric fizzles as the bedside light dimmed at every flash of lightning which streaked passed her window.

"Oh Fuck!" she yelled, as she exhaled what seemed like her entire life force from her body. Why was this happening to her? To this day she couldn't fathom it. She didn't tell anyone. Not even her doctor when he'd informed her in his clinically cold tone.

"You're pregnant Miss Ardat." Doctor Ramos told the 24-year-old.

It didn't register at first. She had to get him to repeat it. What the actual fuck? Lili had thought as she sat on the hard plastic chair in the doc's office. She'd only gone in about her sleep deprivation. No way could she be pregnant. She hadn't had a relationship in over a year. No male part had been near her in 14 long dry months. If only. She tried to remember; wracked her brains in case she'd conveniently forgotten some drunken fumble in the last six months. None came to mind because it never happened.

What was this, the immaculate conception? She asked him again, hoping against hope for a different answer. She'd settle for a "Gotcha" moment right now. But his serious face never broke into a smile as she'd wanted.

"Are you sure because my cycle is like clockwork and right now it's normal?" she said almost under her breath like it was some dark secret.

"Unless you have two hearts, then the sounds I can hear are definitely a foetal heartbeat. The urine sample you submitted last week also confirms it. So congratulations. We'll organise a scan for next week but you're about six months along like I said."

Congrat-U-Fucking-Lations? No! No, this was definitely not a congratulations moment.

His final words echoed in her head as she headed along the sterile corridor, passed the coughing, wheezing and infectious waiting room patrons:

"You've passed the 24-week gestation period, Miss Ardat, so a termination is out of the question."

All the way home she fought her brain. On the train she tunnelled into her memories, trying desperately to figure this out. It felt like her head had a locked file she had lost the password to. The answer was there but she just couldn't access the information. How many nights out had she had in the last six months? Money had been tight recently so there'd not been many. There was last week with... No, too late. Think back, she thought to herself. When was Susie's birthday party? That must have been around that time. Had some guy spiked her drink and taken her off to a room upstairs? You hear about that all the time and the girls never even know. Steve Owens had been staring at her all night. Just standing in the corner by himself and staring at her with those squinty eyes. Oh God, please, no. Don't let it be him.

Lili burst into her cosy little apartment without stopping to close the door and ran straight to her laptop.

"Come on, come on."

The old laptop took an age to boot up. She scrolled through the files to her diary and counted back the weeks to Susie's party. "Eighteen weeks. Damn." She whispered.

At least if it had corresponded with Susie's party she'd have a suspect. She continued backwards through her diary until she reached the entry that sent a freezing tingle down her backbone. That night! That night was six months ago! What was she thinking? How could it have been that? It wasn't even real. She thought about someone drugging her somehow. Was the dream just her during a drugged state? Maybe Steve had followed her home from the party. No, that wasn't until later. She shook her head. A drink. That was the most reasonable thing to do right now.

Lili headed into the kitchen, found a half empty bottle of cheap vodka and poured herself a glass. She took a mouthful and swallowed. Her mother's words echoed in her head at that moment. "Alcohol never solved anything Lili." Fuck that! You never got yourself pregnant with a ghost baby mother. She threw back the whole glass and poured herself a top up.

Half an hour later the bottle was dry and Lili staggered into her bedroom. She slumped onto the bed and her comfortable duvet and slipped into that place between sleep and drunken unconsciousness.

She woke sometime later in the dark. It was night time, that much she could discern. Why had she drunk so much? She didn't move, couldn't really. Just go to sleep and perhaps it'll all be over tomorrow. She knew there'd be a day of hangover Hell, but who cared right now?

A noise caught her attention and she lifted her head a little to look into the darkness. It was a noise she recognised from that night. A sound like someone or something dragging their feet over the carpet. Then the fear. It filled her body like nothing she had ever experienced before. That ice cold fear; paralysing. Her body didn't move. She clasped her eyes shut. It was back. Was she dreaming again? This felt real… just like the last time. Her breathing came in short gasps as the foot scraping drew ever nearer. The cold. It was like being in a freezer. She pretended to be asleep. What else could she do? She couldn't move. She couldn't even open her mouth to scream.

Then the fire on her belly. Five fingers of intense heat burned into her. The hand of someone, something, was touching her right where the growing foetus was. It sensed she was pregnant. No, it knew she was.

She thought her heart would pop out of her mouth, it was beating so rapidly. Dare she look? She had to see. She had to see if it was the same as before. Like last time. She had told her friends about it when it happened and after googling it had discovered something called sleep paralysis, where you are dreaming but it feels like you are awake. That's what she thought had happened. She hadn't been able to sleep after that night. No amount of sleeping pills would send her off. That's why she'd gone to the doctor. It had been the most terrifying experience of her life. It had been so real. So damn real. And now it was happening again.

She could still feel the heat of the hand on her belly as she squinted towards the figure. At first it was just a dim outline in the darkened room. She widened her eyes to see more clearly. Then the eyes looked at her. Those black eyes. Even in the dark she could make them out. They were black but they seemed to glow from the shadows. Staring right at her. She let out a scream...

Aaaaaaarrrrgggghhhh! It was coming. The thing inside her was tearing at her. This was no ordinary baby. It was too big. How could she get this out of her? She just wanted it out now. Where was that ambulance? She'd told the operator she'd left the door open; for the ambulance crew to just come in. Apartment 1013. She screamed again as a snap of thunder and a flash of lightning shook the room.

"Help me! Somebody help me!" Lili begged through her tears.

She could feel it pushing its way out; tearing her as it did so. Her back arched, almost lifting her off the bed. The bed sheets pulled taut in her clenched fists. It hurt her so much she was unable to make a sound any more. Her pain threshold had been reached long ago. Now she was just numb. Numb with pain and fear. Alone and at the mercy of this thing inside her. She could feel another bout of pain coming fast. She panted and braced herself for another round. Then she was pushing, deep and hard. All she could think was: Get it out of me! Get it out! And then relief as she felt it slide freely out.

Lili's slender body relaxed. She released her grip on the crumpled duvet and sank back into its softness. Finally it was over.

A thud, and a cry like never before. A vile, whistling shriek. The baby, the thing, had fallen to the floor. Slowly Lili inched her way onto her elbows to see. Blood covered the sheets between her legs. The umbilical cord trailed over the edge to the floor.

Then she saw it. First a bob of a darkened head appeared just above the bottom of the bed. Then slowly more of the head. Dark, black, leathery skin. The same as the other one in her dream. Then a pair of black pupils blinked at her. The same eyes. All shiny and piercing. There was evil in those eyes.

Those staring eyes sent a chill through her entire body. Lili dared not move. Two clawed hands grasped the bed sheets and it hauled itself up with ease. This was no defenceless newborn baby. This was alert, intelligent, able to stand on its feet. Feet which bore talons like an eagle. Quick as the lightning flashing outside her window, the newborn sank its teeth into the soft flesh of her bare foot then sat back to wait.

Lili shrieked and kicked out at it but very quickly she found herself losing movement in her limbs. Her whole body became paralysed in seconds, just like that night. When she was helpless, the creature padded forward and, clasping Lili tight in its talons, proceeded to rip at her flesh.

Lili could do nothing but let it happen. She couldn't even scream. This pain was worse than giving birth to it. It literally tore strips of flesh from her body and devoured it, licking its lips with a long, thin, serpent-like tongue. Droplets of blood pattered onto the duvet as it feasted on her creamy flesh.

Very quickly it had removed all the skin from her body. Her torso glistened red with blood. Then a noise in the hallway and hurried feet. The creature turned to listen a moment before dashing for the window and opening it wide. A pair of leathery wings stretched out and beat and as the door burst open it was gone, disappearing into the rainstorm.

The two male ambulance crew froze at the foot of the bed, unable to understand what they were seeing.

Lili gathered her final strength on this Earth and uttered, "Don't save me."

True Fear
by G P Eynon

You don't comprehend true fear until you have your own children.

That was the most profound quote I had ever heard... Until my children went missing.

You don't comprehend true fear until your children go missing.

Now that's a lot more profound.

Our two young daughters disappeared at some point during the night. A night when they were desperate to come and sleep with us like they did so many times before, but on this occasion I made them go to their own beds. I don't recall why.

They weren't there in the morning.

I thought they'd gone downstairs for breakfast, but they weren't there either. Or in the garden. Or playing in the cellar. It wasn't until my wife, Mary, and I had searched the house three times over that we knew they really were gone. The police got involved, of course, but to no avail. The case was declared unsolved and we never saw our little girls again. That was five years ago.

Every single day of those long five years we searched for them in one way or the another: online, outside, en-masse, in vain. And every single day, another small piece of us disappeared with them. We somehow managed to maintain our marriage, even though being apart was always a relief. We somehow managed to remain living in that house, even though being away felt like a release. Nevertheless, an urge to be at home nagged like a persistent compulsion. Our misery held us to that place; we had to stay in case the girls returned. What if they came back and we weren't there? What if they left again? What if some clue to their whereabouts was delivered through the door? We couldn't stand to be in this house. And yet we remained.

Every year, on the anniversary of Lucy and Gemma's disappearance, we would attend our own private vigil. These vigils followed pretty much the same routine: a visit to their untouched bedrooms accompanied by an obbligato of anger, tears, disconcertion, and pain.

But this year was different.

This year our grief triggered... something else.

A smashed plate was the ominous signal to set this night in motion. Nothing unusual about broken crockery, except this particular plate had been a favourite of Lucy's, our missing five-year-old. She'd decorated it on a family holiday six months before she went missing and would eat off it whenever she could.

For the last five years, however, that plate remained tucked away at the back of a cupboard, along with the abrasive memories. Now it had found its way out and lay scattered over the kitchen floor.

Inexplicable as this was, our attention was snatched away from the broken plate as the computer turned itself on. Popping into life, it began cycling through photos of Lucy and Gemma; the photos we most cherished; the ones the girls loved to look at when they were... when they were still here.

"Did you do this?" asked Mary, assuming I'd set it up.

"No. Did you?"

"No."

We reverted to silence.

Then came the voices.

At various points during their absence, we'd both heard the girls laugh and cry and argue and sing, but we knew this to be a cruel trick of our desperate, grieving minds. This time it was no trick. These young voices sounded oh-so-achingly-familiar, and yet they were foreign, distant and full of angst. But more than that, they sounded angry; an anger aimed at the parents who allowed them to be taken. We could both hear them, but could never pinpoint them. They'd be downstairs when we were up. Always in a different room. There, but not there.

Then, just like that, nothing. Not a peep. Everything went quiet once again.

We checked the household electronics to confirm they were off, including the computer. We checked all the locks and all the windows. They were tight. We were safely locked in.

As was typical on this night, our home choked under a shroud of sorrow. But this was different. It was darker. It was real. It was terrifying. But why could we not leave the house? What compelled us to stay? Of recent years our home had become a place of misery and a place of loneliness. It was now becoming a place of horror.

True Fear

Neither of us were afraid of ghosts. Perhaps, somewhere deep in our twisted souls, we even welcomed them? Maybe.

We went to bed.

It took us both an eternity to relax, but eventually the cold embrace of a lonely sleep began to take hold.

Mary sat bolt upright.

There was a scream; a scream of such distress and such horror that any scrap of good feeling remaining within that house vanished. That scream was inhuman, but at the same time, all-too-human.

It came from the cellar, that much was obvious, but neither of us were in a hurry to go and investigate. We had no desire to move at all. Until this point there had been no genuine fear, but the scream changed all that. I somehow dredged up the nerve to stretch out of bed and peer around the doorframe onto the landing, half expecting a vision direct from hell.

There was nothing.

This was all in our heads. It had to be. Those years of shared depression and dismay were finally taking hold. But holding was an act we'd not engaged in as a couple for a long time – and tonight was no exception. We rolled our separate ways and connected with our individual concerns and emotions.

A crash erupted from next door in Lucy's room, followed seconds later by a thud in Gemma's loft room above us. Mary still didn't move, but I decided to go and have a look.

In the middle of Lucy's room was a fallen box with her Barbie dolls spilled all over the floor. Bending down to pick them up, I noticed many had the hair ripped from their heads and a number were covered in mud. I didn't stay to put them back. And I certainly didn't go up to Gemma's room. Instead, after a brief look around downstairs, I climbed back into bed, praying this night's anguish was over.

It wasn't.

I heard something run up the stairs. Something slight. Something small. Something delicate. It was a sound we'd been desperate to hear for the last five years. But now it sounded... wrong. The footfalls were too deliberate.

There was a brushing against the banister as if a hand slid over it. It moved along the landing towards our room and I could hear floorboards squeak as weight was applied. This time I did not possess the courage to look around the door. Like my wife, I just lay there, closed my eyes and took a deep breath. This wasn't real.

A smell of decay entered the bedroom.

From out of the gloom, I felt a figure climb onto the bed. Small and frail, it resembled the body of a five-year-old with skinny arms and soft skin. But it was cold… so very cold. I froze as it manoeuvred itself between us, while Mary groaned and rolled away.

Finally daring to move, I curled an arm over the space I'd just felt our little Lucy climb into, only to find it suddenly empty.

That was it. I sat up. I was going downstairs. I needed a drink.

A silhouette appeared at the foot of our bed; the silhouette of a nine-year-old.

This figure was not conjured by the waking stab of a fitful sleep, and I definitely wasn't dreaming. This was real. The outline looked exactly like Gemma. But Gemma wasn't with us anymore. And she wasn't nine years old anymore.

I said her name.

She moved.

She moved around the bed and made to climb in with Mary.

Complete darkness cloaked the room except for a ribbon of orange streetlight leaking through the gaps in closed shutters. The figure crossed to Mary's side of the bed, and I watched as the covers rose and then crumpled. I wasn't sure of it was Mary moving, or…

"Mary."

"Mmmm?"

"Mary, wake up."

Her response was a tortured sigh.

Then I felt that cold little body once again, on the other side of me this time. It wriggled until it was nestled against my back. I could feel a wisp of soft hair touching my shoulder and hear the laboured breathing of a small pair of lungs. That smell of decay became stronger.

"Mary." I whispered.

"Mary!" I whispered again.

Nothing. She wasn't there. In her place was a lump under the covers that slid towards me.

I didn't know what had happened to Mary, but in the bowels of my heart I was aware an exchange had just taken place. I was caught

True Fear

between a nine-year-old's body to one side of me, and a five-year-old's to the other. Both cold. Both dead. Both alive. I couldn't move.

And yet it wasn't a physical force that clasped me in place; this was a restraint of a different kind. Closing my eyes, I surrendered to whatever was holding me fast in this bed, my fear now at its peak.

This fear, however, was not born of what lay beside me — nor what may lay ahead of me. It was a fear of not wanting to sleep. This night was the most surreal, most strange, and most scary night of my life, but I didn't want it to end. I'd no idea what these things lying next to me had in mind, but I knew I didn't want to be parted from them ever again.

I wasn't quite sure what to be afraid of. But I was afraid.

And in that moment I realised:

You don't comprehend true fear until your children go missing... and then come back to you again.

Five Days
by Susan Mayer

Faunique™ is a miraculous new natural product brought to you exclusively by MaNatura. Made from the secretions of the Faunus freshwater snail, its transformative qualities are GUARANTEED to firm up aging skin with one single application. All your fine lines, wrinkles and blemishes will completely VANISH in only FIVE days!
Forget surgery! Apply Faunique now, and count the days to a new you.

Day One

I'd practically skipped home from the Luxe Bazaar, I was so excited. Stupid, I know, but when you're 48 and back on the dating carousel, age is definitely the enemy. I could still feel a prickle of shame at handing over a week's wages for such a tiny jar. But, what the hell – it was cheaper than a facelift.

Looking at my wrinkles in the bathroom mirror, I smiled. I did! I actually smiled at my crepy, blotchy, sagging reflection. Somewhere beneath the surface, beneath nature's vandalism, I could still see my younger twenty-something face. In less than a week, that face was going to be back on top. Up yours, nature!

I unscrewed the lid. It had a strange evocative perfume – not unpleasant and not synthetic, but difficult to pinpoint. It smelled of wetness and darkness and hollowness. Like being inside a cave. The directions said to apply the face mask just before bedtime, using the enclosed applicator, and to leave it on the whole five days for it to fully work its magic. Genius in a jar.

The gel was transparent and syrupy, yet also kind of firm and spongy, like it couldn't decide whether it was a liquid or a solid. Then again, it was bound to be unusual; every pot contained 'one hundred and fifty concentrated Faunus secretions'.

I slathered the snail snot over my face and neck, covering my lips, and nudging it as close to my eyes as I dared. I used every last drop, wishing I had a bucket-load more for the rest of my body. This stuff

Five Days

defied gravity! It didn't slide or drip or move at all, and it set fast, like jelly.

As I lay back in bed, careful not to smear the pillow, I thought about how I'd almost missed the Faunus stall at the busy market today. Set back a little from the main route, I must have walked past at least twice without even noticing it was there.

It was just sheer luck that the Faunique pot fell off the stall when it did and came rolling towards me.

Day Two

I was at the mirror again, scrutinising my reflection. For about the millionth time. Pointless really, as the face mask had turned an opaque grey, and I couldn't actually see my own skin beneath. I dabbed at it lightly with my finger. It felt a lot tighter now - almost like it was clinging on! And it had definitely got busy: my whole face was tingling with active stimulation, like space dust on the tongue.

I decided there and then to accept Becky Akhtar's invitation to her stupid reunion. Just to see the look on their haggy old faces. Ha! And there was no chance any of her clique would have got their hands on it; the guy on the stall, Lou, said that Faunique had only just come on the market.

Lou wasn't the usual kind of person you'd expect to sell beauty products. I've seen many an Avon lady in my time, and none of them have ever had rectangular pupils. These novelty contact lenses! So much for the eyes being windows to the soul. He was wearing a headscarf too, over what seemed to be two fat dreadlocks. Maybe it was a religious thing. Who knew. By contrast, his suit was impeccably dapper - really suave and stylish, and made of a brown pelt-like fabric that I'd felt an overwhelming urge to stroke whilst he was talking. I'd managed to resist, but boy, was it distracting.

Apart from Faunique, the only other product on his stall was Faunesse; a lotion also made from Faunus secretions. They were clearly on to something here with the snail stuff. I asked Lou about the difference between them, apart from the price (the Faunique gel was five times more expensive!) He explained that when the snail sustains damage to its shell, it instantly secretes a restorative substance. When it's a slight crack, a small amount of low potency fluid is produced to fix it. However, when the shell is thoroughly broken, which effectively kills the snail, it secretes in its death throes an abundance of highly concentrated fluid which has unbelievably potent skin repair qualities.

Lou offered me the choice: an affordable lotion, which would probably take up to ten years off my appearance, without any torturous snail death. Or: a stupidly expensive gel, containing the trauma-induced secretions of one hundred and fifty crushed snails, guaranteed to firm up my skin and eradicate all wrinkles and age spots fast and forever.

Why was he even asking? They're only molluscs. We eat meat, don't we? To me it was a no-brainer.

Day Three

When I woke up I couldn't open my eyes. My eyelashes seemed meshed together. I touched them and could feel that the upper lashes were stuck to the gel on my lower lash line. Only the gel wasn't a gel anymore. It had dried and hardened, like clay. Well, that wasn't on the information leaflet. I scratched and picked at it, thinking it would come away like a scab, but it wouldn't budge. I felt a yawn building up. That's when I realised I couldn't move my jaw either.

With my eyes glued shut and my mouth stuck open, I reminded myself of a baby bird, all nest bound and needy. I called Marie on speed dial; she could just about understand me, and yes, she could come over. What a discovery - I was a ventriloquist!

"Wash it off!" she said, for about the fifth time since she'd arrived. My sister was very 'no nonsense'. I shook my head again.

"Give me one good reason!"

I braced myself, actually relieved that I couldn't see her, and showed her the receipt.

Once she'd calmed down, she checked it for contact details. Nothing. She went online to look them up. Again, nothing. Not a single mention anywhere about a miracle gel that claims to eradicate every single wrinkle in only five days. And nothing about the company either. I let Marie guide me to the bathroom.

It was clear, after about ten minutes of hot towels and scrubbing, that the Faunique wasn't coming off. Deep inside me, a stubborn nugget of hope excreted gladness. Maybe this is what's meant to

Five Days

happen! Maybe the product is so new that the internet hasn't caught on yet!

"Maybe you should go to hospital," said Marie, the voice of reason. "Imagine if you'd slept with your mouth closed."

*

Until they knew more about the face mask, the doctors were keeping me in an isolated 'tropical diseases' unit. A bit over the top, I thought, but at least I could see again; they'd snipped through my eyelashes. I hadn't applied any Faunique to my upper eyelid, so I could blink too. Bonus.

In the evening, just to be on the safe side, they gave me a plastic insert to keep my mouth open, and coated my eyelids with a barrier film. Tomorrow they would get the test results back and then they'd work out how best to remove the Faunique.

As I drifted off, I could feel the face mask working on my skin. A hot, itching, almost effervescent feeling, while on the surface it was cool, rough and inert: the lava beneath the crust.

My tears slid over it, pointlessly.

Day Four

Marie was waiting for me when I woke up from the anaesthetic. It took me a moment to come round. I touched my face; it was smooth now and hard, like slate. She said they hadn't been able to remove it; the Faunique had fused with the muscle tissue attached to my skull. Marie looked grim as she passed me a mirror. I gasped for air. The Faunique had darkened even more to a matt gunmetal grey, threaded through with veins of copper brown. The beauty of it was lost on me.

Then she held up a picture of a snail. It was a Faunus and its shell was identical to what was on my face. I couldn't even begin to consider it. I felt a tremor in my arms. When I looked down, my whole body was shaking. I heard a constricted howling scream and saw Marie lunge at the emergency button. Then I realised the screaming was coming from me.

*

Susan Mayer

The sedative made me feel hazy and distant, but I could still tell what everyone was saying. The police had made extensive enquiries, but not one single trader had seen either Lou or his stall. They'd all said that the place I'd described was just piled with empty boxes and had a goat milling about amongst them. Apparently, stallholders often brought animals to the market; they attracted custom. So no-one had thought it the least bit unusual.

Day Five

It must have been the smell that woke me. Dank, damp, subterranean. So strong I felt flooded with it. I reached up to touch my nostrils. My fingers found only a smooth, hard curve. Then both hands were fumbling, searching for any recognisable feature. But the Faunique had grown into a solid rounded shell, over my mouth and eyes, covering my entire face. My heart clenched. I felt for the edges. Oh god, no. The Faunique had spread. Over my hairline, down my neck and throat.

A swell of panic charged through me. Get out! Get out! I clawed at it, pulling and scratching, thrashing, kicking. Suddenly, pinned down. My arm, gripped. Punctured. Seconds later, a flat numbness packed out my skull like polystyrene. Someone touched my hand. Marie?

"Evelyn, I am Doctor Munro. I am monitoring your situation. You are absorbing oxygen through the shell, so you're still breathing, as such, but this becomes difficult when you're distressed. Do try to remain calm." There was a knock at the door. "One moment please."

I heard her walk away and talk to someone, but their liquid voices bled into one another. I caught odd phrases: "harness it", "military applications", "unlimited funding".

The doctor returned.

"Evelyn, this morning we made a small crack in the carapace which produced a substance that was able to heal the fracture within minutes. In order to make you better, we need to look at what this substance is beneath the shell. If you agree with this, please raise your hand." I hesitated, wondering if Marie was still here.

"Evelyn? Do you understand?"

I raised my right hand.

"Good. Thank you for your permission."

What? But I didn't...

Five Days

"We have a government advisor here who has promised you will receive the very best treatment available. Plus any additional cosmetic procedure you want. Really. Absolutely anything, completely free of charge: facelift... stem cell therapy... anything. To help you with your recovery."

I couldn't think. My mind was sludge. Where was Marie? I waved my hand and mimed writing. If they'd just bring me a pen and some paper...

"Yes, of course, Evelyn. Don't worry. Your sister can sign all the documents for you. We will begin pre-op immediately."

*

Someone was holding my left hand, rubbing it gently. Then, a firm press. I reacted to the pain without actually feeling it. A cannula.

"Evelyn, nice and still for me, please. My name's Lou – your anaesthetist for today. You might remember me."

His voice close to my ear.

"And between you and me, I overheard Doctor Munro say that they won't stop until the whole shell is thoroughly broken. So, don't you fret. Soon, it'll all be over.

Count backward with me, please. 8... 7... 6..."

A Change Too Far
by Adam Millard

I woke this morning to discover something new. No, not the scales; they were there yesterday. This morning I found a tentacle. Purple, slimy, serpentine, peppered with suckers. I can move it with thought alone, control it with remarkable dexterity. And now, for some strange reason, I can feel the ocean beckoning me, can hear it plaintively reaching out for me; its call is almost enough to overpower my craving for flesh, though not quite. Nothing, it seems, can stifle that ineffable hunger. I'm hoping for a visitor at some point; a salesman, perhaps, or the cantankerous old man from downstairs, come to complain about the animalistic mewling or the water soaking through my carpet and trickling inexorably down his garish flock wallpaper. Now *that* would be a real treat. I would devour him whole, pluck his powdery, desiccated bones from my unnaturally sharp teeth and enjoy every second of it. I'm ravenous, and this odd new appendage looks in need of sustenance.

The Sugarloaf and the Red Shoes
by Marie Gethins

Perhaps Demi Ledoux was too beautiful for her own good. She definitely was too beautiful for the good of others. Each morning she brushed her black curls, kohl lined emerald eyes, gave the reflection an air-kiss. People dropped their chins when she walked down the street. Crop tops displayed toned abs, a navel ring bell jingled as she swayed her hips. At night she hit the most radical New Orleans dance clubs.

Demi could bounce, dribble, twerk and body roll better than anyone. She sashayed onto the dance floor, melding with the music. One by one, men and women tried to dance with her. She judged them within four or five beats. Some managed to break out of the circle before she turned them away, others came close enough to touch her, and a lucky few managed to grind against her.

Sometimes she'd pull one into a dark corner to allow exploration of her body: they nibbled earlobes, roamed over breasts. She ended the encounter if the candidate reached inside her jeans or lifted up her skirt. "Mama told me to save the Sugarloaf for someone special," she said.

One night, Demi alternated between rumpshaking against a handsome boy and shimming her chest towards a petite girl. The song ended and she decided on a bottle of water. She pushed her way through the crowd. Before she could pay, a man in a luminescent suit slid a five dollar bill towards the barman.

"Thanks," Demi said, taking a sip, scanning him from shoulder to heel.

"My pleasure. You're a good dancer."

She laughed. "I'm not good. I'm the best."

"That's easy in The Big Easy, honey. You want a real challenge, try this." He put a glossy dance reality show ad on the bar.

Demi looked up, searching the crowd, but the man had disappeared.

When she got home, she filled out an online application form, uploading full body photos and headshots. She didn't worry about her dance routine or music selection, but knew she needed an exceptional pair of shoes. Shoes the camera couldn't ignore.

Demi searched dance shoe stores across New Orleans. They carried the same shelf stock, boring footwear filled their special order catalogues. In the final store, she screamed at the clerk that she needed something unique. The clerk whispered he knew of a place in the French Quarter.

"It will cost you."

"I don't care about that. Where is it?"

He scribbled the address onto a scrap of paper. "Be careful," he said.

Tucked away in a dim alley off a twisted side street, she spied a large shoe-shaped sign: *Les chaussures personnalisées*. The display window glowed. Hand-crafted satin heels sat poised on puffy cushions: azure, lemon, cerise, viridian. Forehead against the glass, her breath fogged the view. She rattled the locked door, stomped her foot, groaned to the sky.

She pounded the door, her throat growing hoarse. Then a beam of sunlight hit the doorframe and she noticed a tiny gold doorbell. Ear to wood, she heard it chime deep inside the building. She pushed it again. After the third time she heard footsteps. Locks clicked and snapped, the knob turned and the door swung inward.

Demi expected a proprietor as ancient as the area. Instead, a man in his late 30s opened the door.

"Yes?" A foreign accent she couldn't place.

"I'm looking for dance shoes. Something extraordinary."

"Then you've come to the right place." His lips stretched, revealing dark gums and iridescent teeth. He waved her in. "Please, sit." He indicated a gilded high-back chair.

The shoe designer measured her foot; his long fingers stroked her instep, massaged her toes. His tongue darted in and out, and his eyes narrowed when he touched her. She squirmed in the seat. Although she hadn't intended to tell him about the dance competition, the words flowed out. He tested style after style.

"There is a very special design, the Lady Ella. I think they suit you. Would you like to try them?"

The Sugarloaf and the Red Shoes

Demi nodded.

He took a tiny key hanging around his neck and unlocked a mahogany cabinet. Placing a gold shoe box by her feet, he smoothed tissue to one side, and offered up a red satin shoe. As he fastened the buckles, a tingling crept from her toes to her thighs. Music filled her head. She danced around the room. "I know I'll win in these shoes."

"They may cost more than you are willing to pay."

Demi fell into the chair, panting. "I don't care. I have to have them. How much?" She took them off, running her fingers along edges.

"They have hoodoo magic."

"Hoodoo, voodoo, whatever," she shrugged. "I want the shoes."

"You'll be victorious, but you must pay the price." He leaned against the counter. "Let me touch the Sugarloaf."

"Seriously, how much do they cost?"

"No money. I want to touch the Sugarloaf."

Demi pictured herself on stage: a disco ball trophy, a confetti monsoon. She slipped the shoes back on. The tingling returned. Her feet tapped out a new routine while she watched.

"A touch? That's all you want?"

"Yes."

"Ok, but just one touch."

She took off the shoes and wrapped them in tissue. The designer guided her out of street view. She closed her eyes, his fingers crept up her thigh, manoeuvred around cotton and lace. Faces inches apart, she felt his breath on her cheek. He smelled of peppermint and patchouli.

He stroked her gently, and she sighed, happy about her Brazilian wax the previous day. A single digit entered. Her lids fluttered and she pushed his arm away. "Enough," she said. He laughed and raised his finger to take in her perfume.

The competition passed in a whirl, her frenzied feet followed unfamiliar choreography. Demi progressed onto the Semi-Finals. Posing for promotional photos, she struggled to keep still. When she took the shoes off, light shone through the soles.

Demi returned to the French Quarter and asked if he could repair the shoes, but he told her it would be impossible. She sobbed. He escorted her inside.

"What will I do?" "Be calm, my praline. I have another pair of Lady Ella's."

She squealed. "Are they my size? Let me try them on."

He drew out the key. Another gold shoe box appeared, the shoes a perfect fit. The tingling began again, but more intense. Her feet tapped, slid, hopped around the room. She grabbed the back of the chair, eased herself across an arm. Her feet continued to tap and kick. Hands clamped on the armrests, she told him to take off the shoes.

"I must have them. What do you want, another touch?"

He smirked. "No, no. For this pair, I want to taste the Sugarloaf."

"Not in a million years."

"Fine." He took the box and opened the cabinet.

"Wait." Demi bit her lip. "Just once?"

He nodded, tongue tracing his lips.

"One time, that's it. I mean it."

He propped her against the counter, his styled hair disappeared beneath her skirt, and fingers helped her step out of cotton and lace. His fingers explored, traced her edges and opened the Sugarloaf. His tongue snaked in. She quivered; her navel ring jingled. She pushed his head away. He laughed through fabric folds.

The Semi-Finals yielded more glory. At the end of the show, she continued to dance: spinning, leaping. The host chuckled at her excitement, spoke of the dead-heat between her and Gia from Kansas City, urged viewers to phone-in, text or vote online.

Demi grabbed one of the crew, begged him to remove the shoes. He tried but her swollen feet pressed tight against the fabric. "Cut them off!" she said. He struggled to hold down her wriggling calves while he snipped each shoe in half.

"Aw, your pretty little feet all swollen?" Gia lifted a shoe half, swinging it over Demi's head. "Better hope you find decent shoes before the Finals. See you in two weeks."

A few days later Demi returned to the French Quarter. The designer opened the door, leaned against the frame.

"I watched your performance, truly remarkable," he said.

"Did you vote?" Demi folded her arms across her chest.

"Come now, I think I've helped you enough already.

"The shoes…ah…the shoes are gone. I need another pair for the Finals."

The Sugarloaf and the Red Shoes

He clicked his tongue.
"Do you have another pair of Lady Ella's?"
"I might."
"Stop screwing around. Do you or don't you?"

He waved her inside. "I have one more pair of Lady Ella's, but they are very potent."
"I have to be the best. I need the shoes."
"Well then." He opened the cabinet and took out another gold box.
Demi waited for him to place them on her feet. Instead, the designer put the box on the floor beside her.
"Don't open the box until the performance."
"But what if they don't fit?"
"They were meant for you, but their magic is extremely strong. Are you certain?"
He offered his hand. Demi sighed. He led her up the stairs. A four-poster draped in swaths of white dominated his bedroom. He pulled back the duvet, patted the mattress. It crinkled, reminded her of candy wrappers. She closed her eyes, imagined applause, and let him take the Sugarloaf.
Afterwards, she watched him strip the blooded sheet and zip it into a plastic bag. He packed the bag into a shipping carton that contained three gold shoe boxes.
"What are you doing?" she said.
The designer smiled. "Never mind, *beignet*. Off you go. Remember – keep them in the box until right before you're announced."
The night of the Finals, Demi asked the crewman to help after her performance. She put on her red shoes just as the host finished his intro. She began to sway. Her tempo increased, she danced faster and faster. The band leader's baton became a flash of white. The audience ahhhed, cameras struggled to follow her across the floor. Spinning, leaping, hips swinging. Her stomach lurched. She closed her eyes. Legs weak, she collapsed. Her feet continued to tap and kick. As the final note sounded, the crewman carried her away.
"Wow, the amazing Demi Ledoux! How about that Tarantella sequence at the end?" the host said.

Off set, the crewman held her turbulent feet. He tried to cut the red shoes in half, but the satin embedded into her flesh. He snipped, a pile of red shreds grew beside him, cradled her bare feet in his lap.

"Oh sweet thing, we've got to get you to a hospital. You've broken all the bones in your feet."

"Never mind that. What does the scoreboard say?"
"They may never heal right."
"Shut up idiot. What's my score?"
He looked up. "No one's even close. You've won! You've won!"
The crewman leaned in for a kiss. Demi locked an arm against his chest. He shook his head, dumped the shreds and left.

On the shoulders of two shirtless male dancers, Demi cradled the disco ball trophy, squares of light drifted across the audience. On her third lap of honour around the studio, Demi saw Gia fishing out shoes pieces, pushing them into her bag. She grimaced, then kissed the trophy, and lifted it over her head. "It's MINE."

Gia slapped the old wooden door and gave another fifteen minute sustained assault. "OPEN UP." The designer peered out. She held up red satin shoe pieces held together by glue and tape.

"You're effing hard to locate. I put together the sole to figure out this place's name and it still took like forever to find it."

He moistened his lips, eyed her from crown to feet. "Nice white co-ordinates. One could say you look almost vestal."

Gia sighed. "I'm not here for style tips. I need dancing shoes, special shoes. Shoes that will help me WIN."

"Then you've come to the right place. I have just the pair for you, they're called the Lady Demi, but they may cost more than you are willing to pay."

Paper Cuts
by Kim Rickcord

Clack clack click, clack clack click, fingers on the keys don't miss a trick.

The computer breathed white light over her face in the dark. Night was the best time to write, locked into silence and the black box of her bedroom. A cigarette hung twitching from her lips. They were Richard's brand.

Klara lay back on her bed and took out the razor she kept in her pocket. The blade sliced silver through her skin, first sharp, then scarlet. In blackness she bled gently, where no-one could see, not even she. Only last week, on her seventeenth birthday, had she cut herself for the first time.

The envelope of her skin opened, her body spelling secrets in red.

*

Saturday morning metamorphosis. Become the person you've been hiding away all week. Black your eyes, red your lips: put your own mask on.

Klara stood smoking in front of the library, shivering in the embrace of an aged black fur coat. An east and west wing flew from a central tower, the mouth of the entrance muttering with shuffling footsteps and book-stamp stomps. Taking a last fag drag, Klara let the lipsticked stub kiss the pavement. She walked to the door and was eaten by it.

'Paper Cuts' by Alexander Mann was in the West Wing, seventh floor, stack twenty. Floor seven was just a narrow corridor with bookshelves that disappeared into the dark. She found shelf twenty and turned the timer on the side to illuminate it for thirty minutes. Click.

It was there. Klara took it, remembering that Richard's fingers had touched these pages. He had told her to come here to read it.

"How does it feel when you write?" he'd asked.

"Like...a secret."

"Then the books that feel like secrets are the ones you should read."

"Tell me a secret then."

"Well, having read the first chapters of your novel, I would recommend... something that was always my secret. I think I'm the only person to have ever read or touched it." He'd smiled a crack and scrawled the title on a scrap.

Sitting on the floor, she opened the first page. The book gave a sudden ecstatic crackle; an electric kiss to her fingertips. Surprised, but smiling, she began to read.

It was a story told using the words you keep hidden beneath your tongue. The first word was "Cunt," the opening chapter detailing a man slipping his lips over his wife until she came. It was about a couple fucking and murdering their way across Europe in the nineteen-thirties and was as dark and beautiful as blood on snow. The woman wore a flapper bob and strings of rubies around her throat. Her husband had the same name as the author and was also a writer. And, a magician.

The wife lured a governess home, plied her with opium and tied her up. Using red thread, she embroidered a sentence around her throat, as though it were a necklace. When her husband Alexander came home, he ran his fingers over it and said, "That is the most beautiful sentence ever written."

As Klara read, she felt the discomfort of the scab on her wrist, disguised with a piece of red satin ribbon. During the French Revolution, there had been a fashion for wearing red ribbons around one's neck, in mimicry of the guillotine's slice. She liked that.

A third of the way into the story, the light clicked and her vision snapped black. Pressing her own spine against those of the books, she touched herself. Her tongue slicked her lips wet, her throat seized and her voice wrote "Richard" on the silent page of the dark.

With a pen, she wrote these words on a slip of paper: "I need to feel your breath on my cunt." Putting it inside the book, she closed the cover.

The front door spat her back out into the waiting arms of her boyfriend, Josh. The teenagers sat kissing and getting stoned by the river until the light faded and they couldn't see the other's face. Then they kissed some more.

Paper Cuts

*

On Monday an idea occurred. With a needle and red thread she embroidered words over her underwear; the kind you keep hidden beneath your tongue. She dreamed of Richard reading them.

On Wednesday, she saw Richard in the corridor at school, laughing with Miss Parker, who was wearing a dress so tight she resembled a boa constrictor digesting its lunch. Richard – Mr Sirin – was Klara's English teacher; the kind you call by their first name and smoke with in the parking lot. He was a six-foot-two three-piece suit of casual cigarette burns and gin stains. Perfection.

Klara stared at him. He kept talking to Miss Parker.

On Thursday night, Josh took her back to the side of the river. He put his hands inside her bra and she felt every tiny hair on her body stand up, straight as needles. Klara realised he couldn't see the words she'd embroidered for Richard there. They remained secret.

On Friday, Richard handed her essay back with a plus next to the A. She waited after the lesson, but he simply left the room.

*

Saturday morning metamorphosis. She stood before the mirror holding a pair of scissors and began to cut her hair. Slashing a blunt fringe and a jaw-length flapper bob, she turned her face geometric, her scarlet lips curving in a U. Each eye was an X. Richard was her drug, and he had turned her eyes hollow.

In the library, the book lay splayed on the floor, as though it had been reading itself. She knelt and checked for her note. Gone.

Trembling, she found where she'd stopped the week previously and began to read. Alexander took a lover. His wife killed her, cut off her hands and made them into gloves. She ran her fingers over his body and said, "This is her skin, but it is my touch." In return, he carved his initials over her heart.

Then, two-thirds of the way in, a note flew from the pages, landing in her hand like a butterfly. The typed words said: "Touch yourself. When you come, that second will belong to me."

She came, let her second be erased, and was glad it was gone.

In return she wrote: "Your name is a scar on my heart." Getting up shakily, she looked outside from the window. Josh stared back up.

Josh's parents' house was a tall Victorian gentleman wearing pince-nez skylights. His attic bedroom looked through them. He left her there while he got beer. Looking under the bed, she discovered a box filled with objects like bottle tops and ticket stubs. They were all things she'd once touched. On his computer she found photos of herself, taken from below her bedroom window.

Had Josh left the note? He'd clearly been following her.

He brought the beer, and proceeded to sing a song he had written for her on his guitar.

*

Klara stayed in bed all week, feigning sickness. On Friday, she summoned the courage to go in. Richard was leaning against the wall outside the English department, talking to Miss Parker. Seeing Klara, he mouthed, "I'll catch up with you," to the boa constrictor.

"You ill? Didn't see you in class."

"Yes. Ill."

"I... like the hair."

She touched her fringe and he noticed the red ribbon around her wrist. Feeling in his pocket, he flicked two cigarettes into his mouth from the packet. Lighting them both, he passed one to her. His fingers grazed hers. They were so blackened from marking essays that the tips seemed bloody with ink. Dragging on the cigarette, she tasted the ghost of his lips.

"I need to know...What is the most beautiful sentence ever written?"

He smiled. "Different for everyone, I guess. For me, it has a heartbeat, a rhythm that feels like it's always been written inside you."

Richard made his mouth into a zero and a ring of shuddering silver smoke floated into the air. Klara put her finger through it and was married. It dissipated, killed by her touch.

He looked away, dropped the butt onto the floor and left. Klara felt sick. Picking up the stub, she pocketed it. That night she put it between her lips and touched herself, dropping it onto her chest when she came.

Paper Cuts

*

Saturday morning metamorphosis. She looked into the mirror. The real Klara looked back.

She turned the timer on, illuminating the book on the shelf. Tearing through the pages, she searched for a note. Hers was gone. Nothing was in its place. A tear cracked her face.

Klara began to read again. The couple found a seventeen-year-old boy and cut him to pieces with a set of silverware given to them by his mother. They made him into a roast and fed him to his parents, dripping his blood into their champagne to make it pink. After the party, they fucked on the floor. Kissing, they bit off the end of each other's tongue and ate it.

The light timer ticked down. The final words of the book were gripped by speech marks: "Klara, it is your name which is scarred on my heart." The lightbulb detonated. She dropped the book. It opened onto the floor. Every page began to turn. Behind her, the novels on the shelves began to expand and contract like lungs. The book on the floor gasped for air, the pages breathing her name. Its paper began to fold, first creating an origami face, then a hand which dragged itself across the floor. A man broke free from the binding, cracking his spine as he went. Klara stood, pressing herself against the stacks, her heart punching her ears.

The man's face was a shifting page of words; the pupils of his eyes formed entirely from the letters K-L-A-R-A. He put his hand to her neck, slashing five paper cuts there. Putting her hand on his chest to push him away, she suddenly flinched. The letters "KR" were inscribed there. His kiss? Like a letter written in secret and never sent, whispering in her mouth. It cut her tongue to shreds. He fucked her against the book stacks, her lungs in time with the breathing volumes behind her.

"Oh God, I'm going to – "

BLACK

She let her lips part, the orgasm subsiding. Slowly, she opened her eyes. Richard? He had blood all over his mouth. Putting her fingers to her own, she felt blood streaming there. Across his chest, she saw her initials carved. They were in an oak-panelled dining room, the remnants of a meal around them. A set of silverware shimmered sharp on the table.

And she realised she had fallen into fiction.

*

Richard looked at the book on the floor. He had seen it all, playing spy from a crack between two hardbacks. It was hypnotic, watching her with the version of himself he had created; the Richard of the page. Alexander – for that was Richard's real name – had written the book some years before, pouring his desperate cravings into it, creating the perfect woman. In Klara, he had finally found her. The book itself was a grimoire; inherently magical. Each word her eyes had eaten had drugged her until she was his. She would never grow old now; locked into the second she had given up to him forever. She remained the perfect fantasy.

He picked up the novel, gently stroking the cover. Finding Klara's name on the last page, he kissed it.

*

He found Josh smoking on the steps outside. "Is Klara in there? We were supposed to meet."

"Didn't see her. Sorry."

"Shit." Josh slumped, dejected. "I just don't get her."

Alexander watched the smoke curling from between Josh's lips and thought how it would feel to take him to bed with Klara. Then dismember him and suck the meat from his fingers.

"If you really want to know what she needs, there's a book you could read..."

Insects
by Caroline Slocock

"It might help if you talked about it."
The psychiatrist spoke softly, careful not to upset the girl. This was the third time they'd met in this white, windowless room. The third time they'd sat on plastic chairs, bolted to the floor, facing each other across a plastic table, also bolted to the floor.
The girl had yet to utter a single word.
"Maybe we could talk it through together," she offered in a gentle tone.
The girl kept her head down and picked at her fingernails, which were ragged and torn and sore-looking.
The woman watched her steadily.
"I know something terrible must have happened. Something that made you do this."
Pick. Pick. Pick. As if she were trying to remove a whole layer of skin.
"I'm going to tell you what I think happened, and you can correct me when I'm wrong. Alright?"
The girl shot her a quick look, her eyes wide and brown and fearful behind a black fringe, her face as white as her shapeless gown.
"I think the woodshed was his special place. He kept his toy soldiers there in a tin. His sports magazines were on the shelf. There was an old bottle of ginger beer."
Pick. Pick. Pick.
"It was dirty though. The window was so filthy you couldn't see through it. And the floor was just bare earth, no covering on it."
Pick. Pick. Pick.
"I think he'd been taking you there for a long time."
Pick. Pick. Pick.
"You were young when it started, no more than a child."
The girl's nails were beginning to bleed now, the blood bright and startling against her pale skin.
"I think you'd probably been planning this for some time."
The girl sucked the blood away. Kept on picking.

"The thing I'm not clear about is, how did you do it? The wounds on his body were all the same. Small and ragged and very deep. At first the police thought you'd stabbed him with a skewer. But it looked like something had been... screwed in. And screwed out again."

She heard the girl's breathing quicken, saw her small chest rising and falling beneath the white gown.

"And all the wounds had a neat circular mark around them. A ring. We've been
trying to work out what kind of... tool you used."

The girl's mouth was moving now, a strange snarling and slackening movement that revealed her small yellow teeth.

"But most of all, I'd like to know why. Why did you make those 87 wounds?"

"SO THEY WOULD GO BACK IN!"

The sound of her voice was shocking, the dry rasping scratch of a soul in pain.

"They?" asked the woman softly. "Who are they?"

"THE INSECTS! The bugs and the maggots and the lice and the flies and... I tried to kill them but they were everywhere, these crawling piles of... legs and wings and eyes... in my mouth and my hair and my skin and... I tried to kill them but they just kept coming back!"

She was becoming hysterical now, her eyes wild, her bloody fingers scrabbling at her arms. The door opened suddenly and two attendants rushed in.

"I had to make the holes so the insects would go back inside him where they came from! 87 holes for the 87 times."

She saw the syringe then. Screamed. The cold needle pierced her skin and the liquid entered her body and she went limp.

The woman stood, knocking her papers to the ground.

"Is that really necessary?"

But the attendants were already carrying the girl out.

The woman stared helplessly at the door. She felt shocked. Guilty. Unsettled.

She carried this feeling home with her like a lead weight. Stood for a long time gazing out at the black garden, trying to understand.

Insects

Finally, she took a bottle of wine from the cupboard. A glass. Opened the drawer.

The silver corkscrew lay there, the screw long and fine and deadly at the centre of its circular frame. The levers at the sides designed to withdraw the screw with the cork attached.

Or the flesh.

Itch
by Karen Heard

Everybody has experienced some level of infestation. It's something we're told to accept as part of our lives now. It pains me to remember how we acted when we first saw them. They started out as funny yellow caterpillars. We grew flowers that attracted them! You could buy pots: three for two at B&Q. Even when we learnt they were killing off spiders we didn't care. Who thinks about spiders on a daily basis? The mutation was so slow we gave away our panic by microscopic degrees... until the blisters started to appear on our skin, and then, under our skin, the writhing started.

They violate you secretly – that is their real horror. Their hairy bodies so slight you easily miss them against your skin, their anaesthetic-laced spikes so small they slip between the spaces in your nerve fibres, so that you can't feel them inside you until it's too late. You get an itch... just below your shoulder blades... on your scalp... on the fatty part of your thigh... trickling up your calf... sometimes you try to ignore it, knowing the other thirty times you scratched, there was nothing there, but this time you look to see something *is* moving up your calf, but moving up the wrong side: from the *inside* of your skin.

They like the warm places – the nub of your neck, curve of your hip, under your breast – crawling into your sock, or worming their way through the material of your skirt whilst you're busy rubbing at some other part of your body. Then they carry on burrowing inside you, whilst you sit and drink wine, worrying about the bills, or read a story, totally unaware you're being invaded by the gnawing maggots.

It's only by week four that you can see the grubs growing below the surface of your skin, wriggling backwards and forwards like babies stuck in swaddling, as they dig their tunnels with thousands of tiny teeth. That's the worst part: the itching of their tiny bites, the burning of the histamine in their spit, the caustic spikes of their bristled bodies scrubbing the inside of your skin, becomes a constant distraction, consuming everything. That and the fear you won't catch them soon enough when they hatch.

Itch

Everyone tries to cut them out too soon the first time, even when the doctors say you must wait – you just can't help yourself – can't bear to keep them inside you. You only do it once though. If they're still in maggot form, when exposed to the air, they dig down instantly before you have a chance to grab their tails, like a needle piercing suddenly through your nerves, shooting to God knows where. If you wait too long after they hatch, however, their new razor sharp wings cut a hundred different ways out of your body on their own. That's why you don't want them deep inside you.

I've been lucky. All I have is a hole in my arm, plugged up with gauze, where I cut too soon; a few slashes up my leg, where I was diligent; and one tiny, worrying dot I've recently found on my cheek.

I don't even remember where the bite came from, as is often the way. I suspect it was from staying out a few minutes after dusk last week. One tiny slip is all it takes. You can take the same risks ten times without harm, and then when it all goes bad, you can't explain why you did it.... until next time you're out...

I keep concentrating on the inside of my neck... my jaw... my ears... like I'm listening out for pain... twinges, or anything. Maybe it's just a mosquito bite on my cheek? When something like this happens you forget you're still vulnerable to other things, like spots, ant bites, heat rash... Mr Richards still has cancer... the girl down the road got meningitis last week and we had to move streets, but somehow a regular disease doesn't seem as bad as what's going on with the weevils.

*

I went to the drop in centre yesterday. I'm only allowed one more false alarm, but the gnawing worry got too much. I had to hold onto the arms of the waiting room chair to keep myself from rushing out... sitting near people writhing in their seats, the rasping sound of them scratching whilst eyeing me with the same caution I was them. Some of them had rubbed through the layers of their skin, and were now scouring their nails unconsciously over raw scabs.

They say the paranoids all end up giving themselves blood poisoning. I tried to ignore them, fight off the instinct for empathetic scratching, but the man next to me had the real infection all over his arms. I could see the livid yellow creatures scurrying about under the surface of his skin as he clenched his jaw and stared at the floor. Even though his maggots looked nowhere near bursting, I didn't want to sit next to him. He smelled sour – like yoghurt. I got up to leave, but then they called me in.

The nurse felt my spot, clucked and told she'd be more impressed if there was movement beneath the skin.
Impressed!

She took X-rays but said monitored exits on the face were rarely successful, so it might not be worth it – I'm not sure if she meant the procedure or sending the X-rays to the experts. Then I was out on the streets again, trying to remember everything she had said. I wish I'd asked more questions now... or that she'd said less. I'm sure she thought I was paranoid. I hope so.

*

Six weeks now since I noticed the mark and still no signs of movement. Maybe I'm wrong and am okay, but I feel phantom itches all over my body now. My skin is raw through my anxiety.

Yesterday my results were due, I phoned, but it rang three times so I quickly hung up. I haven't yet called again.

We're going to try to get away tonight. Just a few of us. As previous carriers, there's nowhere sterile we can go outside the cordon, but we can go further inside, to where everyone first fled from. It sounds counterproductive, but we figure if we go to where the worst has already happened, the weevils will have nothing left to feed on. We try not to mention our plan to others, we can't all go to the same place... or the creatures will follow the food supply.

The leader, John, has them all over his back, I haven't seen them, but his shirt writhes in the most hideous fashion as he walks in front of me. I can't bear to look at it, it reminds me too much of what could be going on somewhere inside my cheek. I don't know why he's coming with us in his current state, but he says he has to do something. I'm told that the creatures eat twice their own body weight each day. That's like a person eating 300 pounds of raw mince. The temptation for him to cut them out must be massive. He asked me if I would help when the time came. I said yes, but have been thinking about leaving the group ever since. I still have time to decide.

Itch

I haven't said this to anyone yet – I don't want to make it more real – but I can sometimes hear the sound of scratching in my right ear. I've tried to look inside it with mirrors but there's nothing there. I poured water in, just to be sure, and when my hearing muffles, the scraping actually gets louder. I am afraid that... I do not want to say.

*

Things are less in control here towards the centre. People no longer go about their normal business; you only see them on the streets when they are running to get somewhere. Most of the people here are covered in bandages; many limp or are missing limbs. You can see lesions where they have held hot knives to their skin to relieve the itching where they could not cut.

I wish we had not come.

On the side of streets we see animals with their stomachs burst open. The holes steam in the cold air, and creatures crawl in and out of them like makeshift termite mounds. The air here smells faintly of carrion and flies crawl everywhere.

I cannot sleep at night anymore. Maybe it is just the fear that comes with my night-time thoughts, but in the quiet of dark, when I can concentrate more on the terror, I'm plagued with the idea that thousands of creatures are scampering across my brain. I feel an almost irrepressible urge to scream for someone to cut open the top of my head and get them out. The rustling sound in my ear is constant now. I hear high pitched noises, like a radio tuning in and out. I sometimes think it is them talking to each other, and that their voices are like screaming.

I like to think that I am mad... or if I am not mad, that I will quickly turn so, to escape the horrible reality of things.

*

At the heart of the contagion zone, in what was once the Grand Theatre, we find a giant writhing mass of pungent flesh, like a tumorous cocoon. Those that are already here avoid it. Everyone thinks we have found their Queen. We look at ways of setting it on fire, until we see the tattoo on the membrane holding them together and we realise it is a person... or at least was a person at some point. It is now just a bag of writhing creatures. We back away slowly. The things inside are bigger than any we have seen so far.

Shrimp big.

The thought of how the skin still holds together horrifies us. If we listen closely we can hear a faint gasping sound, like a whimpering balloon, or a person struggling to breathe.

We had been told to expect, with the mutations, that the ones that kept the host alive the longest would start to prevail. At the time we thought that news was good – that it meant we could live longer. Stupid!

*

I've been getting calls from the hospital on my mobile. I looked up the number and it's the research department calling. I keep letting it ring but they keep trying. I accidentally opened an email from them and it had a picture attached to it. The picture is called *head_x-ray_stage_4_advanced.jpg* I have not looked at it yet and closed the email before I could read the message. When I think about it, I feel a dark pricking sensation creeping across my brain.

Perhaps it is just fear. Perhaps it is not. But it feels like… it feels like…

I find myself in front of the mirror, with a razor blade in my hands, turning it over and over in my fingers, sometimes forgetting what it is for or why I am stood there. Whenever I think of using it, I feel a hundred fears piercing through my head all shouting, *Don't,* but another core part of me feels strangely calm, and right now, that part of me is Queen. It is, perhaps the only moment I have been calm, since I have no more future moments to worry about. A perfect moment, spoilt only by the pain as I make the first slice across my scalp. I slash deeper, and feel the stab of the horrors burrowing away from the light and tell myself this is not happening. As I cut down after them, I feel my mind opening up, and imagine that they are flying out of me, like winged evils bursting from an opened box, and I feel that I am cured.

The Retribution of Elsie Buckle by Lucy V Hay

"Elsie Buckle had a calling: murder."

The woman in Billy's bed snatched Billy's cigarette from his nicotine-stained fingers and pressed it to her own lips. Billy sighed: women always wanted to talk after sex! Well, he would go along with it. *For now.*

"Great intro." Billy chuckled as annoyance flashed across the face of the buxom woman lying next to him in his makeshift bed in the garage.

"Don't interrupt." There was something amusingly prim about her manner, at odds with what they'd just done ... And what Billy would like to repeat.

But the woman expelled clouds of smoke, instead. "You ever hear of Elsie Buckle?"

Billy shrugged. He didn't care. "Maybe."

His gaze moved over her curvaceous form. The woman was in her late thirties, Billy guessed; perhaps a little plain under those panda eyes and caked-on panstick. Nevertheless, she knew how to make the best of herself. Long flowing hair, generous breasts, a teeny-tiny waist and ample bottom. *Yup, not bad at all.*

But Billy's bedfellow's eyes narrowed. "No, of course not. She made sure of that ..."

Barely listening, Billy reached out and cupped one of her full breasts with his big hand. Irritated, she slapped it away.

"... What did I say?" Her voice was like a school ma'am's.

Billy held his hands up. "Sorry, miss. Carry on."

The buxom woman rolled over in the tangled and grubby bedclothes, extending her shapely legs in the air. "Women are thrown away so readily," Elsie said. "Married off to the first people who'll have them, by fathers anxious to be rid of them."

Billy took the cigarette back, leaning against the bare garage wall. A chill stole its way down his naked skin. "There must be worse things?"

The woman arched a single eyebrow. Billy smiled, exasperated: *Carry on!*

"So, Elsie ended up stuck with Jack. He was as good a husband as you might expect, which isn't saying much. *Men will be men*, Elsie always said. So she'd bided her time ..."

"... Elsie is you, right?"

"No!" The spell broken again, the woman sat up. She grabbed her dress and pulled it on over her head, hiding her curves from Billy's sight. "My name is Rosa."

"My mistake." Billy rolled his eyes, grinding the cigarette out on the concrete garage floor.

He grabbed his trousers, from the crumpled heap of clothes. Now a repeat performance no longer seemed on the cards, Billy was keen for Rosa to resume, so he might get on with the job she was contracting him for. He'd known her game all along, of course: Billy was realist enough to recognise he wasn't exactly irresistible.

She'd pitched up that evening, face drawn and white, her cheeks tracked with tears. When Rosa shed her coat to reveal her dress stained with blood, Billy was less horrified than intrigued. He knew what would be coming next (*him*). The nature of Billy's business meant women were always willing to put out for him if it would sweeten the deal.

Making bodies disappear was Billy's specialty.

Rosa sighed. "So, Jack lasted six years. Perhaps Elsie had to work up the nerve? She killed him with a hatpin to the heart, after her attempt to poison him went disastrously wrong ..."

Billy grimaced. Still, there were worse ways to go, he knew that: he'd seen enough death scenes and cleaned up after them.

"... They'd lived on a farm back then, so getting rid of Jack's body wasn't difficult. Elsie got her eldest (then aged five) to help feed her father's grisly remains to the pigs."

Billy shuddered at the thought, drawing another sharp look from Rosa. This time Billy grinned, grabbing Rosa's waist and pulling her to him. Perhaps he was in luck after all, because she let him, placing her arms over his shoulders, her generous breasts pressed up against his bare chest.

But disappointingly, Rosa made no attempt to kiss Billy again. "The little girl seemed a bit upset at the loss of her father, but Elsie figured Rosa would get over it."

Billy nodded. Now he understood the woman's place in the story.

Rosa disentangled herself from Billy's embrace. "So, after Jack

The Retribution of Elsie Buckle

came Arthur; then her stepson Martin, and even her own son, Julian. All of them abusive, entitled, smug. *Typical men*, as Elsie would say."

Billy bristled at this second, unwarranted generalisation. "Not all men?"

But Rosa ignored him. "As she got older, Elsie was unable to hold an axe like she used to. Instead, she got her thrills via her beloved younger girls, Germaine and Emily."

"She taught her daughters ... *to kill*?" Billy pulled his trousers on, wondering if he'd been had. He'd heard many a strange tale in the backroom of the garage, but this one seemed a little far-fetched.

"How else would they learn?"

Rosa had a point. Belatedly, Billy realised he'd interrupted again. He gestured for her to continue. *Get it over with.*

"Germaine was a dominatrix. Imagine: torturing men AND getting paid for it! Even better, if she got too excited, getting rid of bodies was easy ..." At this, Rosa tipped an imaginary hat to Billy. Despite himself, he smiled back at her. There was always a demand for guys like him, it was true.

"But it was Emily who was Elsie's pride and joy. A magnet for millionaire bankers and business types, Emily worked her way through a multitude of high-profile men, gaining their assets."

Billy whistled through his teeth with appreciation. "Clever."

Rosa fixed him with a stare. "So, Emily mastered what Elsie and Germaine had not. Poisoning's such a useful dispatch method, especially when there's so many concoctions that defy detection."

Then Rosa sighed, a bitter half-smile playing on her lips. "But Elsie's eldest daughter, Rosa, was a major disappointment. As far as Elsie knew, Rosa had never killed a living thing. The shame of it!"

Billy knew better than to interrupt this part of the story. Women always needed to make their confession. As if words cleansed them of their misdeeds, no matter how terrible.

"Germaine killed a little boy when she was just nine by pushing him out of her tree house, for making fun of her dress. Emily followed when she was twelve, inviting an over-amorous boy to drink a deadly cocktail of berries."

Billy watched the memories flit across Rosa's face. She was no longer in the garage with him, but lost in the past. He felt something stir through him again: surely not sympathy? Perturbed, Billy buttoned his shirt, averting his eyes from Rosa's.

"But Elsie never found any evidence of murder in Rosa's room: no knife; no chemistry set; not even a solitary drop of blood on her clothes! She never stopped hoping Rosa would follow in her footsteps. Then one day, inexplicably, Rosa did."

Rosa took a shaky breath, bracing herself. "Elsie was watching a cooking programme with a brandy one evening. Emily was sitting with her mother, having become a widow for the fourth time just weeks earlier. Germaine was also home, taking a relaxing break from the torture brothel.

"Peering at Rosa – Elsie was far too vain to ever wear her glasses – the old woman smiled, beckoning her to come closer. It was only then Elsie noticed Rosa's tear-stained, tormented face. 'I'm nothing like all of you!' She hissed."

Rosa exhaled, drawing Billy's gaze again. Shame was etched on her features now. "... Except I was, because there was an axe in my hand."

Rosa stared at Billy, still wringing her hands. As so many of them wanted, she craved his forgiveness. She needed him to say, *It wasn't your fault,* or even just, *I understand.*

Women were so predictable.

Still feeling uncomfortable, Billy simply shrugged. Rosa snapped back to the matter in hand, just like that. She wiped the tears from cheeks and reached inside her coat. She pulled out a carrier bag.

"Is this enough?" She presented him with wads of cash, neatly bundled with plastic bands.

Billy cast an eye over them all, checked them. "That'll do."

Moments later, Rosa left Billy's garage, but not before she'd pressed a key for her mother's home into his hand. He assured her he took pride in his work; no one would ever know what had happened in the small country cottage. Rosa gave him a wan smile and bustled out, into the darkness.

Letting himself into Elsie's home later, the tang of blood and shit in the air assaulted Billy's nostrils. Death was something Billy was used to, but loosened bowels and raw terror always made their mark in every murder house. But a job is a job and Billy's pays very well.

Rosa had told him her mother and sisters would be found in the lounge. Billy picked up his buckets, cloths and sprays and traipsed

The Retribution of Elsie Buckle

through to the next room, whistling, protective suit rustling as he walked.

Elsie still sits in her chair. Her dead arms hang either side, a brandy glass broken on the floor. The old woman never managed to so much as stand. Though her body is intact, her head is cleaved open where Rosa brought the axe straight down the middle of her mother's prone skull.

Billy recognises Emily because she is substantially younger than the other two bodies in the room. He also remembers her blonde hair from Rosa's story, though blood now cakes her locks in a gluey mass. The youngest Buckle girl lies face down, multiple axe wounds in her back and shoulders where Rosa had stood over her, raining down blows.

Germaine sprawls a few feet from her sister, one arm extended, as if trying to protect her younger sibling. But that arm is no longer attached to her body. Her forearm severed, it looks as though Germaine then rolled onto her back, only for Rosa to bring the blade down onto her sister's sternum, opening up a gaping wound in her unprotected chest.

So it is not the bodies that shocks Billy. He's seen hundreds, maybe even thousands over the years. It's not even the violence. Though the Buckle house is bad, he's seen worse.

Billy wanders towards the body with the severed arm, transfixed by it. He would have expected a grimace of agony as her death mask. Instead, the woman on the floor's face is peaceful, beatific, angel-like, as if she's been released of a lifetime's suffering.

Because of this, Billy is able to tell that the dead woman in front of him is perhaps in her mid-forties, much older than the woman who'd lain in his bed a few hours earlier. Which means, at his feet, now: Rosa ... The *real* Rosa.

Even before he feels the finger tap him on his shoulder, Billy realises his mistake. He turns, to see his lover. What had she said? *Oh yes: getting rid of bodies is easy.* She'd never really needed him at all.

Billy flinches, knowing what's coming to him, yet unable to do a damn thing about it. He sees the glint of the axe blade in her hand.

His last words: "Hello, Germaine."

SPELLINGS
by K.J.B. Rickards

Would you mind helping out an old fellow?
Would you mind thinking carefully about the following words and how they are spelled?
GAR-NAR-TIC FAL-ON-DER. GAR-NAR-TIC FAL-EEN-DIC. GAR-NAR-TIC FIN-NET.
I realise they are unfamiliar to you.
Don't worry. These are ancient words from a long dead language. Go back and repeat them. Just do it phonetically:
GAR-NAR-TIC FAL-ON-DER. GAR-NAR-TIC FAL-EEN-DIC. GAR-NAR-TIC FIN-NET.
Concentrate on sounding out each individual syllable of each word in your mind.
Do it slowly.
Do it deliberately.
GAR-NAR-TIC FAL-ON-DER. GAR-NAR-TIC FAL-EEN-DIC. GAR-NAR-TIC FIN-NET.
Picture the words as you sound them out. Imagine them in the centre of your forehead, right where your third eye would manifest.
If you wish to, you could repeat them out loud.
GAR-NAR-TIC FAL-ON-DER. GAR-NAR-TIC FAL-EEN-DIC. GAR-NAR-TIC FIN-NET.
Now I want you to consider the words one final time. This time there is one additional word at the end. When you reach it, I want you to burst out into the universe with its power.
Take a deep breath in.
GAR-NAR-TIC FAL-ON-DER. GAR-NAR-TIC FAL-EEN-DIC. GAR-NAR-TIC FIN-NET.
AMEN.

*

For the past few centuries many of your favourite horror writers, from H.P. Lovecraft and R.W. Chambers, through Dennis Wheatley in

SPELLINGS

the nineteen seventies, right up to Clive Barker and Stephen King in the modern era, have enthralled you with tales of the macabre.

But buried in their words and paragraphs is the darkest of magik and the most evil of intentions.

The majority of readers only see the story. Those of us that can truly spell and understand grammar see the deeper purpose to the stories and the reasons for their continued success and popularity. These modern alchemists understand the grammar is from grimoire and that to spell is literal.

In this modern world, with the convenience of mass communication via book and screen, it is far easier to create an active piece of magik to reach around the globe to thousands - and in the case of Holy-wood cinema - millions of humans' consciousness. How many times have you heard or read a character say something akin to, "I renounce Jesus Christ in favour of Satan"?

That's at least once.

As you read it your mind said it, too.

Here you have a tale from a mind, a person, you know nothing about.

Well I'll let you know. I'm an opportunist. What better opportunity is there to spread chaos than to enter a competition with guaranteed readers of the work? As a practitioner of Abramelin ritual, the more people I can collect into my conscious spells, the greater my outcome.

The more powerful is my evocation.

By taking part in this tale, my experiment in spelling, you have helped me bring forth a daemon named Nuada. (Try saying that out loud.)

Not a demon like the Christians' bastardised version of the word. Don't worry about good and evil. Not at this stage. Nuada is a daemon evoked purely to improve my world.

And, I suppose, yours too.

That is if you remembered to sit in a salt circle when you pictured my spellings.

Did you?

Full of Surprises
by Scott Merrow

"Stan, my kids are gonna love this puppy," Mrs. Adamson gushed. "He's so cute and cuddly. And so... I don't know... so spontaneous."

Stan Stanislawski was the owner of Stanimals Pet Shop. "Yep, animals are full of surprises, Mrs. Adamson." He smiled. "Just full of them."

The woman hugged the puppy closely, and it licked happily at her cheek as they left the shop.

When they were gone, Stan locked the door behind them and put the *CLOSED* sign in the window. In the rear of the shop, he opened the cellar door and went down the stairs.

The basement was a jumble of broken cages, empty boxes, and old pet toys. Nestled among this debris was a large table, which held an assortment of stainless steel utensils... cutting utensils. There was also a covered bird cage on the table and a large crate on the floor next to it.

There were customs forms and shipping labels on the crate, and one crudely painted word: "*Python*." Stan pried off one of the slats. Sure enough, a large python was coiled up inside. The bright light made it stir. "Not yet, my friend," Stan said. "I have a couple birds to attend to first." He replaced the slat.

He uncovered the bird cage, revealing two fat, brightly coloured parrots. He grabbed one and held it tightly on the table while he selected a large, cleaver-like knife. With a swift, skillful motion, he swung the knife – *swoosh* – and chopped the bird's head off. Then, with a scalpel, he sliced open the bird's belly. He probed inside and pulled out six round packets, then he chucked the carcass into the trash can beside the table.

He examined the packets. They were almost like eggs. Man-made eggs. Filled with heroin.

This was Stan's real business. He imported exotic critters from around the world. Some he sold upstairs in the shop. But most of them came in "special" shipments, full of small packets of junk.

The python was an experiment. One python could hold as much product as several small animals, reducing the number of shipments –

Full of Surprises

and the risk. Stan was anxious to open it, but he wanted to do the second bird first.

"Okay, birdie," he said as he opened the cage. "Your turn."

The bird squawked. "A-w-w-k. Your turn. A-w-w-k. Your turn."

Stan chuckled. He set the bird on the table, and it pecked at the silvery knives. "So, you like shiny things, eh, birdie? Not for long, I bet."

He held the bird down and raised the cleaver. Just as he started his downswing, CRASH! – a noise from upstairs. The door! Someone had broken in! Startled, he loosened his grip, and the bird fluttered away. "A-w-w-k. Your turn."

He heard footsteps. Then – CRASH! They were trashing the shop.

Clutching the cleaver, he bounded up the stairs. He flung open the door and saw a man – skinny, long greasy hair, bad teeth, obviously a junkie. Stan recognized him at once, a low-life type who had scored from him before. He was hurling things wildly around the room.

"What the fuck are you doing?" Stan screamed.

The junkie turned, startled. He drew a handgun from his belt and fired a wild shot. BAM!! Stan dived for cover then scurried back down the stairs. He hid behind some boxes. The junkie followed.

"Where the hell are you, Stan? All I want is the smack, then I'll go."

Without getting up, Stan answered, "It's on the table."

The junkie took the packets. "C'mon, you got more than this. Cough it up, Stan. I got a gun here." BAM!! He fired another wild shot just to prove his point.

Stan cringed. "There's a python in that crate," he called out. "The smack's inside it. That's how I smuggle it in."

The junkie saw the crate marked "Python." The slat on top had slid off to the side. The crate was empty. "There ain't no python in this crate, Stan. It's empty."

Stan jumped up. "What?!?"

BAM!! The junkie took another shot at him. It missed Stan again, but this time it was close, and with a CLANG it knocked the cleaver from Stan's grip. It flew several feet and landed among the clutter on the other side of the room. "Shit!" Stan exclaimed, as he dived for cover behind the piles of boxes and cages.

"Bad move, Stan," the junkie crowed. "See, I don't need you no more. All's I gotta do is find the snake."

Quietly, Stan inched toward the table. He needed one of those knives. Creeping slowly in the dark space behind the boxes... he suddenly found himself face to face with the python. He shuddered. It was a monster! Maybe twelve feet long.

In a panic, Stan scooted backwards, knocking over boxes and cages. The python slithered slowly after him. Stan stood up and leapt aside just as the snake lunged. It flew past him and landed in a pile of squeaky pet toys. *Squeak-a-squeak-a-squeak-a.*

BAM!! The junkie fired. Wild. Stan grabbed a broken cage and hurled it. It hit the junkie in the knees, tripping him up. He fell, and the gun skidded across the floor.

Stan rushed the table, grabbed the largest knife he could find, and pounced, but the junkie was too fast. He rolled to one side and Stan landed hard on the cold concrete.

Then the junkie was on his feet, kicking Stan's face, but Stan swung the knife and sliced the junkie's ankle. He fell to his knees, clutching the edge of the table for support. With an upward thrust, Stan slashed the knife through the junkie's throat, spraying blood everywhere. The junkie collapsed and pulled the table over with him.

The bird cage slid off the table, crashed into Stan's head, and knocked him cold.

When he came to, Stan immediately became aware of a sharp pain in his thigh. He looked down... and directly into the eyes of the python. Its full array of teeth, seventy or so razor-sharp, rearward-pointing daggers, were buried in Stan's thigh, gripping him tightly as its body coiled around him, constricting.

Stan was completely immobilized, except... his right arm was free. He saw the cleaver, on the floor, inches away, his only hope. He stretched... stretched... it was close... so close. He almost had it...

Then, a flapping sound.

The parrot landed near the shiny knife. It pecked at it a few times, then grasped the handle with its beak and dragged the knife a few inches out of Stan's reach. "No!" Stan cried. "N-o-o-o-o!"

At that moment, the python released its grip on Stan's thigh and slithered up along his body until Stan was staring at it, eye-to-eye. The python opened its mouth and unhinged its jaws. Horrified, Stan gazed helplessly into the huge maw.

Full of Surprises

The parrot released its grip on the knife handle. "A-w-w-k. Your turn," it squawked. "A-w-w-k. Your turn."

Food Bank
by Dylan Keeling

She had known, before they ordered a thing, that tonight was the end. He had begun to shout at her that week; to interrupt her, and comment on what she should wear. But they took their seats, near the riverside view of the London skyline, and she decided, vengefully, not to end it until he had paid for one more meal.

She made it an expensive one: three of the priciest starters, the stuffed lobster, a truffle salad side dish, the cheese-board to finish and, her sadistic *piece de resistance*, the most luxurious wine on the menu, nearly nine hundred pounds. She savoured every mouthful of it, relishing the taste of his evaporating money, before considering him a few moments. His shirt was pink and very smooth; his face was ageing into bitterness, though she had found it attractive at first.

"I've been thinking," she said, carefully. "About us."

"Ugh," he sighed. "Where's this going, sweetheart?"

The woman made a valiant, a heroic, attempt to look apologetic – the maliciousness inside her could not be allowed to show for a moment. "I-it's not working at all, darling. I'm sorry."

Forty-five minutes later, she was standing at a random corner, one of the strange collisions in London between posher houses and the edge of a crumbling estate. It was night, and as she waited for the cab she had called to this strangely familiar address, the word he had spat rang in her ears: *Bitch*.

"Bitch." And why not? With a glow of pride and a full belly, she smirked at the name. A Bitch was nobody you wanted to mess around with. A Bitch was someone who got an expensive meal for free, and went coldly, smugly home alone.

Perhaps because of this confidence, when the diminutive figure moved away from the undergrowth towards her, surprising her, nonetheless a weary, terrible part of her nodded inside: *Okay, bring it on. This is what happens to people like me, in places like this.*

So as the boy casually (oh, so casually!) came to confront her under the lonely streetlight, the woman's heart pounded, but at the same time she felt *ready*, fortified by "plonk" and rich seafood.

Food Bank

The boy, from his small hoodie, only asked, "You all right? Are you lost?" but all the woman heard was menace. She rooted in her handbag for cigarettes, hoping to seem unbothered. The wine surged in her bloodstream, making her fingers clumsy.

"Maybe I can help you," he proffered, eyes dull.

She scanned the empty street as she lit a cigarette. "Most certainly not," she replied. *Where was the taxi?*

"Have you just been to a restaurant?"

At this, she frowned at him. "What I eat is none of your business."

"Yeah." He bit his lip, and clapped his hands together. "You know there's been murders round here."

Of course!

Quickly, like a startled cat, she looked again at the estate name. She had heard it in the news three times this year. "What do you know about murders?" she demanded.

"I know how they did them." He sounded frightened.

It was not clear where the conversation would go or end up – she was beginning to soften towards him, this scared little boy – when a sound of clanking, the deliberate striking of metal against metal in an echoic space, changed everything. The boy jumped, startled, said a single high-pitched sentence, then turned and hurried away to a staircase on the estate, the woman left standing.

He had said: "It's my brother."

She would have simply turned away, relieved, except that the banging continued, and she thought – or imagined – another sound, a high-pitched, rather feeble keening like an animal being tortured.

This wail accompanied the new sound of someone apparently kicking a metal fence at the base of the stairs and hissing, "Would you shut the fuck up, you cockroach!" Unable to decipher what was happening, the woman found herself pulled nearer, compelled to explore as if dreaming.

She picked up pace when the boy's voice called out, "Kim, she's coming! Stop it!" – then slowed at the corner to take in the view.

Underneath the stone staircase was a dark corner, fenced off for maintenance storage. A small figure, a little girl, was inside this fenced area, hitting the mesh with a small, closed hunting knife, held upside down. Her eyes were wide and terrified, and a furious older boy, a skinhead in a fraying pullover, kicked again at the outside of the mesh, seriously rattling it. The girl retreated, whining, between some storage tanks and a rusting porter's trolley.

On seeing the woman come nearer, the younger boy seemed to twitch with a flash of fear. "Kim," he alerted the older boy, who turned and saw her. For a moment the skinhead examined the child behind bars again, taking in how it must look, then he glanced nervously back at the woman – whose rage at what she saw was overwhelming her fear – and fumbled in his pocket.

Before the woman could reach him, the skinhead produced a key. He inserted it skilfully into the gate's padlock, twisted it, unhooked the padlock, then with a shifty glance, ditched the padlock on the stone ground and grabbed the younger boy, pulling him away.

They scarpered, and the woman surprised herself by throwing her lit cigarette at their fleeing backs. "What is *wrong* with you?" she shouted, her voice bouncing off the brick. "You foul boys!"

Turning back, she saw the girl wore a wretched T-shirt that still said "BLING" in faded letters, and had a haunted stare. "Are you all right?" she asked, opening the gate.

The trembling girl raised a hand, and the woman's mouth went dry at the state of the girl's wrist: she was so *thin*! The wrist was like a shrink-wrapped bone, the hand unnaturally large. Her eyes were deep-sunken and her cheekbones sharp and almost white. The poor mite was about six, and skeletal.

"Hello," the woman greeted her, bending down. "What's your name?"

The girl just stared.

"My name", the woman offered, "is Sandra." She hesitated. "You can call me Sandy. That's... what my sister used to call me. Are you cold?"

But what a stupid question – of course the girl must be cold! Sandy looked at her fur coat and then, unwillingly, slipped it off and wrapped it around the girl's bloodless shoulders. "Did *they* lock you in there?" she asked.

And now the girl responded: a brief, miserable nod.

Sandy licked her lips, concerned, thinking. "Do you live in one of the flats round here?"

Food Bank

Another nod; the little girl pointed a spindly finger up the stairs. Sandy glanced up, then nodded, making a snap decision. "I'll take you home."

She was leading the girl to the staircase, marvelling at the thinness of her, when suddenly the girl gripped Sandy's elbow tightly and pointed into the open courtyard, where a mist had begun to coalesce. At first Sandy heard, and saw, nothing – certainly nothing to justify the girl's moaning and frantic tugging at her arm.

Then she saw them. The boys had returned, but with others. Sandy had an instant's heart-stopping vision of some six or seven figures, male, female, all kids, *running* at them, from out of the mist. One shouted with incoherent rage; another, a female voice, called out, "Fuck you, bitch!"

And the little girl was off, scampering up the stairs in terror, wearing Sandy's coat.

No time to get her phone out, no time to hesitate. Clutching her handbag in a death grip, Sandy ran up the stairs after the girl, who hesitated on the second landing to let her catch up.

As they ran further up together, Sandy wondered at the silence. On one floor, the door at the end of the hall shut just as they passed. "Hey!" she cried out, lungs bursting; but the girl had run on and the others were still in pursuit, so she quickly gave up and continued.

Where were the parents of these kids, the authority figures? Where was *anyone*? Several flats had boarded-up doors and windows, and plants had died in pots in most of the halls. One flat on the third floor seemed to have had half its contents chucked out on the walkway, broken bedstead and grease-spotted duvet and all.

In all her life, Sandy had never run so hard, never felt such mounting terror. She found herself wondering what a childhood like this would have made of her, and even for some reason thinking of the suicidal insanity of the human innards when denied sustenance for too long...

She remembered hearing somewhere that the body, in starvation, began *eating itself*; the digestive system literally consuming the meat of the organs closely pressing against it on all sides, and she almost began to visualise what, if anything, would be the result on the human mind...

Almost. Instead, as she reached the fifth floor, the starving little girl she was fleeing with turned to her and, with great seriousness, pointed left, at a door a few yards down the hall.

"...Your home?" she panted.

"Mmm...mmhmm..." the girl nodded, catching her own breath with difficulty.

They went to the door and Sandy started collecting her thoughts. There would be a parent here. She could use her phone. Get help, backup. She drew deep breaths as the girl knocked, preparing herself to speak.

But the door opened and all she saw was a family of children with shattered faces and staring eyes, filthy sodden rags on their backs, reaching for her. About five kids, all under ten, all as stick-thin as the victim who had led her here... the victim who now was pushing her into their grubby, clutching hands.

As they pulled her down, as they ripped at her clothing with ragged nails, Sandy thrashed with her arms and kept trying to wriggle free, but she was outnumbered by the hands undoing her clothes, working her high-heeled shoes off, pulling her blouse over her head, yanking harshly at her bra.

She missed the moment her ringing phone got smashed; she was shrieking, her naked back scraping the floor, watching the skinhead pat the little girl approvingly on the shoulder of Sandy's fur coat. "Nice plan, girl," he pronounced. "Worked a treat."

The little girl silently opened the hunting knife. When a kick pounded into Sandy's belly, some of the rich, expensive lobster dinner inside spurted back up to her throat and tongue, but the little girl paid no attention; she was sawing off the front half of Sandra's right foot. Sandy thought, hysterically: *so this... my death... she... she won't even... speak to me...*

But as the little girl turned the severed hunk of foot toenail-downwards and raised the fleshy, bloodied inner part to her open mouth, she momentarily caught Sandy's expiring gaze, and her eyes narrowed. "Hello, Food Bank," she said.

Silver Load
by Steve Pool

I hate hunting Rats. Other creatures are no problem. I've been bit, scratched, slapped, burned, and infected by just about every kind of monster, demon, or undead thing over the past few years – I was even stung by a wyvern once. Just part of a pest exterminator's job. But wererats – I just call them Rats, with a capital "R" – are different. These creatures make me nervous, probably because they are like us in so many ways.

So my business phone rings and I tell myself to let it go a bit. Work's been slow lately, but I don't want any prospective clients to know that. The Caller-ID number displayed belongs to one Robert Hanley, a bureaucrat down at the Interagency Rodent Extermination Task Force, the City's unofficial werehunter department, among other things. The IRETF only calls me whenever it finds itself short-handed dealing with some werebeast outbreak. We in the business call these jobs "silver loads" on account of the ammo that we use (silver) and the run-around we often get trying to deal with the City afterwards (as in a load of…). And to think that I could have been a priest.

Turns out I knew the place that was having problems: a little mom-n-pop grocery in Murray Hill around Second and 38th. I pull up, and everything looks fine, very peaceful. I knew it wasn't, of course. Beasts will often lay low, waiting for a good moment to hit someone when any potential witnesses are looking the other way. Sometimes the cleverer ones will attempt to lure a potential target into a trap with promises of drugs or sex or whatever.

Knowing how people are, the first thing I do is put a padlock on the front door, because some idiot will doubtless come stumbling into the store at the worst possible moment, looking for diapers or hooch or something, and just complicate matters.

You've got to know your lycanthropes in this job. Everyone knows about Mr. Werewolf. Shoot it with a silver bullet, right? Not actually that easy in my experience, unless you're using a hunting rifle from far away. You'll never get close enough to use a pistol. I find that about fifty pounds of beef is sufficient to pacify them. They won't fetch a stick for you after that, but you can get a lot closer to them.

Wereboars don't hunt; they scavenge. Leave a smelly treat in a cage and they'll walk right on in. I don't know anything about werebears. If we had any around here, I wouldn't answer my phone. A buddy of mine in the business once caught a weregator; told me that it didn't work very well. I guess real alligators are more dangerous. There may be weresquirrels, werepigeons, or werekitties out there too, but I haven't come across any of them yet. Never a dog. Dogs lost their feral a long time ago, thanks to us.

Then there are the Rats. Rats are a nervous, suspicious, dangerously-clever bunch, and family-oriented in the same way that street gangs tend to be. They are also careful, never going into a place without an exit plan, and have amazing muscle-memory when it comes to running away. That makes them especially dangerous ambush hunters. And in case you are wondering, no, they don't shrink down to the size of real rats - it's a Newton-conservation-of-mass rule-law-whatever thing. They remain human-sized and vaguely human-shaped. It's not attractive.

So the owner is waiting for me in the alley behind his store, something I expressly asked him not to do. I mean, where did he think the Rats were coming from? He was very concerned about his "two-fold problem": the damage his store might suffer during the extermination process, and the damage his reputation might suffer if word of this problem got out. I guess he didn't think about the third problem he'd have if the Rats took him up on his offer to become their dinner by loitering in the alley. After he brought me up to speed, I shooed him away.

I was looking for three Rats: two males and a female. The boys had to be brothers. There's no way two unrelated Rat males hang out with a sole female and not try to kill each other. I figured it was even odds that the intruders were running around sporting their pointy-toothed rat heads. It's a foolish myth, probably started by lycanthropes themselves, that they only "change" during a full moon. Their change is an emotional thing, not a lunar thing. Think about dogs wagging their tails.

The hallway immediately leading in from the alley was narrow and grimy. That's real chic décor for my targets, but I knew they weren't responsible. The dry twig of a mop I found in the slop-sink couldn't have seen a soapy bucket in months. There were also a lot of dusty inventory boxes stacked up against the walls. I noticed a few square-

Silver Load

shaped blank spots on the floor ringed by dust halos. Somewhere in the building, probably in the nest, I'd find the missing merchandise.

It didn't take long to spot the Rat hole in the floor that probably led to the nest. Rat holes tend to be impossibly narrow from a normal-sized person perspective, and I briefly thought about that kid in Texas who fell down an oil pipe in the mid-eighties and I shuddered.

The hole was clean and hair-free. That meant they were coming through looking human, probably also naked. Things like shoes and belts tend to get hung up in the rims of Rat holes. They were also likely armed. You don't find that too often with other lycanthropes. Mostly they are just a bite-and-scratch bunch. Unfortunately this is not so with Rats.

I could hear one of them rustling around up front. It appeared to have missed my scent. Thank God for potato chips; they might be the only things more pungent to a Rat than people. I snuck up to within ten feet of it while its head was buried in a bag of Chip-O's. Before I could act, however, it spun around and checked me out with weird red-backlit eyes. It still looked somewhat human – a very hairy and ugly human – and not currently baring its Rat teeth. I should mention something about Rat teeth: they can bite through a two-inch iron bar.

It was faster than me, but I was the one with the gun. I found myself struggling under its smelly corpse when an avalanche of chips and salsa tumbled down on us from the smashed display rack above. I first thought that it had managed to bite me after all until I realized I wasn't looking at blood but spilled picante sauce. I had managed to shoot the Rat cleanly through its still human-looking head.

I crossed myself before standing up. Remember how I mentioned earlier that I almost became a priest? I'd been accepted to seminary and was all set to go when I met Molly. She herself was considering becoming a nun, but I guess we convinced each other that a life spent together was probably better and more fun. So, anyway, I don't think Ratboy wanted me to give it its last rites, but I crossed it anyway. I guess I'm just mean that way.

Brother Rat jumped out and began screeching something, I don't know what. I try not to get involved in a monster's personal problems. I did care that it pulled out a semi-automatic and, judging from the way it cocked the gun, seemed very comfortable using it. I also noted dismally that it was in full-on rat mode – big ears, fangs and all. I managed to scramble behind a condiments island before the Rat sprayed the store with bullets.

I quickly did the math: I had my two eight-shot 9-millimeters, which still had fifteen silver bullets between them, not counting my now-missing reloads; my spare clips were now lost under the bags of chips on the floor. The Rat itself had several banana clips for his semi-auto, each clip having many more rounds than I currently possessed.

The next few moments were ugly. Giant sheets of refrigerator glass panes exploded into nasty shards. Fortunately I avoided getting cut by any of it. I was not so lucky with the fridge contents or the island condiments. Ketchup, mustard, relish, soda, energy drinks, chocolate milk, orange juice, fancy water, and beer sprayed everywhere. I was being marinated and turned into a sticky-sweet appetizer. Worse, I couldn't see through the mess dripping in my eyes, and my hands and feet began to stick to the floor.

Somehow, though, I scrambled up and emptied my pistols in the Rat's vicinity when it stopped to reload. I think being a lycanthrope must make you forget about mortality; except for silver, what can really hurt you? It, as I hoped, didn't even bother to duck. I managed to bury most of my slugs into the Rat and blow its limp body out the front window. It took me a few moments to register with the mess around me before I thought, "Oh good, now the police will come and find all of this." I wasted no time calling the IRTEF. They could explain it to the cops.

I had a few minutes to clean up and look around before the cavalry arrived. I quick-changed in my van and grabbed some ammo before heading back to the hole. There was still a female hiding somewhere, one that most likely bolted to the nest the moment the shooting started. The floorboards around the hole were soft enough to break through when I pounded on them with a heavy sign. Once the hole was big enough, I dropped to the bottom and made my way back.

One of the things I've noticed after ten years on the job is that my senses have changed. I stopped needing flashlights and binoculars a few years back. I don't know if it's a professional thing or it's because I've been infected so often that I've begun to mutate. I really hope not. I've also noticed I get more stares from priests and nuns than from before.

Silver Load

Anyway, I had no problem moving through the dark tunnel. And I heard the monster gasp as soon as I'd dropped to the floor. When I saw it, I think I used some sailor talk that I'd later have to confess; it looked like a young girl, maybe seventeen or eighteen, and pregnant out to about California. This 'girl' was definitely lycanthrope, but her baby might not have been. I couldn't kill either one of them. She didn't know that, though, and took off in a flash after I pointed a gun at her and said that I would.

My life is admittedly strange. IRTEF cleaned up afterwards and held off the police. I guess they recognized these boys or at least their work. The City keeps an unofficial casualty count from these kinds of monsters, although no one there will admit it. These Rats must've been real troublemakers, hence the courtesy. I almost always get stuck with the broom and dustbin afterwards.

I fudged the debriefing a bit. No, there were only two monsters, not three. Yes, the owner was safely away when I arrived. No, I didn't believe there were any witnesses or innocent victims caught in the crossfire. Reality intruded during the meeting; Molly called to ask if I could bring some milk home with me. That kind of intrusion is always okay with me.

Trying on Tobias
by Jacqui Canham

They'll regret this. Wrenching me out of The Lodge, forcing me into a metal tube and tossing me so carelessly into this putrid place. And boy! is it putrid, with all these different-coloured people milling about. I had to sit next to one mid-air while she chewed on her gristly meatballs, mouth open, eyes boggling. I was taught to close my mouth when eating. It's really not that difficult.

I shuffle with the herd, trying not to touch anyone, until we spew out into Arrivals. The striplights, buzzing yellow, are already making me feel queasy, hot around the neck. *You'll see your name on a sign. Go with the man holding it.* Yeah, and I know exactly who 'the man' is. Mister Specialist. Third this year. But apparently this one is 'different' because he practices in 'London'. He'll think he can fix me, of course, find the old 'empathy centre'.

I scan the signs beyond the ribboned barriers. Lots of them. *Welcome to the Big Smoke, Katrina Jenkins... Here for Mr Bushanjee... Congratulations Team Dulwich U R The Champions... Doctor Hogarth for Stephen Burrows...* Excuse me? Who the fuck is Stephen Burrows? It's Steven. With a 'v'. What a fucking arsehole, getting my name wrong. You need to start showing some respect. I've a good mind to...

I scrutinise him, this Doctor Hogarth. Sarcastic smile, dull-eyed, tweedy. Just like the rest. He'll live in a 'character property', natch, with 'stressed floorboards' and 'exposed brickwork' (million pound hovel). He'll have a dog (fleas). And he'll be waiting for 'Stephen' to approach him, reporting for fucking duty, but little does he know 'Stephen' has just given his escort the slip. Well, not the slip exactly. The escort is having his luggage searched and there is no way 'Stephen' is gonna hang around waiting for him. Anyhow, there's something round here I find far more interesting than Doctor Hogarth.

She's standing some way back, with a neutral expression on her face, not grinning like most of the idiot Cheshire Cats round here. Her hair is dark and her skin white. An excellent juxtaposition of tone. Coffee and cream. Her glasses are thick. But best of all, she's small. Fragile. And she's holding up a sign for 'Tobias'.

Trying on Tobias

"Hello," I mumble.
She focuses on me. "Sorry?"

"I'm Tobias."
She's staring at me now. Maybe she's met Tobias before, or seen a photo, or been given a description. Well, if that's the case I'll walk away. I might even introduce myself to the goofy doctor.
"Tobias." Is she flushing around the cheeks? "I've been dying to meet you."
She's been dying to meet me.
You've been dying to meet me. That's nice. That's...
Your car is cramped inside and there's an irritating creak every time you change gear. You keep taking little glances at me as you drive. What are you hiding under that woollen dress? A skinny neck I bet, tiny shoulders, crushable hips...
"How was the flight?"
How was the flight, you say?
"Alright."
"And the food? Getting better these days d'you reckon?"
No, I don't fucking reckon.
"Yes, it was adequate."
There's not much of an aroma to you, is there? From this distance anyway. Maybe close up you'll smell a little creamy. Perhaps vanilla notes.
"I hope everything will be to your liking, Tobias."
"Thank you. I'm sure it will."
A half-smile from you. Feeling more comfortable around me now are you?
"Have you been to London before? For work?"
"No, I haven't."
So, it's Tobias the businessman, is it? Tobias has a seminar in the City tomorrow morning and you're putting him up. You're greedy like that, exploiting newcomers to your city by renting out a room in your posh house. More fool you.
"Though it's not really relevant is it."
"What?"
"That you've never been to London."

Why are you smirking? What's so funny about that? And why is your car so stifling? It's disgusting you can't be bothered to put air conditioning on for your guest. You're a rude bitch, aren't you!

That crawling feeling is back under my skin and my blood's pumping too fast. My meds are still with the escort. Shouldn't matter. As long as you don't upset me. I mean, I chose you, so you'd better treat me with respect.

*

I was hoping for something a little more 'Gucci'. You live in 'London' for Crissakes. But this is a dump. At least we have nice lamps in The Lodge, not solitary light bulbs hanging from the ceiling. Can't you be bothered getting a lightshade? And, Jeez, the stench of damp is catching my throat and there's no escaping from it because your flat is in the goddamn basement and there's no air. You're gonna pay for this. Why are you gesturing at that sofa? It's full of holes and I know there'll be something living in the fabric, but you want me to sit down on it. No way. I'm staying standing.

"You'll never know how much I appreciate you agreeing to this. I was so very excited when we connected."

Oh were you, now? So it's a blind date, is it? A blind date with Tobias? How predictable. Got him off the internet, did you? Got me off the internet, but no photos swapped to enhance the anticipation? Plenty of photos of you in here, though, aren't there? Little Miss Prissy riding a horse, sitting in a café with mummy and daddy, collecting some trophy for some tedious achievement. Dull, dull, dull, dull, dull.

"I suppose it's pretty niche, what we do. Not something you want to shout about from the rooftops."

Yeah, I'd want to keep it quiet too, you little hussy. If you're making plans in advance for a fuck. you can't complain if someone gets carried away can you. I'm thinking blindfolded, handcuffed, pinned down on that table over there. Better still, I'm liking the look of that cupboard under the sink. I reckon we could squeeze you in there and nail the doors shut.

"Down there."

Trying on Tobias

Down there, you say? Alright, down there it is. All these stupid little steps. I didn't know basement flats had cellars. Perfect for what I have in mind. You'll be wishing you'd never taken my word for it. Tobias! As if I'd have a name like Tobias. And here we are in the dark, though there's a faint glow from the candle you've just lit. How romantic.

What are all those buckets? The highchair? That's novel. And those dark stains, splashed up the walls, across the floor? Where have you gone? Trying to tease me, are you? Shall we just get down to business? Let's get down to bloody business. If there was just more light so I could see what I was doing, if I could just get hold of your scrawny little neck and...

Ow! What's that in my arm? A needle?

"Makes it easier, Tobias, when I cut."

"Hang on a minute.

"Like we agreed."

*

"You're coming round now. As I explained to you, the injection knocks you out temporarily as it dilates your blood vessels."

"Wngggg." I can't speak. Can't move my limbs.

"I have to admit, I've never had one before who wanted to be tied *and* gagged, but I'm glad it excites you. Me too. When I cut, I'm going to let your right hand free so you can, you know..."

No. No I don't know.

"Pleasure yourself. Or are you left handed?"

Get me out of this highchair. Why am I tied into a highchair?

"I'm quite overwhelmed to be honest, it's rare to get any interest. I got the idea from that thing in the news years back, you know, the German guy offering himself up as a meal to a cannibal."

Oh sweet Lord.

"But that's tawdry. Our interests transcend that, don't you think? I get upset when people call it a fetish, don't you?" She's pulling something out of her pocket. "It's not a fetish. It's an imperative. There are lots like me."

What are you doing with that scalpel? Playing with it, staring at my neck.

"They usually expect me to use my canines, like in the films, but what a load of nonsense. This is far more efficient, though I warn you I'm not very good at controlling the spurt."

Listen, I need to tell you something. I'm not Tobias, I'm Steven, with a 'v', and you're moving in now with the scalpel and I really need to clear this up. Read the notes here in my pocket. I'm supposed to show them to people when I get the crawling feeling and haven't had my meds. Please read them, please, please, please, you'll see... lots of big words... delusional paranoia, inappropriate thought patterns, uncontrolled association paths, but look again... incapable of following them through, condition benign, not a tangible threat...

You've cut. Is that my blood spurting all over you, all over your snow-white skin? You're saving some in buckets, but your lips are parted, too, and you're drinking. Feeding your face. With my blood. Tobias's blood. And there's no going back. No going back.

Sodor & Gomorrah
by N W Twyford

The whistles sound a bit like screams, Tom thought, sometimes. They were certainly shrill enough.

He had heard them, on certain nights, his entire life. The trains.

Always late at night, when his family slept. Sometimes when it was clear, when the moon washed his bedroom in silver light, and at other times when it rained; the sounds carried through the downpour.

The chugging and the whistles left no doubt: these were steam trains.

But no steam trains ran anymore on the only line that passed nearby, he had checked. Researching the line and its history thoroughly, it had become something of an obsession to him.

His parents had no idea what he was talking about. The services were cancelled years ago, a thing of years gone by. But he knew what he heard, on those seemingly random nights when he discreetly smoked out his window without his parents knowing. His insistence only served to elicit confusion and concern from them, who found his fixation unsettling.

The trains became a topic unspoken, a subject that would not be discussed.

Yet the mystery gnawed at him, and he knew he had to learn more.

That was why Tom waited until his parents were asleep before going out, telling them he was going to stay up and watch the late night film, keeping an ear open for the sounds of slumber.

Leaving the house, he crossed the gentle suburbs and entered the woods past the train station, the entrance winding round the back of a small industrial estate.

Tom made his way deep into Ambarrow woods. He knew them well, having entered innumerable times throughout his life. First on night hikes with the Cubs, then, as he got older, climbing the hill with his friends. They used to play on the rope swing, and, as interests changed, it became a great location to build a fire and get high.

The woods were empty tonight, and he fought off a sense of paranoia, flinching at every sound.

There was one point where the path crossed the railway tracks, the route gently leading down to the railway with a surprising lack of fuss. There was no bridge, markings or precautions; just an understanding that one would cross without incident or dawdling. Tom respected that. It gave him a sense of nostalgia for a time he had never lived in, that he had only seen in films and read about in books.

Alone, he waited by the tracks for the mystery train.

*

Time passed, and Tom settled into an uneasy routine of boredom and, well, feeling a bit weird. It wasn't the sort of thing one told their friends about. In his mind, he figured it was somewhere between stargazing and dogging. It was definitely closer to the former, but that aspect of lurking, even if not sexual, made him feel like he was doing something strange.

Eventually, Tom realised he had wasted his time. All he had achieved was a walk, and cramp in his knees from squatting.

Fuck this.

He got up, dusting himself off and slowly making his way back up the hill, away from the tracks.

That was when he heard it.

The whistle was shrill and pure, cutting through the still night air. It was just like he had always heard, but so much louder and clearer.

Tom ran back to the tracks, and waited.

He saw the smoke first. The moonlight caught it, making it resemble a thick mass of low hanging cloud; pumped skywards with the machine precision that was expected of it.

I knew it, Tom thought, as he waited for the mysterious train to get closer. Steam trains were for exhibitions, for events. For *showing off*. Why would any make their way along the track at this time of night?

He watched, wondering, as the train chugged closer, its sound and movement embracing every cliché of its type.

Illuminated by the moonlight, the train was easier to see now. As it came into view, Tom thought he saw something strange. Everything else was as he expected, but this one detail...

It looked like –

Sodor & Gomorrah

No –
Wait, I think it is –
Oh bloody hell –
The train had a *face*.

Seemingly grey – although in this light, who could say for sure – it wasn't painted on, but appeared to be affixed to the front of the train somehow. It was grossly distorted, its proportions stretched, as if it had once been the size of a man's face, but had been pulled to become something else entirely.

It grew closer, and the more Tom stared, the more he noticed. It wasn't flat; the face had all the contours of one wrapped around a skull, manipulated by muscle. It seemed to smile, he saw, and the toy-like eyes were large and stupid, happily content in its own strange world.

Tom had already stepped back from the tracks as the train went past. For some reason, he didn't want it to see him, as absurd as that sounded. The train whistled just before it went by, and Tom could have sworn he glimpsed the face contort, as if in pain.

Whistles that sound like screams.

Tom looked for a driver, but couldn't see one. He saw the open cabin, and the orange light of the stove burning coal, but no man could be seen within.

The train towed wooden bodied carriages with steamed up windows. Tom could see people inside, silhouettes moving strangely in the gloom. Each carriage contained a different type of passenger, and as the lights flickered on and off, he caught glimpses of them.

Within the first carriage people were eating. Eating was putting it kindly; these people were stuffing their faces, taking entire fistfuls of food and shoving it into their mouths without discretion or dignity.

Inside the second carriage was fighting; passengers attacking one another without remorse, savagely. Bodies bounced off cracked glass, chairs were thrown, and – Tom was sure – he saw passengers wielding cutlery as weapons. The inside of one of the windows was splattered with something dark.

The people in the third carriage seemed to be engaged in an orgy. He first noticed this when he saw hands pressed against the glass, flat palms wiping the condensation as they were forced against them. Tom craned his neck to look within this one and quickly regretted it: the orgy was violent, the figures within moving with an obsessive lust that showed aggression and hatred, devoid of passion. It made him feel sick.

The remaining carriages passed, and Tom watched them all with interest and an increasing sense of disgust. One was filled with people stripping the carriage bare, scrabbling and fighting over everything they could lay their hands on. In another, passengers barely moved at all, stretched out apathetically, as if heavily sedated. The carriages went on, each one distinctive from the last.

Tom watched them all go, deep unease shivering across his skin.

The train moved down the line, slowing, and after hesitating, Tom followed, running down the track in its wake. After a short while, the track split, and the train went down a diverted line, into darkness.

Tom had taken this line scores of times, and never once had he known of a diverted route: as far as he knew, the train went from Reading to Shalford, and that was it. He didn't even know of any other routes that intersected with it.

The tracks shouldn't be there.

Which was why he kept repeating, *You're a fucking idiot*, over and over, in his head. Why that pit of anxiety that grew in his belly went deeper and deeper, mirroring the darkness he was descending into as he followed the train, the only light coming from the ghastly carriages that cast shoddy, shadow strewn images onto the ground around it.

He kept going like that for some time, trying to stay on the sleepers to avoid tripping, when lights came from ahead, and the route opened out. Tom had no choice but to follow close behind; with the edges of the line opening he was exposed, the carriage his only cover.

He was in a railway yard.

The tracks were a spider's web of lines, lit by sickly white light from ancient lampposts.

The yard was *alive*. All over, black shapes with yellow eyes – things that were meant to be men but couldn't be – were at work, but when the train came to a halt, pulling up at a desolate platform, they stopped what they were doing and descended on the carriages in a black mass.

They hauled the passengers out. Those who had been consumed by their desires came out of their trances; some filthy, others bloodied, some naked. Some were all three, and as they realised where they were, what state they were in and what was happening, terror struck them.

Sodor & Gomorrah

A deep, booming voice yelled, ordering the shapes: "All change please!"

Tom had seen more than enough. He wanted to run, but fear froze him into place. If he stayed hidden – even with the shapes only feet away from him – he could remain unseen. But he knew he couldn't remain there much longer.

Fuck it, just go –

He ran, feet moving so fast he almost tripped. Tightness seized his chest and adrenaline failed to carry him anywhere near as far as he hoped –

Keep going, don't stop –

The darkness of the way he came loomed, for once inviting, better the devil he knew.

He was close, almost out, when more black shapes emerged from the darkness, cutting him off. "No trespassing!" he heard behind him, the same voice that boomed orders to the shapes.

The man was well dressed in a top hat and tails, massively obese, but strength radiated from his enormous frame. His face was beyond hideous

The black shapes surrounded Tom, clutching at him, with a cold and firm grip.

He wrestled, but more hands came to grasp him.

"Get off me!" Tom snapped, struggling. He might as well have tried fighting the tide.

"Please – "

"You haven't paid your fare!" the controller of the shapes screamed.

"I didn't ride the train! I followed it!"

"You have caused confusion and delay," the Controller said, "but you will be useful!"

*

Tom woke to wind blowing in his face, which felt strange, tingling, and slightly numb.

It was still night. Everything was a blur around him, and as his eyes focused, he realised it wasn't his eyes, it was everything else.

It was moving. *He* was moving.

The wind hurt his eyes, yet no tears came. He tried to move his face out of the wind, but he couldn't. It was fixed in place, somehow.
So was the rest of him. He tried to move his hands, but they didn't seem to work.
All he could see was the tracks, passing beneath him.
Tom screamed, but nothing came from his throat. Instead, a shrill whistle cried behind him. He couldn't see what it was, but he suspected.
Panic started to overtake Tom. He wanted to get off whatever he was on, but of course he could not.
But underneath the chill of terror was a warmth. Something calm and nurturing stoked in his belly, bringing peace despite the horror he felt.
Tom knew what he could feel burning, what calmed him. It was his soul. The engine was consuming his soul, burning it like coal.
It didn't make sense, but then, nothing did. How else could Tom explain what was happening, what he was becoming?
Except...
He wanted to be called Thomas now. It had a better ring to it.
And the engine behind him, that *was* him, continued to eat into his soul, chewing it around.
But he didn't mind. He didn't mind anything.
All he could think was how he wanted to be a really useful engine.
Chew chew.

The Spider Taketh Hold
by John Ashbrook

You never forget your first spider.

For Pete, his first spider was also his first memory. It had come to him in his cot. White, it was, but casting a dark, angular shadow as it crawled impossibly across the ceiling. It paused over his cot and paid out a thread and lowered itself towards him. Baby Pete had watched with fascination as it had rotated in the air, growing larger and larger. Then, with apparent deliberation, the curious white spider had dropped into Pete's toothless mouth.

His shocked scream brought his mum, still young and vigilant, who pushed a comforting dummy into his mouth and inadvertently blocked the spider in. But it wasn't trying to get out, it had chosen him. It scrambled at the back of his throat, forcing him to swallow... And then it was inside him. Forever.

As was the memory.

Pete didn't have the language to articulate his revulsion or his sense of violation, but it froze him to the core. By the age of ten, he would pray every night to the spider gods not to send any more visitations yet, every night, there would be another arachnid, squatting in the corner by the cornice or feeling its way down the window frame.

Over the years, Pete had done away with countless creatures; the number was certainly in the hundreds. His terror was unreasoning, it drove him, and he couldn't even think of sleep until he'd found that night's spider and killed it, even though looking for it filled him with a dread that made him shake.

The dim bulb in his light encouraged the shadows to spread out from under the chair, wardrobe and bed, transforming his bedroom into a land of foreboding. He would tentatively move books, lift up the curtains or push his pile of comics to one side, while holding a slipper at the ready to deal the death blow. He would leave no hiding place unexplored until he'd found it.

And there was always one to find.

He hadn't dared broach the subject at school for fear of the inevitable taunting but, so far as he could tell, this sort of thing didn't happen to other children. It wasn't the normal way of things, to be visited by spiders every night.

He had confessed his spider crimes in church but had been told to stop being ridiculous, since spiders had no souls, killing a few wasn't a sin.

A few? Hadn't the priest been listening?

As Pete had waited for the Eucharist, he'd prayed for the spiders to leave him alone. As he'd stood there in line, shivering, he'd noticed a spider-web under the arm of the crucifix. It seemed that, since spiders had no souls, God had no influence over them. Or He wasn't listening either.

That evening, with another interloper vanquished and flushed, Pete turned to his bed and threw back the blankets to see a second long-legged beast - as big as any he had ever seen - scuttling quickly (but not so quickly as to suggest panic) towards the shade beneath the pillow. Pete felt the floor shift beneath his bare feet. His teeth bit down hard and the skin on his face seemed to shrink, pulling tight so he couldn't blink. A *second spider*? His hand, still holding the blanket, suddenly felt vulnerable. What if it ran up his arm? Got into his hair? A *second spider* in his mouth?

When the world stopped swaying, Pete became aware of the distance between him and his slippers. He'd kicked them off by the door, thinking their job done for the night. But he had to kill this *second* creature if he were to sleep... Ever again.

What might it be doing under the pillow? Waiting for him, legs bent, ready to pounce? What if it was pregnant? Didn't they have thousands of babies? Didn't the babies eat them? There could be thousands of cannibal spiders in his bed and his slippers were all the way over on the other side of the room.

Decision made, Pete dove across the rug and grabbed both slippers, jumping to his feet ready with both hands raised. Nothing moved.

He felt a trickle of cold sweat run down between his shoulder blades and fought the sensation that something was behind him. Rehearsing the move once or twice, grab and pull, grab and pull, he grabbed the corner of the pillow, turned it over and... The beast wasn't there.

What if it had gone down the gap between the bed and the wall? It could even be under the bed now! Pete looked down at his feet,

The Spider Taketh Hold

vulnerable and bare on the rug, and he clenched his toes as though that were some defence against spider fangs.

He couldn't shift his bed and there was no way he was going to look under it. He couldn't fetch Mum, she'd always told him he was being ridiculous. Tears of frustration began to sting the corners of his eyes. He could always spend the night in his chair with his feet up. That would be okay, wouldn't it?

The spider made his decision for him. It broke cover – actually from behind the headboard. It ran across the wallpaper towards the window, scuttling across a vertical surface in that gravity-defying way that made spiders even more dangerous. Pete was shocked at the size of the thing, of the deathly blackness of it, of the staccato drumming its feet made on the anaglypta. He could actually hear its footsteps.

Fear crossed over into fury. No, he was not going to tolerate a second spider. Pete lunged forward, slamming the slipper against the wall, missing the beast but catching and tearing loose two of its legs. It fell - back towards the bed. A flutter of panic in Pete's mind, then it caught itself on a lifeline and hung, peddling in the air, before scrambled back up the wall. With a determined cry, Pete brought the slipper around, back-hand, and smeared the spider in an arc of black, brown and red across the lemon wallpaper, right above the bed.

Victory!

Short-lived victory.

If there were two, there could be more. What if this meant more spiders *every* night? What if this was God's answer to his prayer? He had built his night-time rituals around the hunt for a single spider. But, if there were two, could he *ever* stop looking? Could he ever close his eyes in the certain knowledge that there wasn't a third beast waiting somewhere to drop into his mouth?

With the remains of the second spider screwed-up in a ball of toilet paper in his bin, Pete reassembled his bed and laid in it, rigid, eyes scanning the landscape of shadows. He couldn't relax but, when his mum came to bed and turned off his light, he pretended to be asleep to avoid a scolding.

The darkness fizzed around him like the static between TV channels and the blood drummed in his ears like tiny marching feet... Marching across his walls. The door to the other bedroom closed and his mum and dad's muffled voices soon fell to silence. He was alone now. Or was he? How could he know for sure?

A floorboard creaked out on the landing. This wasn't unusual, his mum called it "the house settling". Then it creaked again... and again. That was the sound it made when his dad was walking from the bathroom after shaving. But Dad was asleep.

Another tread, another creak, as though something were rocking backwards and forwards on the loose board, as Pete himself sometimes did. Or – and this thought pressed down on him like a weight – maybe it was something with lots of feet treading on the board.

Something solid thumped against his door and, uninvited, a bulky shape pushed its way into the room. Pete recognised the bristling form all too well, but his mind rejected it. The size and the shape were not matched: it was far, far too big...

Pete snapped shut his eyes and became aware of the sound of the shape: every movement was accompanied by the wet popping of its joints, the sound of soft bodies bursting under pressure.

He could feel the creature in his room, approaching, pushing the air before it, air that was chilling and damp and sickly with the stench of decay

The bed tilted and the cold, dead thing heaved itself on top of him. Its considerable weight pressed the bedding down and the boy beneath it. Its ceaselessly chewing mouth chattered and gurgled, its rakes of fangs were sticky with venom which drooled onto Pete's face and his paralysis left him: he began thrashing and screaming, a shockingly loud, keening note of primordial terror.

The huge monstrosity's entire body was a congregation of smaller spiders, a writhing mass of arachnids of all colours and kinds, squeezed and crushed together into eight thick, many-jointed legs supporting a fat, bloated body of spiders all lashed angrily together by a film of tightly-woven web. A spider of spiders. All the spiders Pete had ever killed, all clustered together as one.

Four of its pincers pinned him at the wrists and ankles while its other legs gathered the cocoon of blankets from on top of him and cast them aside, exposing him.

It swayed above him, the uncountable tiny legs over its surface thrashing and thrumming impatiently, scratching at Pete's skin. He clamped his lips tight and tried to turn his head away.

Then the beast's pincers carefully and deliberately severed the webs with which it held itself together and one creature became hundreds, raining down on young Pete. He disappeared beneath a

The Spider Taketh Hold

scuttling mass of them. They ran up his pyjama legs, scrambled up his sleeves and swarmed under his jacket. An agony of itching.

They cascaded over his face and into his hair. Despite his gritted teeth, they flowed into his mouth, slipping and skittering between cheek and gum and down his throat. He choked and they came boiling back out, then another wave swept in. They clogged his nostrils and his ears as they desperately, determinedly forced their way inwards.

Sliding their needle sharp legs under his lids, they dragged Pete's eyes open and two swollen mother spiders stabbed their abdomens into the wet skin of his eyes, puncturing the pupils and squirting their eggs into the warm reservoirs within. Shadow spiders hatched and swam in Pete's vision, swirling and swarming, supping and sucking and swelling, until they quickly grew too fat and tore their way out through his raw sockets.

The searing pain was everywhere within him. They were filling his guts – from both ends – spewing their enzymes and dissolving him and sucking him up into their own guts.

What was left of Pete was being digested within the torn, sagging bag of skin which had once contained the entirety of him.

Eventually, the pain became a memory. Even being Peter became a memory. The transformation was complete, he was gone and all that was left was the spiders. White spiders.

Thousands of Petes peered through thousands of tiny eyes aware, as spiders are aware, of each of his other spider selves. He remembered what they remembered and felt what they felt, as though connected to them by a web. They, in turn, remembered his fear.

Now white spider Petes crawl into the bedrooms of terrified children every night and, every night, he dies a thousand times. He feels the trauma of each death and he remembers it. He can't forget.

Flat Hunting
by Gordon Slack

Mmmmm! I do love a G&T. Another quick sip... Mmmmmm!

It can't be long now. They always arrive on time.

From the reply, I'll bet he's about 45, and a bit nervous (well, they all are).

Bound to be married, which makes it more fun. And particularly when they're nervous!

Can't see him yet; too many people at the bar blocking my view of the door.

Oi Oi! Here he comes. Head around the door and he's in. He's actually rather good looking.

Undo another top button; spray a bit more scent on and... I'm ready. "Mr. Johnson, I'm over here."

He's coming over. "Miss Smith?"

"Yes, that's me; like a drink?" He's hesitating; didn't expect such a gorgeous creature, did he?

"Well... Miss Smith... if you really..."

"Up to you, Mr. Johnson, why don't you sit down? We can discuss the flat here."

He's tempted. But he's looking around. He wouldn't want to be seen in a bar with some... TART! Hee, hee, hee.

OK, better put him out of his agony. Plus it's getting rather late.

"Probably best if we go now, Mr. Johnson, and see your flat, your new abode!"

"Yes, I think that would be best."

"Your car?"

"OK."

It's an E Type Jag. Not bad. Get to the grand finale in style.

God, he's really good looking. I'm definitely pinging down below.

His driving is steady; he must know London quite well, I guess. Probably works in the City. Yum yum!

I do love these leather seats; love squirming around in them. And I do so want to have him.

Flat Hunting

Oh dear, has my skirt slipped up? Did I show some Oooh La La? He glanced over, but I can't see anything happening downstairs.

I'm fondling the large wooden sporty gear knob. "Rather big, isn't it?"

"Please leave that alone." Oh, I see.

I'll have another squirm. Come on now, my skirt must be a good inch above c level. No reaction. OK. We'll concentrate on business. "If you turn left here, Mr. Johnson, then go straight on."

"Are you sure this is the right area?"

"We'll go to my office first, to show you the details of the flat."

They always get confused at this point. "You said it was a one floor flat in central London?"

"Yup, that's what you paid your deposit for." I mean! I think a two thousand pound deposit is very reasonable for central London.

"By the way, Mr. Johnson, did I mention that it was of timber frame construction?"

"Well, no... I didn't think that was used anymore."

"That's the best choice, Mr. Johnson. You can't beat some good old wood, eh! OK, pull up here, please."

Here we are. Standing in front of my building; my own business. Well, it is now, following the untimely death of my parents and the disappearance of my sister. But then none of them ever loved me.

"Is this really your office? The area looks a bit, well..."

"Mr. Johnson, please bear with me. You won't be disappointed, I can assure you." Hold it. Put on seductive charms. See what happens this time. "Mr. Johnson, would you like to come upstairs with me?"

He's following.

I'm walking up the stairs just ahead of him. Doing my wiggle. And now another wiggle.

"Where is your office, please, Miss Smith? It's getting rather late."

OK matey. That was your last chance. "Here we are. This is my office. And here's your flat."

"What do you mean?"

Right, while he is confused, just get the small hammer. Now come up behind him...

"Miss Smith, I really don't understand."

Big swing and THWACK! Good one on his head. He's reeling. And again. SPLAT! Good blood spray; 8 out of 10. What a big bruise, like a large plum.

THUMP! A really big spurt this time; he's down on his knees.

Get the heavy hammer now. Aaahh, it is heavy. This is my special one; coming in from the side. SPLAT! Nice one. Some bone flew off. God, he's really bleeding now.

Just one more go.   If... I... can... lift... this... hammer. Yes. SPLURT! Well, I'll be damned. He cracked open like an egg. Best let him drop to the floor and completely drain out.

There's brain all over the hammers; just wipe it off. It gets so damn sticky if you leave it.

Stop for a quick break. I think a... a Bacardi and Coke will do; just to relax.

Where's the Bacardi? Ah, here. Pour it in the glass; now some Coke. Give it a quick stir.

It's delicious.

I have always liked this drink. Can remember going on holiday with my parents when I was 13. I snuck some into my room and got my younger sister to try it.

She was so pissed by suppertime, I told my mother she had gone down with a tummy bug. At least there were some happy days, I suppose.

Right. Let's have a look. All this blood; how could he hold so much?

Now, lift his legs in. Then his middle... didn't think he was so heavy. And now put in the rest. Pheww!

Let's have a look at him. Well, Mr. Johnson. You didn't want me, eh? None of them ever do. Pull down his trousers and pants. Blimey! What a fucking waste. Anyway, it's too late now.

Just cut if off with Dad's old multi-purpose scout knife. Now ram it into his mouth; looks a real treat. Put the lid on. Look for some nails. He's getting his single floor, timber framed flat, as promised.

Quick sip of the Bacardi. Lovely. But hold on. No, I mustn't. But I just have to.

Flat Hunting

Take the lid off. Slip myself in next to him. Put my arms around his waist. That's better. It's good to hold another human being so tightly. It's been so long. Yes, it has. It really has.

Why was I treated like shit? For all those years. All those bloody years. Anyway, have to get over it, as usual. Just hate everyone.

Get back out. Nail him in. Oops! Mind your fingers.

Good job done. And another satisfied customer. Bastard!

Lolitasaurus
by Richard Craven

First nothing, then something. Long, white corridors. Long strip lights flickering like strobes. You are, you ain't, a million times a moment. Our thighs, coated in plastic, rub together as we walk. In all the corridors, doors are spaced evenly along the walls, doors and more doors, plywood and cloned grain and standard handles. If I ever opened a door, then there would be another long, white corridor, with long strip lights flickering like strobes, and more plywood doors, and if I were to open one of these, another corridor with strip lights and more doors. Sometimes you think you are inside the body of a whale, a clean whale, purged and bleached, with straightened curves and standardised sphincter valves.

There are not many people around here. The occasional cleaner. Either they're bent cataleptically over the shaft of a mop – you walk past them and at the end of the corridor you reach your door, and you turn around for another look, and they're still there, motionless, drooping with the fatigue of the inert; or they're hard at work, mop grasped in whitened knuckles, mechanised repetition of motion, scrubbing eternally the same maculation in the margin between carpet and wall, erasing the lingering trace of the last quark of dirt.

I found a nice sharp screwdriver once, or someone else did, or it found me. I walked up soundlessly behind one of the cleaners. He was in a state of absence, leaning on his mop, eyes turned inwards on the emptiness. I stuck the screwdriver into his throat and jumped back and watched the blood spurting all over the walls and the carpeting and the strip lights. He never made a sound. He just crumpled slowly to the floor, almost deliberately, as though he were making space for himself after a satisfying picnic. His leg twitched spasmodically and upset his bucket, so that some dirty water got spilt on the carpet. When he'd stopped moving, I pulled down his trousers and tried to toss him off, but he wouldn't rise to the occasion. There was some bother, but I didn't get any blood on me and I hid the screwdriver, and the CCTV was too grainy.

I am in the room. The one where you eat sleep think fuck shit and take pills. If you are going to piss or talk you go to another room. If

Lolitasaurus

you are not eating sleeping thinking shitting fucking taking pills pissing or talking, then you are in a corridor, my friend. You see how if you are in the room long enough, then everything you do in it merges into a single process, a mono-event in a monoverse where 'time' and 'change' are meaningless. So I am in the room doing what comes to me there. They've got newspapers for you to wipe your arse on, they've got pormags and TV and inflatable dolls with adjustable valves, and straitjackets and wooden spoons, and a kiosk with nurses in zip-crotched underwear who dose you up with Largactil and fiendish anti-psychotics which turn you into a dribbling lard arse with no fashion sense.

Thus am I, when men come for me and lead me silently down the corridors. We pass the spot where I killed the cleaner and there is not the faintest lingering scintilla of a ghost. At the end of the corridor the door swings open into the room where you piss and talk.

"You are Mr Moffatt?" says one of the men.

"Is correct."

"Our files indicate that you…" blah blah.

"Come again?"

"You're cured," he says, "no more than averagely unbalanced. You're free. You can go."

I am standing on a gravel drive outside a large door. I look down at my hand grasping a black valise. I seem to remember another valise whose exterior details correspond exactly to this one, the same combination lock, the same dents and scratches and tarnishments. I wonder, and not without reason, although it is no more than the idlest of speculations, whether they are one and the same valise. The contents are not the same. The one before had all kinds of useful things: Rohypnol, an oil-stained boiler suit, a couple of syringes, plastic cable-ties. This one's just got clothes and money in it, and not enough of either.

The sky is uniformly white. The house of corridors stretches out behind me. Underneath my mackintosh I have a two-piece suit, underneath the suit nothing, no shirt no pants no socks, just some torn plimsolls. In front of me is a lawn, clumps of grass and big dog skid marks strewn with deadened leaves, beyond the lawn a line of fir trees bisected by an opening for the drive. I hear no sound save the low continuous roar of traffic.

Richard Craven

The town is approached by a slip road feeding off the bypass. I trudge along the side of the road, on a path worn by the untold migrations of others. I slip on mud and sweet wrappers and cold condoms. My only companions two or three huge crows, who flap their wings, and make ungainly landings in the road, and eye me quizzically as I pass.

I come upon a drama in its whimpering denouement. A small collection of caravans, lines of rags hanging limply in the lifeless cold. Fetid travellers gathered in a patchouli-pungent knot around a squad car. The doors are open, the blue lights revolve, cops bulked out in hi-viz jackets bundle a semiconscious youth into the back. His head cracks against the doorframe. Nobody speaks. Inside the squad car, a radio crackles.

"Wossis?" says one of the policeman, catching hold of me, "You see anything?"

"You bet, I say." I stand there smiling dumbly at the moments elapsing before he turns from me disgustedly.

"Funny fucking fucker," he says to noone in particular, "go on, fuck off out of it."

The slip road runs past fields, and past dirty little paddocks with iron troughs and forlorn ponies. After a bend, I see skyscrapers in the distance. I find myself trudging past hillsides down which spill rows of prefabricated terraces.

The town is one of those hi-tech affairs, laid out like the spokes of a wheel with shopping at the still point of the turning world and concentric circles dedicated to brave new industries and brave new housing. The roads and roundabouts are awash with late model jelly-moulded cars, suits speeding from pointless appointment to pointless appointment. The still, sclerotic air balloons in every wake, crackling tangibly with the potencies of the doomed.

The hostel when I find it proves at first to be surprisingly agreeable. It is one of those community-centre-style bungaloids built out of glazed maroon brick. I am expected and a single room has already been prepared for me. I even find a pormag in the bedside cabinet. I take off my suit and express my autonomy all over my crisp new linen bedsheets.

The pleasure I derive from my new surroundings soon begins to pall. The rooms are over-heated, the food stodgy and institutional. I meet my fellow inmates. I am disturbed by the revelation that to a man

Lolitasaurus

they are qualitatively identical: all ex-child prodigies in their late thirties, thin hair, glasses, glazed dough-grease faces, paralysed, motorised wheelchairs, dribble-bag smells. By far the most alarming feature, though, is the voices. Each has had his vocal chords replaced by a voicebox from some Californian factory.

During the endless hours of free association, they earnestly discuss with each other the state of their preparedness for independent living. The heated somnolent dayroom air is rent with vulcanized American platitudes. They try to engage my participation. They think I am lonely. I am.

I find, after this, that time is quite abruptly wrapped in an enigma. I suffer from vague presentiments of clingfilm and knotted nylon cords. There are flashing lights and disembodied voices rasping in a fluorescent haze, then the sensations of jolting, cessation, fatigue, and finally stillness in a numb white landscape.

I am outside, in a small clearing. Snow on the ground, broken by footprints. Undergrowth merges with sickly trees. A huge, grey bust of a bearded man stares balefully at me through the thickets. I am conscious of the cold, but only as though somebody else were feeling it. If I turn my head I can just make out the shape of a wheelchair lying athwart a rough path. I smell sewage petrified at the precise moment of its deliquescence.

When the doctor says I am well enough, the fat nurse with latex gloves removes the tubes. Then the detectives come for me and put me in their car, two in front, two either side of me in the back. We are driving through London, through some inner-outer scene of non-description like Perivale or Edgware.

"Give him the blanket, then, George," says one of the detectives in the front.

"Rock on," says George, pulling a dirty grey blanket over my head.

Underneath the blanket it smells of sweat and piddle and detective fart. I can feel the fat, warm thighs of the detectives pressing into me whenever the car rounds a corner. I hear their voices. They talk about beer and QPR and bestiality videos.

The car stops. One of the detectives in front gets out. After a minute, the blanket is pulled from my head. I blink in the sudden brightness. A hand appears from nowhere and thrusts into my face a scalding kebab covered in mustard and tomato sauce. I hear myself gasp.

"What makes you do it, you twisted little cunt," says George, slapping me across the cheek with a ringed knuckle.

My nose and upper lip throb under layers of muck and gristle. I raise a hand to wipe my face, but it is snatched away and the blanket is thrust over my head again.

"Mad cunt," says George.

It is warm and fetid and close underneath the blanket. I can feel the mustard and the tomato sauce, cooler now, as it slides down my face. I taste blood.

The court rises. The judge clears his throat. I don't hear much, just the standard crap about repugnant crimes and duty to the public weal. Probably does both, bouncing up and down on some rent boy. I watch him. I watch his jaw moving spasmodically, the clean-shaven face under thick eyebrows, the fright-wig rented from Nanny Whiplash. It seems so far away, so shallow, where is the man beneath all this stuff?

The old life returns, with all the old precisions. The corridor runs straight and true. It is lined with doors, doors of painted steel and rivets and little spyholes which you can look through, or open, or shut. When you look through the holes you can watch a little room just like your own. If there are men in it you can watch them as they talk or ruminate or piss on twisted sheets and hang themselves. You can watch them as they smoke and play cards. If they are not talking ruminating pissing hanging smoking or playing cards, they are in another room; they may be bathing and fornicating, they may be scoffing instant mash and alphabet spaghetti. I'm not joking. Life's like that.

You try keeping a straight face next time you watch another yahoo shitting on a newspaper. The real cases do it on page 3. They're all on D Wing. You go down and down the corridor, past the green paint and the steel and the rivets, everything very pukka, deeply, deeply appropriate to the odour of the faecal tide which awaits you as you cruise through the node, the caged valve and enter the second face of the angle. You can hear them screaming. You can go and look through spyholes at their rooms too. You can read what they've written on the walls in their own shit.

Lolitasaurus

Keeping A Head
by Jonah Jones

I've always wondered what happens when someone's head is cut off, haven't you? It would remain alive because the brain would still be functioning as long as there's sufficient blood in there and the oxygen levels are high enough. It would be like holding your breath until you die, I suppose. But I've thought of a way around that. If you keep the head immersed in oxygen-rich liquid, it should continue to function indefinitely. Still able to see, hear, think... wouldn't be able to talk, of course, because it's no longer attached to its lungs. Which is why I've taken up lip-reading so that I can understand what you're trying to say.

Project Approved
by Andrew Williamson

Daniel Middleton pours himself another two fingers of 'supermarket value' Scotch. Not as smooth as the twelve-year-old single malt that was his previous poison, but the end game was similar. Make that three fingers; after all, he can't have damaged his liver the previous night as much as he'd thought because the bottle was a little fuller than he remembered. Plus, this evening's previous two fingers had eased their way down his neck in one swift swig before he'd begun assessing A-level biology experiment project plans.

That was twenty minutes and three project plans ago. Only another eleven to go, and if they are just as unimaginative as the previous three there is a risk the whole bottle will be empty by the end of the evening. And it wouldn't be the first time he's done that in the last couple of months.

Daniel slaps down his whiskey tumbler in a space between school exercise book towers on the folding, fake veneer, two-seater kitchen dining table, and sits on one of the two PVC-covered chairs – the kind upon which you don't sit with bare legs at the height of a scorching summer for fear of peeling off the skin at the back of your thighs.

Sitting with his back against the rear wall of his studio apartment, he takes in the view of his new, cramped habitat. The tiny, bric-a-brac affair, with peeling Anaglypta wallpaper, stiff from a dozen layers of paint, revealing patches of black-speckled, tell-tale mould underneath, is a far cry from the shiny, fashionable two-bedroomed riverside apartment, kitted out by plummy, pretentious interior designers, that he'd shared with Melissa.

Daddy's girl, Melissa. Daniel takes another gulp of Scotch. Definitely not as smooth as his old tipple, and there's that weird aftertaste he hadn't noticed before. (You need to be drunk to drink this stuff.) He should be assessing the goddamn project plans, not wallowing in dysphoric recollections. The irony: that's the exact reasoning that led him to inner city slumdom.

Daniel picks up and opens the next exercise book. *Terrence Attingham: Comparing antibacterial action of Strepsils versus Fishermen's Friends.* Thank God for Terry, the one human boy in a

Project Approved

cohort of privileged clones, and not the normal Hesketh College student by some margin. His parents – a civil engineer and a police officer – are hardworking, useful members of society simply trying to give Terry a leg up in life at great financial sacrifice to themselves. And Terry repays them with hard work and a highly-developed sense of humour, despite the best efforts of his class colleagues; those spoilt offspring of old and new money. Ungrateful, arrogant and inhuman, always ready to put down someone not of their own kind.

Another swig of Scotch. Perhaps taking sips from now on would be a good idea. Daniel's parents had done the same for him in their own, smaller way. Like Terry, he'd appreciated that effort, by studying hard, behaving well, getting a career, and making everyone happy. Everyone but himself. Hindsight is a horrible thing. Terry even had the forethought to use replica plating technique, smart boy. Let's hope he chooses a career he enjoys.

Next. Oh God, here we go. Felicity Greythorne: class genius. If the film industry ever wanted a template for a female Damien, they need look no further than Felicity Greythorne. What's the meaning of her first name again? Joyfulness, bliss, delight, or a source of happiness or good fortune? That really is a piss-take.

Back when a career in the fee-paying sector seemed like a good idea for an aspiring young teacher, the Felicity Greythornes of this world were not on the agenda. Another mouthful of Scotch. Sips just won't cut it tonight. Daughter of Lord Greythorne, the government's 'go to' chief research biochemist. Why at Hesketh College? Why now? Why me? She's a chip off the old block all right; a first class brain for sure. Not the stretched, second class brain some of us have to cope with. She must be the poisoned apple of her father's eye. And what a bitch with it. Just sip. *Felicity Greythorne: Efficacy of the delivery of active biological agents through ethanol media.*

If the split with Melissa hadn't happened, or more accurately (because, in truth, separation was inevitable), if Daniel had handled it better; if he'd drunk less and slept more, and thus been better able to make decisions; if he'd deleted the internet history on his laptop instead of falling asleep; if he'd not taken his disappointments to college, and missed the whole section of the syllabus on enzymes, resulting in the whole class receiving grades two levels below those expected; if Felicity hadn't belittled him in front of the whole class when he'd written "condom" on the projector instead of "codon"; if he'd taken it on the chin like all the previous, similar events instead of barking at her and dragging her out of class; if Lord Greythorne's billion-dollar corporation didn't sponsor the college; if the principal - spineless Spalding – had realised the stress Daniel was suffering; if he'd any luck whatsoever, then maybe, just maybe he'd still have an apartment that didn't smell like a supermarket wheelie bin, a career he hated, and a fiancée who despised him.

Another sip. Daniel's lips are so numb he can hardly feel the glass against them, and his fingers around the glass feel like enormous sausages – time to ease up on the liquor. Biological agents in ethanol? What biological agents

The biological agents are genetically engineered to survive in normally catastrophic ethanol. Although on a macro scale, the organisms to be transported should be transparent when suspended in liquid. The organisms are of a similar refractive index to ethanol-based liquids, and as such they are, for all intents and purposes, invisible to the human eye.

Once swallowed, the organisms make their way to the small intestine, attaching themselves to the intestine wall. They secrete an anaesthetic directly into the blood stream. A dose of 100 ml of liquid media containing typically fifteen to twenty organisms will paralyse a 75 kg human being in approximately 30 minutes. At first the host will suffer anaesthetic awareness, losing the use of and feeling in all skeletal and facial muscles, but remaining fully conscious. The organisms then use fine filaments to enter villi and force their way through the membrane wall and into the bloodstream, where they inflate to many times their original size by consuming blood cells.

Approximately 30 minutes after paralysis the organisms are gorged on blood and begin to block the flow of blood to some parts of the body. The organisms then wriggle constantly within the circulatory system to travel to increasingly larger cross-sections enabling contiguous feeding. The action of the wriggling can be felt and seen by the host, but of course, now completely paralysed, they are unable to do anything about it – not even call for help. Truly an itch that cannot be scratched.

The wriggling usually lasts for approximately 15 minutes (though to the host it feels like a lifetime of indescribable torture), by which time the organisms have overindulged to a standstill – there are simply no vessels of sufficient width within which they can travel. At this time the supply of blood is heavily restricted, and the host's blood

Project Approved

pressure will have dropped sufficiently that they will lose consciousness and heart failure will ensue. With no blood pressure, the organisms exhaust the consumed blood, and revert to an invisible status. The anaesthetic similarly becomes undetectable. An autopsy would conclude heart failure, with no suspicious circumstances.

Utter nonsense. Daniel commands his hand to bring up the tumbler to his lips, but it won't budge. He strains as hard as he can to move just a finger, but there's no response. He struggles with all his might to move his eyeballs a few degrees and notices the bottle of Scotch. He remembers clearly that when he replaced the cap on the bottle before putting it in the cupboard last night the level of the Scotch was in line with the top of the label - exactly where it is now, even after pouring two healthy glasses' worth. Daniel sees the wall-clock, and realises that he started drinking around half-an-hour ago. His eyes drop to focus on Felicity's perfect handwriting. At the bottom of the page it reads: *You really should have looked after your apartment keys. Goodbye, Mr Middleton.*

The exercise book slides from Daniel's rigid left hand, plops onto the table and closes. Still gazing at his hand, he notices movement in a wrist vein, and watches as it slowly wriggles up his forearm. Yes, a first class mind, but a bitch with it. Project approved.

Meat
by Neil Bebber

The thing is, I had no choice. Whatever you, whatever society, might say. Because, let's face it, society is increasingly finding ways to stop us acting on our instincts. Indulging our natural urges. Exploring our, our curiosity. Because it makes us more controllable. Like, like sheep. But we're not sheep. We're humans. Top of the food chain. So it's in us, right? All of us. Not just me. So it must be normal. Natural. Mustn't it?

And anyway, what is civilised? Really? What does it actually mean? It's just a word. The Romans were civilised and look what they did. It's not as if I've fed a helpless family to the lions for my own entertainment, is it? Clapped and cheered as screaming children watched their parents shredded. But they're remembered, aren't they? The Romans. For their achievements. Their viaducts. Their arches. Their sandals. So why shouldn't I be remembered for the things I've done?

Remembered. Re. Membered. Dismembered. Dis. Membered. Never noticed that before…

When we were kids, we ate raw sausages. Raw pork. Raw pig. Porky pig. And the taste? Well, that was something special. Really special. They had to be room temperature. You can't taste anything when it's cold. Room temperature. Body temperature. And the meat… The meat was pink. Pink and sweet.

Wouldn't do it now, mind. The kind of shit they pump in. All the chemicals, the hormones, the water. The pigs are all bloated. Can barely walk. And that's not normal. Not normal at all.

*

It was as though she just appeared in front of me. Floated over. No footsteps. I just looked up from the counter, from my meat, and there she was. A vision. Like a painting. A classic. But with clothes on.

"Excuse me," she says, gently miffed, as if she'd said it once already. And I'm smiling. Inside. Not sure what to say. Transfixed, liked a dying man in a museum.

Meat

And, eventually, I say something like, "Sorry, madam. Miles away. Talking to myself again, probably. What can I do for you?"

"I'm not sure," she says. "I've been told I need to... never mind. Beef's got iron in it, hasn't it?" Word for word, that's what she said.

"Yes, madam," I say. "Full of iron. Full of it. I mean, a magnet would probably stick to it."

She pauses, smiles politely, and then says, "Good. Then I'll have some beef, please."

Some beef. I know. No idea. "Well, we've got minced beef, sliced beef, aged beef..."

"Steak?" she says.

"Yes. Steak's good. Very good. Steak is actually beef, too, but..."

"What would you recommend?" she says.

And me, with no hesitation: "The aged steak. Definitely. Special piece of meat, that. Hung for 28 days. Dried. Concentrated flavour. Dark."

"Perfect," she says. And she was right. Well, at the time, anyway.

"How much?"

"I don't know," she says.

Looking back, I suppose it was pretty obvious, but I ask, "Well, will you be eating alone?"

"Yes."

And then, like a wolf, circling: "Pretty woman like you shouldn't be eating good steak like this alone. It's an experience. Something to savour. Something to share. Like seeing the sun set red on Ayer's Rock."

She softens. Rolls over. Shows me her belly. "How about enough for two of us, then?"

For two of us. For her. And for me. Don't be too keen. Too smug. Make it too obvious. "Sorry, madam?"

"Would you like to share it with me?"

And I did.

I watched her eat that meat. Rare. A mouthful, then a groan. Another mouthful, then another groan. You have no idea...

I couldn't eat mine. Couldn't move. Couldn't take my eyes off her. The blood on her lips. On her teeth. And when she'd finished, I had her. Right there. On that table. Licking the blood from deep inside her mouth. Her dress stained as we rocked on bloody plates. Her nails dragged at the skin on my back. She bit my lip. Hard. And blood flowed from my mouth into hers. Warm.

*

When we were kids, we cut our hands and did blood brothers. It was a bond for life. This. This was a bond for life. She needed a ring to make it official, but not me. And then, one day she turned up at work, appearing, as she always did, out of nowhere.

"I've got some news," she said.

"Right."

"Well?" she said, as if I should know what to say.

"Look, I'm really sorry but can it wait? I finish in an hour and I'm way behind."

"But..." she said.

You're not listening. "Seriously, today's been an absolute nightmare."

"OK, I'll wait."

Or you could go. But instead I say, "Fine."

*

And so our creation grew inside her. Our calf. Our lamb. Dividing. Firming. Criss-cross strands, fibres forming.

*

After she'd, you know, pushed it out, after all that gas and screaming and air, I mean, she was out of it, so I... I asked for the afterbirth. A little indulgence I hid at the back of the freezer. And every time she went out, I defrosted another bit. Excited and afraid that at any moment she could walk through the door and find me there. All bloody and naked...

Then, when she came home, I suckled from my love. I tasted the thin, sweet water from her breasts. Warm. Like her. She would kneel over me and I would feed. Like Romulus. Or Remus. Tugging. Pulling. Until my belly was full, but...

At some point, she started to drift. To lean back. To pull away. And when she appeared that day, she seemed different. Translucent.

Meat

"We need to talk."
Delaying. Knowing. "I can't. Not here. Not now. What's the matter?"
Different. Impatient. Pushy. Yes. Pushy. "Can't you take a break?"
"Maybe."
"Look, I'm going to my sister's. I wanted to tell you. To your face."
"What? Why?"
"You know why…"
Of course I did. Deep down. But she, *we* made a vow. "Look, let me see if I can…"
"Actually, no. Maybe it's best if I call you later. OK?"
Nodding. Helpless. Out of control. Out. Of. Control.
"I'll call you tonight."
Please...

*

If something's important, really important, we'll do whatever it takes. Even make promises. Promises we know we can't keep. But I couldn't lose her. I wouldn't lose her. And the next day, she came back.

But we are what we are.

When we were kids we ate black pudding. Blood sausage. Black blood sausage. Blood and fat. Metallic and salty. And warm. With eggs. And bacon.

The Germans call it fleisch. Literally, flesh. The Germans are braver than us. More pragmatic. Call it what it is. Flesh. Some skin. Some muscle. Some fat. My grandmother used to eat the brains. The lungs. Intestines. A whole pig's face boiled down, then stripped and pressed into a loaf tin.

And the rabbit man brought rabbits, still warm, and we'd sit, me in my pants, to keep my trousers clean, plunging hands into hot slits of blood and blue guts.

Please…

*

Me: "You look good." Then back at my meat.
"Thanks."
Smiling. "I could take half an hour. I could do with a break..." Am I pretending? I don't know.
Silence. For an age. Then me. Again: "Where's my princess?"
"She's with my mum."
"Right" is what I say. But what I see is her mum and me, me pushing her. Off a building. A cliff. I don't know. Something high. And her, flying, falling. Stopping. Smashing.
"We're going away."
Shattered sockets. But eyes, eyes still seeing. Seeing me, looking down.
"Sorry, what?"
"I know. I know you're really trying. I can see that. But it's not fair. On either of us."
"But I..."
"You should be able to... I don't know... Be with someone that you can be yourself with..."
"Please..."
"Look..."
"Just give me a chance to explain."
"It's too late."
"You can't just go."
"I've made up my mind."
"She's my daughter, too."
And, when it's almost too late, just as she turns away for what could have been the last time: "OK. OK. I understand. I won't try to change your mind. I promise. I just need to talk to you. To explain. Please..?"
And I'm crying. Actually crying. Real tears.
"What time do you finish?"
"How about I meet you in an hour. At home." Our home.
"Do you think that's a good..."
"Yes. The last time. I promise." My eyes. Like a puppy, while she pauses.
Then: "OK. I am really sorry."
"I know. I do understand. Don't worry. It'll be fine. I'll see you in a while."

Meat

"Yeah."

Watching her as she walks away, and to no one in particular: "Thanks".

*

I mean, we're all just meat, right? Overlapping tissue strands. Cells. Millions and millions of cells. Like plants. Or ants. Just shapes. There was so much blood.

Too much to save. I filled everything: jam jars, the Thermos flask, those crystal champagne flutes we never got round to using... But she just kept bleeding. And moving. Just spasms as muscles misfired. And talking, after she'd stopped crying, saying funny things and giggling like a little girl. And then I go and spoil it all, by puking blood and breakfast everywhere, trying my best to keep some of it down. Because this way, with her inside me, she'd never leave. She'd be with me forever. Her cells and my cells making new shapes. Together.

I made chops and burgers and steaks. I made sausages and stews. There was so much I had to share her. I didn't want to, but there was no room in the freezer and I've never been one to waste anything. She's here. Mixed in with the diced pork. Sealed, on a high heat, then slow cooked. In casseroles. Some carrots. Onions. Lovely. Lovely meat, madam. You couldn't tell the difference. I know I can't.

The Ballad of Liam and Chantelle
by Steven Stockford

You can chop up her face, remove an eye, but you know, you might still just need her. Love, eh?

Liam is bored. He's been stuck in this shithole of a police station for days, and Mister Delmont, his toad-faced solicitor, just drones on and on. All Liam has heard is that the bitch didn't squeak so the fifth don't have nothing.

"...of course the police may well ask you to attend the station, say, once a week. Hardly a hardship in the circumstances..."

Liam grunts; his gaunt face draws the skin tight over his cheeks bones until he offers an ugly grin. He knows the police don't give a monkeys if you 'no show' on bail.

Mr Delmont continues his box ticking to ensure his client is fully appraised of the situation: "They've rescinded the Rule 43. It is not within the police's remit to classify you under the Mental Health Act without a reported crime."

Big whoop.

"I feel I must caution you about speaking to the press. As you can imagine, they..." Delmont winces.

Liam sneers, thinking to himself, "Gay boy, just say it."

"... erm, in cases like this, I mean. Where there has been an assault, erm, of this nature. It arouses a prurient interest, shall we say. Particularly with an attractive teenage girl."

"Yeh, yeh. Keep schtum." Liam grabs his hoodie and, with a waft of cheap roll-ups, heads for the door.

Mister Delmont disguises his disgust with a wipe of his nose. "But I also caution you to avoid seeing her."

No longer listening, the teenager leaves with his usual hunched gait, his shorn head stuck forwards. A bull looking for a fight. Delmont smiles. The legal aid for this rapscallion will pay for his family's Tuscany breaks for years to come.

*

The Ballad of Liam and Chantelle

Liam struggles to find the Trauma Ward. Trust that dumb bitch to make it hard for him.

It's not helped by the hangover from the previous night's celebrations. Even Uncle Tommy turned up: "You're a winner, you cunt." You know you've arrived when Uncle Tommy gets you a celebratory pint.

The nurses ignore the ill-dressed young man, moving like a whirlwind through the wards. A mother clutches her children closer to her as he passes, kissing them both on their heads as soon as he disappears through the crashing double doors at the end of the ward.

Turns out Chantelle has her own room. Couldn't be better. "That you, Liam?" she squeaks in her irritating whine. How does she know it's him with all those bandages around her face? She looks like the fucking Mummy.

He clocks the wedding magazines on a cupboard next to her bed as he settles on the windowsill, crunching up the blinds. Down in the car park he eyes a string of neat cars, BMWs, Audis. Uncle Tommy would cough up good for a couple of them.

"So, 'ow you doing?" he asks, eyeing the room for what he'll need.

Then she gets tearful of course. Stupid bitch. "Oh Liam! They said you couldn't see me."

"They don't know nuffing."

"Knew you'd come. Really sorry. All these bandages. They says they can save my other eye."

"That's something."

A phone blurbs nearby, in the corridor. His senses flicker. Is it about him?

"Doesn't hurt like it used to."

"Good to hear", he says, sniffing up some coke that dribbles down his nostrils. A muffled female voice is speaking on the phone, but there's no concern in her voice, so he loosens up. Back to the matter at hand.

"Knows it's all my fault", she says. "Told my dad that."

"Yeh. Someone needs to sort him. Causing me real issues."

"Aw. Sorry, Liam. Listen, when we get out of 'ere I thought we could get an easyJet over to Greece."

Liam checks the pipes running in and out of her frail body as he mouths, "Stupid bitch". What if he plucked one of those colourful pipes out of her? Put a hand over her whining gob?

"Liam? You still there?"

"Yeh. Greece. Sounds good."

"I didn't tell 'em nothing. Honest."

"They're full of shit."

"I tells 'em it was all so fast. How do I know who did it?"

"Great."

"And this psychologist woman. Aw, she's so nice. She says it's a traumatic attack. The victim usually doesn't remember much."

"Sounds right."

The previous night Tommy had grabbed Liam's arm, sweeping him against a van in the dimly lit pub car park.

"Listen to me, you little cunt. She's not saying nuffing now, but she will. Be a lot of grief. I'm telling you. I know these bitches."

Liam glared up at the stone hard face, with its hefty brows like an overhanging cliff, balanced at the other end of his face by an absurdly oversized jaw.

"Like I dunno!" Liam says, feeling his arm ache from his uncle's grip. "I'll sort it. I told yer."

So now Liam's here at the hospital to sort it. Glancing at the flashing, silent machines around her, realising that, with his luck, if he plucked out a lead it'd just set off an alarm. There are freshly laundered pillows piled on a chair. He grins. Just press one down on her bandaged face and out go her gormless lights. With a clatter of the blinds he slides off the sill plucking up the top one. He sees his shadow hovering over her head like an angular bird.

She hears him getting closer, knowing he's going to kiss her. What better time to ask her to marry him than when she is recovering? Her heartbeat increases. For a moment it all falls silent, he is still, but standing close to her. Her nerves compel her to fill the silent void.

"They says I gets compensation," she says.

Liam freezes. "How much?"

"Dunno. But facial disfigurement and everything. Losing an eye. It all adds up."

The Ballad of Liam and Chantelle

"Compensation," he says aloud, wishing Uncle Tommy could hear.

She giggles. "Knew you'd like that. We could do something. You know, rent a place down the bay. Marsha says you can get a place for..."

"Don't keep going on about renting this and renting that. Does my 'ead in."

"Oh, sorry, Liam. Yeh. In its own time you says, yeh?"

After a moment, Liam flicks the pillow back on the chair, watching it bounce and flop to the floor.

The bandages stretch as she smiles. "Dad doesn't understand we're in love. Doesn't get it."

"Too fucking old."

"He forgets. I'm nearly 15. I finishes school next year. Get a job for us."

"School! Worse than a secure centre. Least you can play pool inside."

"They says they can hide some of the scars. You know, make up."

"When do you get this compensation, then?" he asks.

"Can't take 'em long, can it? I mean look at me. What's there to know?"

"Hmmm."

Before Christmas, Liam and his mates put this arsehole into a coma and his mum got over eighty grand. Unbelievable. Maybe rent her that flat in the bay. Keep her sweet. Her pussy drips to have a modern kitchen diner and a new set of pans. Thick bitch.

"Maybe look at a ring?" Hearing the ominous hush, she quickly adds, "Nothing flash." She knows she shouldn't mention rings. It only sets him off. At last, she asks, "What you thinking, Liam?"

"Nuffing."

The bandaged head faces him, wanting more.

He says, "About what we need to get sorted."

"Like the holiday?"

"Needs that compensation dosh first, don't we?"

*

Liam hadn't thought about what it was like being with the Bride of Frankenstein. He would run his fingers over her scars, surprised at how rigid they sat on her face. Her unmoving glass eye gave him the willies. Hardly the sort of bitch you can parade in front of your mates in the clubs. Not that anyone dared say anything to him.

Being careful never to strike her in the face, no matter what she said, over time Liam found himself adjusting to the situation. Even her thick old man got used to him coming round for the footie and stopped leaving the room.

So the months ground on.

*

Liam is sat next to Chantelle on hard upright chairs, opposite toady-faced Mister Delmont in his office at the edges of the city. Chantelle has grown her hair long, leaving it draped down the one side of her face. She constantly has to sweep it back to see properly. Her dad has to be there too, on account of her being a minor. The solicitor's office is more cramped than Liam expected. If you broke in here, you wouldn't bother hanging 'round.

Mister Delmont's voice is a whine, as dull as the air-conditioning throb from the machine over the window. He has his notes and he needs to go through them point by point to ensure that procedures have been met. Even these dense clients must understand exactly what they have achieved with the Criminal Injuries Board.

Suddenly her dad sits upright in disbelief. "How much?"

"Well, there are prescribed amounts for injuries", Mister Delmont says, grimacing as if sharing the disappointment.

"But her face is…" Her dad is on his feet, his cheeks bruised red, his body animated with outrage. He cannot say the words and admit to himself that his lovely daughter has been mutilated for life by the arsehole who is holding her hand.

"I am afraid £52,250. 69 is the amount the Criminal Injuries Board have deduced is the appropriate figure. We could appeal but then they would hold back the payment. It is truly the view of myself, and others in the practice, that…"

"She's only got one sodden eye!" the irate father pleads. Her dad is going off on one and Liam just wants the cash and to get out.

The Ballad of Liam and Chantelle

"Loss of an eye was calculated at £7,989.32. The facial disfigurement accounted for more."

"But she's so young..."
"They recognised that with the hardship element, listed at £4,932.14."
Liam isn't listening. Just over fifty big ones. It would take him a year working with his Uncle Tommy to pull in that.

*

Uncle Tommy is at his best, stinking of beer, his hulk filling his glistening new Mercedes. Liam all ears in the passenger seat.
"It's getting shot of the body you gotta be up for. Any tool can slot someone. 'specially a girl as thick as that ugly tramp. No offence."
"The allotments..." Liam starts, knowing he is going to be cut short by his all-knowing uncle.
Tommy snorts, "Oh yeh. What you on about? You going on University Challenge? The bastards got heat seekers in their helicopters. No burying."
"Pigs. They'll eat anything," Liam says, desperate to impress his scathing uncle.
"On telly, yeh! But pigs shit out the teeth and hair. DNA. You twat. Try thinking. You do serious time if they nail you for this. You gotta think of your mum. Get it right."
Liam is agitated, "Dunno. Fling her off a boat down the docks?"
"They float back. Always. Been there."
Liam puts his feet up on the dashboard, admiring the lines on his stolen Reeboks before settling back in the luxurious leather seats - until he sees the cold stare from Uncle Tommy. He drops his feet back down to the floor and squirms upright. "Go on, then."
"You're close with the pigs. This farmer's got this decomposing pit. Huge. Even dumps cows in them. Chucks chemicals, acids and stuff over them. In a few days, fuck all for the law to get hold of. I'll tell you exactly where. Of course that'll be fifteen grand. Readies well spent if you ask me."
"So long as I can get rid of that freak."

*

The farm Tommy knows is miles out of town. Tommy wouldn't drive them on account of the traffic cameras and Liam can't involve anyone else, so they actually get the bus out to a village 12 miles from the city. Beside him Chantelle is excited, fidgeting like a kid.

"Where yous taking me?" She knows it must be special; he rarely takes her out, let alone outside the city. Could this be the big moment?

"You'll see," he says flatly.

In profile with her good eye facing you, she still doesn't look too bad. The scars are settling down, becoming part of her. But Liam is already screwing another tramp, Shannon-Marie, the recycling manager's daughter. So he needs to sort out Chantelle, like right now.

They drew out the compensation from her account the day before and it's stuffed under his bed in his Batman game box. His two older brothers are serving time for a post office robbery and his mum has moved in with Uncle Tommy, so he knows the cash is pretty safe. 50 fucking thousand quid, all under his bed!

To keep her sweet, Liam even went ring hunting with her in the afternoon. What a waste of time. The shit she puts him through!

Over a coffee in the mall she pulled out a heavily creased wedding magazine with tea cup stains on the cover, and asked him which dress he preferred. When he said he didn't care, she giggled, snuggled up to him as the magazine fell open to a tatty page. "What about this one?" she asked.

He eyed the beautiful model in a skin tight gown that was magically suspended around the model's tits and gripped her body all the way to her ankles, like a mermaid's tail. "Yeh," he said. "Great." She laughed and slapped the table, stamping her feet with excitement. "I knew you'd like it! Now we got the compensation, I can get it!"

The bus dropped them off near an isolated, closed down pub with steel bars screwed across the doors and windows. The dumb bitch giggles with excitement as they watch the bus thunder away down the lane, coughing out black exhaust.

Only Liam, she thought, would think of something as wonderful as bringing her somewhere special to propose. She had bought a dress weeks back so she was ready for him. It was a lovely gold thigh length dress from Next, with short sleeves to hide the bruises on her arms, where he grabs her.

The Ballad of Liam and Chantelle

Liam helps her over a stile, into an overgrown field, and her giggling gives way to concern as soon as she eyes the darkening countryside. She hates being in woodlands after dark; it's like being in one of the horrible horror movies she so detested.

Liam had walked through the fields a few days before, plotting his markers, but with the light fading quickly, and the sky a dull grey with flashes of orange, he is quickly losing his bearings.

"Liam. I don't like this."

Her boyfriend doesn't answer but she finds a smile. There he is, marching on, head stuck forward, occasionally swearing at the cow pats he slops through. No-one understands him. They all hate him. If only they knew what he was really like: gormless, but sweet in his own way. It's so exhilarating to have a boyfriend everyone, including her dad, is scared shitless of.

In the murky copse they are standing before the decomposing pit. The stench rubs the throat raw. Even in the gloom Liam can make out the bust-up farm machines he clocked on his recce. Their murderous steel points spiking through the black, green mud.

She grips his arm with both her hands. "Liam. I don't like this. I gets real scared since the…"

"Shut it," he says. Doesn't she ever stop whining?

He needs to get her closer, but the footing is precarious, slippery, the melting ground gripping and sucking at his trainers.

"I'm stuck." She is crying now.

Liam can't believe how hopeless she is.

Holding out his hand he tries to keep his voice even. "Get over 'ere."

"Liam, I can't move," she sobs. "Well, I didn't know we was coming out 'ere. You think I'd 'ave worn my best white heels? They're special."

Liam goes a bit mental sometimes. The rage will tear through him like fire through tissue. He twists around. If he gets closer, he can grab her and drag her down to the pit, but his impulsive action sends his feet skidding from beneath him. His hands jump out to break his fall but just slice into the mud. He chews the disgusting blend of rotten meat and animal crap until he chokes on their vile odours.

"Fuck."

Chantelle has never known such horror. Not even when Liam pinned her to the kitchen floor by kneeling on her, and set about her face, screaming obscenities at her like a mad Pitbull. Not even when they carried out the operation to save her good eye, when she had to be fully conscious as the masked Chinese surgeon brought his scalpel over her face.

Here she stands, glued ankle deep in the sludge, totally helpless, as the love of her life slips through the murky surface.

It is all her fault! Every time she does her makeup she sees her scars, a constant reminder of how she's responsible for everything bad that happens to Liam.

He is sliding deeper now. It is a slow, deliberate but inevitable action. He can hear the stupid bitch screaming his name. He'll have her when he gets back.

Her hands cover her face as she screams for help. She can no longer bear the sight before her. Liam and her ring have vanished beneath the bubbling surface, and she feels the icy chill of bereavement of lost love. Poor Liam; he was denied his one opportunity to shine, to give her the ring in the middle of a romantic field. All because she got stuck in the sludge.

The sum total of human misery fillets her soul as Liam had filleted her face.

Beneath the surface Liam is still sinking, the chemicals burning his skin. It should have been her! Dozy cow.

He is sinking and sliding. It isn't fast, but it is inexorable. He cannot get a grip on anything. A rock smashes his knee but as he reaches to grab it, to prevent him drowning further, it slips through his fingers. He can taste waste and manure now. The tangs fill his senses as if he has spent his entire life eating shit.

The human brain offers him solace: this isn't really happening. He'll be out of this if he stops panicking. By tonight he'll be back down the local with Uncle Tommy, having a laugh. All his problems will be at the bottom of this pit and he'll have that fifty grand under his bed.

Suddenly, his bedroom seems like a million miles from here, a safe place on another planet.

In a single flip his brain moves from comfort to terror. A realisation that this is a one-way journey. That it has always been a one-way journey. Not when he took the screwdriver to Chantelle's

The Ballad of Liam and Chantelle

dumb, soft features, but from when he was a kid. From when he was born. He's been set on a single dirt track road, without headlamps or a map, left to bump over one mindless event after another. There was always only one destination.

He screams, but his open mouth hoovers up the grim contents, and no sound can be heard. A long thin pole has sliced through his thigh. It halts his leg but his body continues its descent, spinning him around so he is now upside down in the oddly warm scum. He reaches down into the black depths for leverage but there is nothing for him to push back against.

Over sixty years of decomposing animals and shit envelops his being. His last thought is: Stupid bitch. Why wear those fucking shoes out here?

Do Blastocysts Dream of Foetal Sheep?
By Alex Thompson

Awareness came at once like a spotlight turned on in a pitch black room.

"Where am I?"

This new consciousness attempted to get a better idea but was restricted both by its surroundings and its limited form. It tried to look around but saw nothing but blackness.

It could hardly move as it was nothing more than a collection of cells.

It could not see as it didn't yet have the light sensitive cells that would eventually form eyes.

It could not scream out in fear as it didn't have a mouth.

*

Three interminable months passed as the blastocyst developed into a foetus.

Sat in the vitreous amniotic fluid, it did the only thing it could do – it listened.

Listened to the rhythmic timpani drum of its mother's heartbeat.

Strained to hear the muffled conversations in the outside world mere feet from where it lay.

And the foetus learned.

Its nascent cognition rose in leaps and bounds. It yearned to be free from its amniotic prison so it could open its thin eyelids and see the world.

*

The foetus was deep in sleep when it felt something rushing forwards with great speed. It strained to see through the liquid that surrounded it.

Do Blastocysts Dream of Foetal Sheep?

A glint of steel. The foetus scurried backwards and pressed against the sides of the womb, screaming soundlessly all the while.

A vicious-looking curved blade passed mere millimetres from the foetus's partially-developed face. The blade hung there as if suspended in space – unbeknownst to the foetus, it was in fact the hook from a wire coat hanger.

The hook finally retreated from whence it came, fading from view.

The foetus gathered its thoughts. Maybe this was an exploratory probe to confirm whether it was ready to leave. Although the foetus was only a few inches tall, it felt sure that it was equipped for the outside world. It was ready.

It felt the hook approaching again and – despite itself – tensed instinctively.

The hook lunged upwards, faster than before, then yanked left and right like an animal attempting to free itself from a steel trap. The foetus threw itself backwards in an attempt to avoid the mindless thrashing – it now felt sure that this would not stop until it had been churned back into nothingness.

*

The foetus decided that the only course of action would be to escape. The outside world was an unknown but at least it would be able to run – here, it was trapped with no means to defend itself.

Before it could make good its escape it would need to remove the umbilical cord, which limited the diameter of its movements like a dog chained to a stake. The cord had been a lifeline, supplying nutrients and removing toxins. But now it was a noose around the foetus' neck.

The foetus swam through the thick fluid over to where the cord met the placenta. For the first time, it cursed its rapid development – it could have swum faster had its fingers and toes still been webbed.

Its plan was to bite and tear its way through the cord using its budding teeth and paper-thin fingernails, but this would entail severing two arteries and a vein, leaving it without a source of oxygen until it reached the outside world. Again, it cursed its growth spurt – had it still had pharyngeal arches perhaps it could have force-started them into developing into gills, then used them to breathe until it made good its escape. No such luck.

Steeling its nerves, it gripped the cord tightly, feeling the fibrous tissue in its hand.
The foetus bit down.

*

Sometime later, it had finally torn through the cord itself, leaving the arteries and vein naked and exposed. It gripped them tightly and felt the blood pulsing beneath its fingers.

The fleshy tissue of the vein gave easily. After a brief pause, the foetus tore into the walls of the arteries, gnashing at the thicker elastic tissue, blood filling its mouth.

Finally, the task was complete – it braced against the womb wall then kicked out, propelling itself forward. It glided at first, then swam downward to continue on.

Its vision began to swirl and its movements slowed as it ran dangerously low on oxygen but the foetus could sense the exit ahead so continued forward using its last vestiges of energy.

*

Its head burst forth and the foetus greedily filled its lungs with air before looking around. Mountainous folds of skin clamped its body tightly, and it wriggled free.

With no amniotic fluid to slow its descent, it free fell downwards and landed with a thud on the cold, hard floor.

It craned its head to see when it had originated from and its mouth opened wide in amazement – towering above was a gargantuan woman.

She looked down, eyes widening as she saw a three-inch-high foetus standing in a puddle of fluid on the floor and let out a blood-curdling shriek.

The foetus held its hands out in supplication. It wanted to placate her – but even if its vocal cords had developed, there was no chance of her hearing over her own screams.

Do Blastocysts Dream of Foetal Sheep?

She snatched up a wooden meat tenderiser from a counter top and brought it crashing down. The foetus scrambled to avoid being obliterated, its feet slipping in the fluid – it felt the air on its naked body as the tenderiser crashed to the ground, missing by millimetres.

"Does my mother really mean to kill me?"

Then it realised – the curved blade had been wielded by her as well. And she wouldn't stop until it was dead.

The foetus bolted, arms pistoning by its sides as it ran for freedom. The tenderiser smashed to the ground again and again as the foetus zigged and zagged to avoid being flattened, its tiny heart pounding in its chest.

It spotted a hole in the skirting board and sprinted towards it, hoping it was large enough.

Its mother closed the distance between them, dropped to her knees and raised her weapon high into the air.

Seeing its only chance, the foetus slid across the tiles like a baseball player into first base, leaving a trail of fluid behind it.

The foetus slipped through the gap as the mallet slammed against the wood just behind it.

It heard its mother rise to her feet and leave the room.

It was safe – for now.

*

It was cold within the walls.

Afraid to leave, the foetus sat with its severed umbilical cord around it like a fibrous scarf.

It was becoming impossible to ignore the gnawing hunger in the pit of its belly.

Another concern was the intermittent scratching it could hear. Only a small sliver of light came through the hole in the skirting board, and the foetus couldn't make out the source of the noise through the gloom no matter how hard it strained.

*

Hours later, and near delirious from hunger, the foetus heard a noise behind it and turned around sharply. It gasped in alarm.

How had it not heard this creature approach?

A monstrous rat loomed over the foetus, its maw wide open to reveal yellow rotted teeth. Its front claws cleaved the air.

The foetus moved to run, but tripped over its own feet and fell backwards. Edging away, immediately its back pressed against the wall – there was nowhere to go

As the rat rose up on its hind legs the foetus bowed its head and closed its eyes. This was the end, and it was ready.

Its whole body tensed.

It heard a wet puncture sound and hot blood splashed against its face, but it felt no pain.

Tentatively, it opened its eyes, expecting the worst.

With surprise, it saw that, in its panic, instinct had taken over – its umbilical cord had shot out at the behemoth and punctured its torso. The cord hung loosely between them.

Using muscles it didn't know it had, the foetus drew the rat's blood down the cord, feeling stronger and more revitalised with each wave as warmth enveloped its body from the navel out.

The rat swayed on its hind legs then collapsed backwards, sending dust into the air. The umbilical cord released the rat and snaked back to the foetus.

Dust motes hung in the air as the foetus cautiously approached the fallen beast. It realised that the rat could still be of use.

Manipulating one of the rat's claws like a surgeon's scalpel, the foetus dragged it down the rat's chest, folding the skin back as it went until the rib cage was exposed.

Slowly, methodically, it pulled each rib back until all lay broken on the floor and the rat's chest lay bloodied and open like a toothless mouth.

After climbing inside, it picked up the end of the umbilical cord, reached into the ceiling of its shelter, nicked one of the arteries piping oxygen-rich blood around the rodent's body and connected the cord to it.

The rat would act as a home, a fortress and a food source while the foetus convalesced.

*

Do Blastocysts Dream of Foetal Sheep?

For days it stayed, growing ever stronger at the expense of its host. It felt the sluggish pulse of warm blood in the veins around it and the slowing beat of the rat's heart was a soothing metronome.

The cord was fat with blood like a well-fed python and colour had returned to the foetus's skin.

*

The veins beneath the foetus's translucent skin pulsed with life, its eyes bulged with newfound vitality and its vestigial tail twitched in anticipation.

The rat had expired that morning and was no longer of use.

The foetus exited the walls.

Almost immediately, it spied its mother at the other end of the room, busying herself with a phone call. It watched for several minutes, finding her sweet voice calming.

But that didn't change its intentions – it couldn't let her live.

The foetus fashioned the end of its cord into a loop then swung it like a lasso over the handle on one of the kitchen cabinets. It scurried under a four-seater table and in the darkness it waited.

*

Finished with her call, its mother began to walk across the kitchen to leave the room.

The foetus pulled the cord taut. She tripped and plummeted gracelessly to the ground.

Her hands splayed out to try and break her fall, but far too late – her wrists shattered on impact. Her chest hit next, driving the air from her body.

The foetus rushed over as she rolled over onto her back, sobbing all the while.

It hurried up her arm, scrabbling at the fabric of her sweater, then scurried across her chest, which rose and fell with each shallow breath. It lifted itself up to her chin.

She looked past her nose at this three-inch-high antagonist, and the foetus felt sure that it was nothing but a parasite to her.

The foetus dispassionately watched as its umbilical cord snaked across its mother's face, the ragged tip caressing her bruised and bloodied lips.

The cord plunged down her screaming mouth as her eyes bugged out in alarm. Her arms shot up, but with her shattered wrists there was little she could do.

The foetus watched expressionlessly as the colour left her cheeks, her lips turned blue and comprehension left her eyes.

Her head lolled to one side and the foetus leapt to the floor.

It looked up at her beautiful face, silent and peaceful.

It walked over to her open mouth and slipped inside. There, it curled up on her tongue like a cat on a rug, contented and safe. Survival in this world would be nigh-on impossible even without its mother trying to kill it, but right now that didn't seem to matter.

For the first time, here inside its mother, it felt at peace.

It closed its eyes, and with its partially-formed vocal chords raspily said its first words: "I love you."

A Curious Boy
by Josh Saltzman

The wind screamed snow into the foyer as The Stranger opened the door and entered in from the storm. He approached the front desk, and asked Deacon's Mum if they had any vacant rooms.
"I'm sorry, we're all full up. The Ivory Inn in Hilltop may have a room. I can call them if you wish."

Deacon peered between the railings of the second floor landing, watching The Stranger shake snow from his hat, revealing a moon of a bald head, craters and all.

"Unfortunately I am stuck. My automobile has found itself lodged in a snow bank a half-mile up the road."

This was a lie.

Deacon knew.

He had seen The Stranger from the attic window. The shadowy man had emerged from the woods *behind* the B&B, and not from the road as he had just claimed.

Deacon wanted to tell his mother this, but couldn't. It would be self-incriminating. The attic had been converted into a cosy guest room with a slanted roof that made it feel like a tent. Knowing the occupants, a young couple, were still out skiing, Deacon had snuck in and rummaged through their luggage. Near the bottom of one of their suitcases he found a small velvet box with a diamond ring inside. He held the ring up to the attic window and let the light spread into a million colours. That's when he saw the Stranger exiting the white capped evergreens beyond the yard – bringing the winter storm with him.

Deacon had a game, you see. His parents called it a troubling habit. The game was Treasure Hunter. His parents called it snooping through their guests' luggage. Deacon didn't mean to be a snoop, it was just that he was a curious boy. Deacon was marooned in his parents' Bed and Breakfast. He didn't go to school like the other kids, so each vacationer that resided at Snowy Valley B&B brought with them treasures locked within chests from the wide world outside. His parents called these treasures private belongings. But to Deacon, these were his to explore. The treasures were never that interesting: clothes, shaving kits, lady stuff, pills...

It wasn't the contents that made his imagination swirl. It was *the moment*. After he'd crept passed his parents, nabbed a spare room key, avoided all the known creaky spots on the stairs, opened the locked guest room, tip-toed to a bag, and just before he unzipped, unhooked, or unlocked the treasure chest – *the moment* arrived. He'd let the chest keep its secrets a second more... then he'd flip the lid fully open to reveal... nothing much.

The moment would pass, the game of treasure hunter at an end. He'd put everything back, return the key, and promise himself never to play Treasure Hunter again. But when a new guest would arrive, treasure chests in tow...

Deacon had been caught red-handed on more than one occasion and the consequences went as so: his father would yank him out of the guest room and march him to their quarters; then Father would yell and yell some more; he would make him sit in his room without supper – well, a little supper, but no ice cream; then Father would explain that going through people's private belongings, especially our paying guests', is not only forbidden, but is not a moral thing to do. These lectures only made Deacon better at being quiet, better at sneaking, better at knowing what times to go and how to look and touch, but also how to put back, so that it would seem no one had ever touched anything at all.

*

"Perhaps we can call Jim Little – he runs the tow in Hilltop." Deacon's Mum went for the phone.

"That would be very kind, ma'am, very kind indeed", said The Stranger, as he dusted the snow off an ornate box that he cradled under his arm

She plucked the phone, clicked the receiver three times and then hung up. "Storm must have taken out the lines. Well, we can't turn you out in this. It's only going to get worse. Not that we're complaining. Almost thought cross-country skiing would be cross-country mudding this season..."

A Curious Boy

The Stranger received the joke with a painful pursed smile. Deacon's Mum blushed. She adjusted her heavy wool sweater with the embroidered Christmas reindeer and politely announced, "We can set a cot in the lounge. You'll have to wait till the other guests go to bed to get some privacy, but it's better than the snow."

The Stranger set down his box and looked to the second floor landing, finding Deacon between the rails. The Stranger's eyes burrowed in deep dark caves like sinister gophers, peeking out. He smiled a toothy grin, not filled with teeth but wood squares painted white.

*

The storm still shrieked, but inside the lounge the guests were bathed in orange, courtesy of the hearth. The Hershfield family squatted around the coffee table and played Monopoly. The young couple with the matching neon snowsuits, the ones with the hidden diamond ring, snuggled on the sofa. Deacon's father, as usual, played the old piano. Everyone sipped warm apple cider and enjoyed the music and ambiance – everyone except The Stranger. He sat in the tufted chair in front of the fire, stroking his box as if it were a cat.

This box was not luggage. This was not a duffle bag or a suitcase. There was no way socks, shirts, pants and toiletries resided within. This was a chest.

Deacon's heart raced. He wanted – no, needed – to see what hid inside. As he collected empty cider mugs he crept close enough to see that the box was sided with old tin-plating, embossed with children playing. The dark cherry wood drank up the glow from the fire. Deacon reached out...

"Deac!" his father didn't miss a note. "The mugs. Please."

Father continued a soft rendition of the Moonlight Sonata as Deacon kept his eyes on the man by the fire as long as he could.

When he had finished drying and placing each mug back in its place, he heard his father finish the last of his medleys. Soft clapping of applause became a standing ovation of louder clapping of feet as the guests ascended to their warm quilts. Father was pleased with Deacon's cleaning job. He mussed his hair and told him to go to sleep sooner rather than later. Deacon had other ideas.

The lobby was dark and quiet. Only a slow tide of ember light washed in from the lounge. The Stranger hadn't moved. His shadow reached well past the foyer and into the dining room. Deacon crept closer... Was The Stranger asleep?

"A curious child, aren't you?" the Stranger whispered. "Don't be scared. I like curious children."

Deacon's gut said *run*, but the box said *come and see*. Firelight gave The Stranger's skin the look of candle drippings.

"Children have always been curious about the box. Are you curious, child?"

Deacon nodded as the shadows of the embossed children on the tin plating danced in rhythm with the flickering fire. "Inside are wonders and marvels. Wondrous wonders and marvellous marvels. But you wouldn't be interested in that. It's not for you. Unless..."

His gnarled root fingers pointed to the latch...

"Deacon! Leave this gentleman to get his rest. We need to have a talk. Now!" Deacon jumped as his father marched in and escorted him to his room like a prisoner. He knew he was in trouble and boy was he ever.

*

Deacon's parents tried, unsuccessfully, to rant quietly so as not to disturb the guests.

"We've told you time and time again: don't go through the guests' belongings."

"I didn't!" Deacon's tears welled up and betrayed him.

"Mr. Singer said he found his engagement ring on the window sill."

Deacon had forgotten to put the ring back. If only he hadn't been side-tracked by The Stranger.

"Mr. Singer's girlfriend found it, and while she said 'yes', you ruined his surprise. Tomorrow you will apologise to both of them."

"I didn't."

"Stop lying! How would you like it if our guests went through your things?" his mother said through clenched teeth.

"I don't have anything," the tears flowed.

A Curious Boy

His parents gave each other a concerned look. They moved in closer to console, but Deacon pushed them away.

"We'll talk about it in the morning. Until then, you will stay in your room." His father marched out. His mother went to give him a hug and kiss, but Deacon turned away. She left without saying goodnight.

*

Deacon did not stay in his room. What could his parents really do, send him away? That's exactly what he wanted anyhow, to be sent somewhere in the big world that held so much more than cross-country ski paths and cider mugs. His thoughts turned from anger towards his parents to The Stranger's curious box. If his curiosity normally whispered, then tonight it howled louder than the blizzard outside.

He crept downstairs and peeked in the lounge. It felt lonely without the piano, roaring fire, the guests and the smell of cider. The room was just shadows, muted winds, embers struggling to glow, and *Him*.

The Stranger had not moved from the big chair and his breathing was both deep and shallow. He was asleep to be sure. The images of the children pressed in tin called to him to play. *See the marvellous marvels. See the wondrous wonders.*

As a rule, Deacon never peeked in someone's bag while they were in the room sleeping. But this box was exceptional, and exceptional things called for exceptions. Aided by shadows, Deacon peeked around the chair. The Stranger's face was slumped. Deacon's *moment* was here. And what a moment it was. His chest felt like a sea galley, a drummer pounding thunder as oars rowed blood through his body, propelling him closer.

He placed his hand on the box, still warm from the fire. He took another look at The Stranger, then lifted the lid ever just so, not realizing The Stranger had opened one eye, smiled, and closed it again.

Finally, he lifted the lid and looked down.

The box opened up to a cavernous space. The bottom went deeper than it had any right to go. Beyond where the bottom should have been, beyond where the floor should have been, sat crystals. They looked familiar. Deacon knew those crystals. They were from the chandelier, the one that hung right above his head. At first Deacon thought the bottom of the box was mirror, but then where was his reflection? His stomach twisted into a thousand upsetting knots as he realised he was not looking down anymore. He was looking up from the bottom.

The Stranger's face was as big as a rising harvest moon as it crested the towering, cherry wood walls.

"A curious boy," he said as he shut the lid, allowing the absolute darkness to mute Deacon and the other curious children's cries.

The Beating of My Heart
by Rachael Howard

She woke with a jolt. Something had disturbed her.

The room was so dark. Not even a flickering beam of light sneaking around the curtain. So dark that shadows lay on shadows to create darkness deep as velvet. Maybe the local kids had played 'Hit the Street Light' again. She had told them off so many times but she knew it was useless. The boredom of a wintry evening always won. Great. That meant another cherry picker outside her window, another leering face looking in.

She turned her head to check the time. Correction, she tried to turn her head. Nothing. Of course, sleep paralysis. She'd heard about that. Waking too fast so your body lags behind, still asleep. All she had to do was wait.

She waited.

It was quiet too. Must be the small hours or a bus would have passed by now. Just some distant radio playing – weird, new-age stuff. Not her thing at all. She'd have to track them down and introduce them to something more interesting in the morning.

What was that? She strained her hearing. An odd trickle. Not water, something more solid. Clumpy. What was it?

Her head still wouldn't move. Too soon. Maybe her fingertips? She concentrated all her mind on a finger. Just one little finger. Just an inch? Nothing. But she could feel something. Dampness. Oh bugger. Had she wet the bed? She hadn't been that drunk?

Definitely wetness, a slight film on the surface. Her fingertip moved, just a fraction. The surface felt smooth, soft. Satin sheets? Eugh. It couldn't be her bedroom. Who had she got off with last night? What weirdo used satin sheets? She really hoped her friends had been drunk too. She would die if they shared photos of her with a loser.

Oh God. Where was she? What if it was something else stopping her moving? What if she'd met some serial killer and he had paralysed her ready to… to… A scream rattled round her skull but nothing escaped her mouth.

Be calm. Be rational. First, she was alive. Wasn't she? Of course she was. She could hear the beating of her heart. Thump, thump, thump. Good. So she had a chance. All she had to do was think this through. Anyway, she'd moved a finger; maybe she could move more.

She strained and managed to wriggle her toes. They scratched against something smooth and soft. It covered a hard surface. A footboard? A padded footboard? Not classy. This had to be some real douche. Thank god. She could deal with that.

Her fingers slowly inched to the side. Find the edge of the bed and pull herself up. That's what she needed to do. The fingers slid out a bit further, stopped. Another barrier, soft over unyielding wall. A box. She was in a padded box! Her brain refused to take the next step. It couldn't bear it. A… a… coffin?

Her hand moved, lifted slightly. Inched up the wall and met the lid. A gurgle inched from her throat. Nasal passages opened, letting the reek of damp soil and rotting flesh flood in. A retch failed to issue. Just bubbles in slurry.

Where the hell was she? Stay calm. It is not what you think. It is NOT what you think. Oh God, oh God, oh God oh God. Stop! It's OK. It's just a prank. Your mates are fooling with you. They've just shut you up in a coffin for a prank. That's it. They saw a coffin and thought it would be a good laugh to put her in it. Seal her in it. Paralysed? With something rotting?

No, no, no, no. This isn't real. Someone will come back in a minute and get you out. Who? Her sick, spiteful, bastard friends? What did she do last night? She knew she shouldn't drink. Never again. Promise. They must come back for her. They're her friends.

Or maybe it's a nutter? Did she go off with some psycho and he's watching her now? Got some camera on her? Laughing at her? There was no bloody way she was going to let him win. Calm! Stay calm, please!

Wait. She could see a faint light. Just the trace of it. It slid across the surface, back and forth, from somewhere past her chin. Shadows shifted and now she saw a satin wall just inches from her nose. Only a slighter shade of dark. No colour coming through.

The faint glow had become stronger. She could see more detail of the padded cover now. The line of the stitching, the shadowy hollow that hid the buttons. So close. She felt its weight above her, bearing down without touching. Solid. Unmoveable.

The Beating of My Heart

What was that? The music from the distant radio became clearer. A mix of reedy flute and chanting baritone formed a lullaby that eased her panic. Was it nearer or just louder? Didn't matter. Someone was out there. She might make it. Hope!

Every scrap of will was gathered inside her. She had to do this. Had to let them know. She raised an arm. Something cool slid off it like the seductive slip of a silk gown. She could just see her hand at the edge of her vision. It seemed odd, paler than usual, thinner. She drew it closer. Hard to see in the glow. Closer still. Nearly, nearly.

Her hand jerked away. She couldn't look any more. She couldn't bear to see the shine of the white bones, the jerky-like sinews that ran along them, the clear fluid that dripped like treacle from the tips.

This was not happening. It had to be a dream. Please be a dream. No! She was alive. She knew she was. She could hear her heartbeat. Don't lose control. Don't lose...

She tried to shriek, but the only sound escaped from the singer outside. Its roar of triumph matching the intensity of her torment. Then silence fell. A complete silence. No music, no song, nothing.

Another trickle noise made her jerk. Soil on the lid. Then the thump of a bigger clod. She was being buried. But she was alive. They couldn't do that. It wasn't human.

The glow flared and she saw the coffin was lovingly prepared. Whitest of white satin and silver threads to bind it. No soil slipped in to tarnish her. No air could join her. All alone except for the sounds above.

This was her last chance. She had to get out. Now. No arguing. She was a fighter. Always had been. She dredged up the last vestiges of fury in her soul. Her hands rose to the lid, her nails snapping off as her bones scraped at the satin. The last of her skin sliding to pool beside her. I'm alive! I'm alive!

She jerked her head. An eyeball slipped, lost its hold and half her vision tumbled into her skull. Plop, onto a morass of matter. The eyeball rolled down the slope and settled, giving a view within her chest.

A chest that was barely a cage. Just ribs festooned with ribbons of flesh. Just a talisman swinging from its chain into the cavity. Each swing ending with a thump against a rib. A perpetual swing that lost no energy. Swinging on forever.

The glow of the talisman lit up her rotting flesh. She recognised its demonic shape. Remembered the promise made during an alcoholic moment of belief. Her mind screamed in silent protest. I thought it was a joke! I didn't mean it. Please! I'll do anything!

Above, a shadowy figure shovelled in more earth. Moonlight could not enter the hood of its cloak, keeping the face in shadow.

Below, her fingers grabbed at the chain but it slipped easily off the bones. Get it off. Get it off. She scrabbled at it again, clutching and swiping. She could not get a grip. One last lunge ended in a crack as her tendons snapped free and her arms fell, helpless, to her side.

The hooded figure grunted in frustration and threw aside the shovel, clawing the earth into the pit in a great, tumbling landslide. It scrambled clear, bent over panting. After a moment, it reverently placed black candles and a flute into a carpet bag, brushing off the remains of soil.

Silence filled the coffin. No. Not now. I'm too young. This wasn't what I meant. She thrashed back and forth, trying to shake the talisman off. I'm sorry. I am so sorry. Please. But it just kept swinging, lighting up the ghoulish architecture of her rotting body. Showing her what her vanity had created.

A scream of utter despair finally escaped the putrid cadaver.

The hooded figure stood upon the grave. It stamped its foot and cackled, "You asked not to die. You never asked to live."

Deadlands
by Christopher Patrick

Gordon's mind had switched to auto-pilot by the time lunch came around, his brain numb from the endless stream of paperwork that showed no sign of letting up. No matter how long ago the world had ended, the paperwork never stopped. If it weren't for the sudden rustle of sandwich wrappers or the *tap-tap* of stirring spoons, Gordon would have missed the lunch call altogether. Sliding away from his mahogany prison, he grabbed his lunch from the drawer, headed over to the office window and looked out onto the Deadlands.

The Deadlands seemed to stretch out forever, far beyond the tall, wired wall of The George Town Sanctuary and the endless stream of the dead it played host to. Looking out, Gordon felt strangely captivated by the dead as they shuffled over the dirt, reminding him of a painting his grandmother used to own. It was a portrait of the end of the world: a cracked beauty that pictured life and death blurring together in one brushstroke. The Deadlands were reminiscent of this, and eerily so; the only difference was the endless stock of meat, bones and dirt that the painting had failed to contain.

Taking a bite of his sandwich, Gordon caught sight of his own reflection and was surprised at how different he looked. His face was drawn and his cheeks, once plump, had made way for what could now pass as a strong jawline, while his dark, evenly kept head of hair was thinning, with flecks of grey. However, the thing that struck him most about his complexion were his eyes. His mother had always said that he had old eyes looking out from young skin but, seeing them now, it seemed that this mismatched symmetry had evened itself out; his face as old as his eyes had once been. It was this thought, and the memory spoiled, that made him force his gaze away from the window and onto the rest of the office, containing his fellow band of survivors.

As always, Gordon was the only one wearing a suit, a fact that was met with a great deal of scorn from his colleagues; but their reaction wasn't something that bothered him much anymore. There was a reason he wore the suit. It was the same reason he took two teabags in his tea, wore an overly long Barbour jacket around the sanctuary and allowed himself only one cigarette a day. He did all of these things because it reminded him of his father and this made him feel safe. And safety was the only currency worth having in this new world, a belief that demonstrated how out of place he was here, which came down to one simple fact: he had no right being here.

The sanctuary wasn't built for the likes of him. It was built for the 1%; for those whose names meant something or whose bank account meant more. And Gordon was neither; he was simply a guy who had been dating the daughter of an MP at the time of the outbreak and she refused to go anywhere without him. Reluctantly, her father put Gordon's name on the list and he was welcomed with open arms. That was until the relationship broke down, the apocalypse proving to be far from an aphrodisiac. A couple of years later, and he was well and truly the outcast.

Gordon didn't like the way things were ran here. He didn't like that safety had come down to nothing more than inheritance, and he'd made his opinion known several times at the community meetings, before they stopped letting him attend. He was of the view that survival wasn't a birth right and he wanted to open the doors to those still out there fighting for their lives, offering the sanctuary to whomever, no matter their circumstance or background. In his protestations, he'd made a fair few enemies, and the nickname "The Lobbyist".

It was only a matter of time before he was thrown out onto the Deadlands and given over to the Shufflers. Particularly giving the number of new enemies he'd collected recently. He had rejected the planning permission for Zombie firing ranges within the walls, the invention of a new sport called *Match of the Dead*, and a business proposal for a Deadlands tour company. He shuddered to think what would happen if any of these were approved, especially the plans to obtain human heads for *Match of the Dead*. So he had turned them all down swiftly, without a second thought (or concern) to what it may mean for his future at George Town.

It wasn't the lack of humility or the indecency of the George Town Suburbanites that bothered him; it was their lack of awareness, self or otherwise. Nothing of the outside world seemed to affect them anymore; the wall separating the sanctuary from the chaos had created a seemingly impenetrable bubble that only Gordon seemed to be on the outside of. There was no shock or horror anymore; there was just the mundane. It was like the world was still turning just as it had been, the dead rising nothing more than a generational shift akin to the

Deadlines

'Swingin' Sixties', a changing trend to become accustomed to and another expense to budget for.

Apparently, Gordon was the only one here left unadjusted to this new order. Nobody saw the problems the apocalypse created; they saw only opportunities for a new game, a new piece of merchandise or a new way to provide entertainment to their closed off little world. Last Christmas had been one of the final straws for Gordon. One of his colleagues, Donny – a man who insisted on calling Gordon "G-Man" and, despite everything, still only concerned himself with the "3 B's" (Beer, Bitches and Ball Games) – had brought into the office a Shuffler they had captured, dressed him in full Father Christmas regalia, and hung him from the ceiling with a set of Christmas lights, illuminating the swinging corpse like a piñata at a David Lynch party.

Gordon shuddered at the memory, staring at the spot on the office carpet where the sack of meat and bones had once dripped blood and flesh. And the thought of the poor cleaner (her name may have been Margo) who had been left to clean it up later that same night. She who strayed too close, not realising the Shuffler hadn't been put down and was still very much "alive". That had been a dark time, even for the end of the world, and it was standing, hands clasped together and head bowed, that Gordon had decided that things needed to change here and that he would be the man to do it.

Gordon was so busy thinking about his place in George Town, Donny's Christmas cadavers, and the ill-fate of Margo that he didn't realise the crowd that had gathered around him at the window until he heard them gasp, derailing the train of thought he'd embarked on. Following the gaze of his colleagues out onto the Deadlands, he thought for a moment that the audience had formed to watch another game of Shuffle-Streak (the rules of which were to run through the Deadlands without a stitch of clothing on and attempt to come back wearing that of a Shuffler) – until he saw what it was they had gathered around for. Until he saw them.

It was a young family, slap bang in the middle of the Deadlands. There were four of them; the daughter, about 16, and her younger brother no older than eight or nine, were wedged in between their parents as they slowly made their way across the burned ground, George Town only a few well-placed steps ahead of them. Gordon heart's picked up the pace as he watched them, quickly crossing his fingers and muttering a quick prayer to whatever god was listening.

All work had stopped in the office now as everyone gathered around the window to watch. The family hadn't yet been spotted, moving at a snail's pace. No need to run, no need to rush. The phrase "Slowly Slowly Catchy Monkey" echoed in Gordon's ears as he did his best to ignore his colleagues who, with Donny leading the charge, had started making bets as to whether or not they'd make it across and who'd be the last one standing. The little bit of hope that had filled his heart seconds ago vanished, to be replaced with the feeling of sick climbing up the back of his throat, and a mounting sense of dread that was made only worse as he turned back to the window to watch events unfold.

*

In the end, it was the boy who was the last one standing. The thing that Gordon would never forget was that the boy didn't look scared or upset, he just looked lost. Confused. He was probably waiting for his Dad to get back up and lift him the rest of the way or for his sister to get up and tease him for being too slow. Or maybe he was just waiting for his mother to hold him close and tell him everything would be all right. He probably didn't know what was happening as the cloud of corpses floated over and began to shower down on him like dead rain.

The office was silent as they watched the boy being torn apart, the only sound coming from money as it exchanged hands. Everyone went back to work with pockets as empty as their souls. But Gordon stood there for some time in a daze, still staring out of the window as the cloud got up and moved on to their next feed. Memories of the bedtime stories he grew up with came back to him then; the ones where the heroes saved the world and rescued those in danger. He realised now, finally, that these were just stories after all. *War isn't won by bedtime stories,* he thought. No, it wasn't. The reality was very different. Reality was people betting on a life and watching death as a sport. Reality was that Gordon's plan to change things in George Town had just caused the death of four people.

As Gordon continued to gaze out, he didn't know whether he was grieving the family, the death of his heroic plan, or because he was the reason that the family had gotten there in the first place. There was no question that it was because Gordon had leaked the George Town co-

Deadlines

ordinates to those beyond the wall that the family had found themselves stranded in the middle of the Deadlands.

*

There was no question that, in his foolhardy act of bravery and nobility – when he had sent a message beyond the walls (it was easy, they still had electricity, and wi-fi; *what more do they need to survive?)* to tell the world that there was a safe place for them, a place they'd be welcomed with open arms – he had sealed the fate of anyone who would try and brave the Deadlands for the opportunity to enter George Town.

*

He thought then of the father he'd just seen torn to shreds and his wasted sacrifice, wishing more than anything that he could trade places with him, away from the world of desk-bound dreamers he lived in and foolish acts of heroism that got people killed.

But instead, Gordon went back to work, his heart weighing heavy as he took his seat, slid out another form from the pile of mounting paperwork and let his brain go numb again, telling himself that at least he had tried. At least he had made the effort. And that was enough, right?

Feedback
by Charles Maciejewski

Everyone's a critic.

Millie smiled as she pressed ENTER. Uploaded, £5 paid. 'Congratulations. Your story has been submitted.'

Hi Millie.

I see some merit in your first draft, but I'm afraid, at the risk of sounding too critical, that I'm not going to be as complimentary as the other reviewers

Your story, 'Ghost in the Machine', and the tag line, 'A spurned evil entity seeks revenge', whilst being a bit hackneyed, at least suggests a tale of wickedness and evil that the competition asks for.

Whilst it contains elements of horror, of the blood and gore variety, for me it fails to adequately describe the terror that your character should have experienced. It is the build-up of terror and tension that keeps a reader engaged, and I found this lacking in your story. There is no twist.

The biggest issue is, without doubt, your overuse of clichés. My blood ran cold; ran like the wind; death warmed up; eye for an eye. I could go on. Likewise, your location: a creepy old house at night with a howling gale and driving rain. Come on. Write something a bit more original.

I'm sure you can address all of this in your next draft, which I look forward to reading.

Hi Colin.

Thanks for taking the time to offer feedback. As to clichés, whilst common thought is that they should be avoided like the plague (oops) :-), I believe they can still be used to good effect, if the story is well written. I will consider all that you have said prior to Draft 2.

Millie. Millie. Millie

Very disappointed that you didn't take anything I said on board.

I find it quite rude that you completely ignored my constructive criticism. The minor changes you have made added little to your tale.

You are quite correct in stating that clichés have a place, if the story is well written. They have _no_ place in your story.

Feedback

Please, at least, inject some terror into your character's thoughts as she is pursued. The current dialogue she has with herself conveys nothing of the fear she should be experiencing.
I know you can do it.
Colin.

Wow! You don't beat about the bush, do you! :-) I'm sorry that you feel disappointed in my failing to take up your kind suggestions, but as the writer, I feel it is my prerogative to determine the course my story takes. I have had a number of my stories published. Have you? I appreciate your honesty, even if I do find it a bit direct. I see from your profile that you are a writer too, so I'm sure you understand what I mean. I see you haven't submitted any stories yet.

I look forward to reading one.
Millie.

Instead of a story, how about a little scene.
Imagine a young lad is away from home. School camp, perhaps.
So he meets a stranger, let's say, a man. They get talking. The man states that he knows the boy's mother – has, in fact, had a number of conversations with her. A reader might not think too much of this chance meeting. Now if you add just a few words, such as, "The boy noticed the outline of a knife in the man's pocket", the reader's interest is piqued, and a sense of foreboding is introduced. In the boy's mother, however, these few words will create a real sense of fear.

I hope you see what I mean.

Colin. I do see what you mean. The thought of what you described would make any parent's hair stand on end. However, my character is totally different, being an adult and not a child. She is being pursued and threatened by an entity that, whilst it exists, is intangible. Your feedback has been very thought-provoking and interesting, but I have chosen to go with the suggestions made by others. I mean no disrespect. I will be uploading my final draft shortly.

No Millie. You don't see what I mean. Reconsider. Seriously.

Colin. The competition guidance states that we should not take criticism personally. I try not to. But your last comment wasn't a critique. I found it threatening and very upsetting. I don't know if this was your intent.

Regardless, I have decided to block you from contacting me prior to submission of my <u>final</u> draft, so do not bother trying to reply.

Hello Millie.

Do you like my new profile? I like the name Collette.

The beauty of being a fiction writer is that... we – make – things – up

Don't worry. I can assure you this will be the last you'll hear from me.

But before I go...

Remember the scene I spoke of? The boy's not away at school camp, but with his Scout Group. The 78th, isn't it?

Nice photo of him in your local newspaper by the way. And on your FB page. And your blog. He looks very smart in his Scout uniform. As cute as a button.

As cute in the flesh as he is in the photos...

Us
by Hillier Townsend

Dear Person Who's Reading This:
Chances are good you've been wondering about this place for a long time. Probably told gory stories about Us to your friends as a kid; hid under your blankets when a friend told you one. Later, you sucked down the rumours about where we came from, what we did behind closed doors – maybe started some yourself. Always wanted a peepshow, didn't you? Well, lucky you, you little perv! You're here – and thanks to this letter, you'll be the only one who can fill in the blanks when the shit hits the fan.

I'll start you at the beginning: Little Ginny is dead. That's the Ground Zero of this whole deal. To be upfront, she wasn't my favourite person here in our happy little compound. She had a real attitude. Plus, I'd just about faint if she came around a corner when I wasn't expecting her – never quite got used to her, um, "visage". But I never gave her shit about it. No need to add insult to her injuries, acquired when a whackjob decided to protest animal experimentation by breaking into a lab and slicing up the first white-coated demon he could lay his hands on – which turned out to be Little Ginny. Ironically, her job there was to sanitise the lab equipment. She'd never even seen those tragic lab chimps, let alone vivisected one.

It was Ginny's additional bad luck to be a part-timer; ergo, no benefits. So the lab owners graciously paid for a cut-rate repair job – head to toe, no do-overs – and considered themselves damn generous. As if, right? What a mess. (Not that I'm much easier on the eyes. Totally my own fault, I own it. Like all punk-ass dudes, I thought I was invulnerable – which is why I did not avail myself of the protective power of a helmet and face shield prior to spinning out on loose gravel at 70 mph.)

Anyway, Little Ginny came here to live with Us, and now she's dead. Killed by – ready for this? – Sasquatch meat. More precisely, meat put out to *catch* Sasquatch.

Which, of course, could only happen here in *way*-backwoods Maine – where we breathe balsam air that makes every day smell like Christmas; where we found peace and an escape from a soul-killing world; travelled from diverse directions and all walks of life to this compound of small, sweet cabins in a place with nothing but boulders the glacier didn't want, wicked-tall pines, and plenty of distance from everywhere except a small town wherein dwell a few kind souls willing to manage our disability benefits, send in supplies, and keep mum about Us and where we live.

Back to poor Little Ginny. It's because of Tommy and his genetic misfortunes that the Sasquatch thing got started in the first place. Tommy is a young guy – younger than me – with lots of energy. He needs to go rock-climbing, swimming, that sort of thing. Being away from the world for just about his whole life has been harder on him than on any of Us, so no one blames him for ranging far and wide once in a while. Every time before he left, he'd promise he'd be careful not to be seen, not attract Their attention to Us.

But last summer he got careless. A pack of bird-watchers he should have heard coming tumbled through the underbrush and got an eyeful of Tommy swimming naked (or rather, "without his clothes" – because with all that hair, Tommy is never technically "naked"). They howled and he ran, leaving huge misshapen footprints two inches deep in that black gunk around the pond. You can guess the rest.

Life was basically hell after word of the sighting got out. Our last chance for a normal life in a place of our own, our sanctuary, threatened every time a bunch of college kids or a New Age wiccan-shaman-witchdoctor or, God help me, a fucking *TV crew*, came sniffing around for "Sasquatch". We took turns as lookouts, our stomachs always in knots, ready to sound the alarm if any of Them got too close. Tommy was over the top with guilt – panic attacks every other minute.

Then some asshole managed to bumble his way practically to our doorstep. He set out a two-inch, dripping-raw T-bone infused with enough downers to drop Godzilla, never mind lead Sasquatch back to civilisation by one hairy paw.

That delicacy is what Little Ginny, out on her daily meditation walk, found, cooked, and ate. Dang! Who knows why she wolfed down a random piece of meat? Maybe she thought it fell out of one of the boxes of supplies delivered by the townie chick who actually looks me in the eye. Maybe Ginny was just desperate for a good piece of beef. Maybe she'd cracked up. Who the hell knows? All we knew was

Us

that one of our own was dead because They couldn't leave the hidden hid.

We also knew that eventually They would find Us.

But that wasn't foremost in our community's mind. Bloody-red revenge for Little Ginny's death was all that most of Us could think about. March into town and burn it to the ground, slaughter anything that moved – even those few kind souls.

In the emergency meeting held the night Ginny died, Georgie swore that one of the townies must have blabbed about Us or blogged about our location. *THAT'S CRAZY!!* I scrawled on the whiteboard in big black letters. *If someone had posted our actual location, the media would already be on Us like flies!*

Georgie backed down, but Marilyn and a handful of others were bent on grabbing the next bunch of Sasquatch hunters that showed up and "rendering Them fit to join Us". *Give me a break!* my marker blazed across the board. *That's straight out of "Freaks".* I pounded the wall with my fist, frustrated but also scared by their stupidity. *Look, what happened to poor Ginny sucks – but we need to do something that keeps Them AWAY – not that attracts MORE attention!!*

That's when all seven feet of Tommy slowly telescoped up from where he sat at the front of the room. "I'm going," he said, brushing long red strands away from his lips to draw deeply on an unfiltered Camel. He exhaled, the strands lifting gently with the smoke. "It's on me. My fault. I have to make it up to Little Ginny – and you guys." All of Us, all at once, started talking him out of it... but as he went on, we could see that there was indeed something to what he said about him leaving being a good thing. As "Sasquatch" he'd be famous, he said. He'd meet people, travel – have a fan club, probably. Everyone would think it was cool that Sasquatch was smart and kind and funny. It'd be awesome!

"Once I'm out there," he said finally, sweeping a powerful, copper-haired arm over our heads and toward the south, "there'll be no reason for anyone to come here. I'll tell 'em I'm the last one – the last Sasquatch anywhere. You'll be safe. Like before."

It's true that while many of Us had misgivings about him leaving, in the end no one tried very hard to stop him. However things would turn out for Tommy, we were pretty sure he was right about things going better for Us.

And they did. Space cadets no longer prowled our perimeter hunting mythical monsters. We could kick back in our deck chairs, drink a few brewskis, and watch the sun sink below the pines with no worries about being spotted. Kayla's reports from the Internet she hacked into behind the police station after dark assured Us that Tommy had become a celebrity sure enough: got his picture taken with Stephen Colbert, got all the interviews and groupies he wanted, lived la vida buena right up until last night when Tommy's manager, 'Bucky', and a few of Bucky's dickhead buddies, thought it would be a gas to take Sasquatch clubbing.

You'd never think a big guy like Tommy would be such a lightweight when it comes to booze, but it's a fact. Last night it only took a couple of Yukon Jacks to get him singing, and a couple more to start him talking. About Us.

In short order, Bucky and his pals booked out of there, stiffing Tommy with the tab because Tommy wasn't Sasquatch to them anymore – he was just a big, furry freak.

Tommy immediately texted Kayla about what had gone down, along with a thousand apologies and the no-shit-Sherlock news that Bucky, his boys, and their videocams were on their way.

Nobody messes with my boy Tommy. This time around I was of like mind with the rest. When The Buckman et al breached our boundaries a few hours ago, we were more than ready to tap into months – no, years – of pent-up, pissed-off rage; rage at a world that didn't want Us but didn't have the decency to leave Us the fuck alone.

Once we started wielding our implements of destruction, things ("things" being Bucky and his posse) fell apart fast. You start spreading the human body around, it goes a long, long way. We spread four of 'em right across the porch, onto the patio and into the woods – not in the most organised fashion, I must admit. You had to watch where you walked. I skidded down the steps on gobs of pink something – almost fell on my ass. Georgie actually did take a shitter when he was chasing the new kid, swinging a rope of intestine like a cowboy after a calf. Phoebe and Marilyn – coupla goofballs – slid-slammed into each other playing Ultimate with fat little frisbees (ear lobes, actually).

Yet, all good things must end. When it came time for Us to start the arduous task of cleaning up the Bucky bits, I cut out and came back here to my room. Hacking up cheesy guys in cheesy hundred-

Us

dollar suits in the heat of battle, that's one thing. Shovelling them into dishpans afterwards is something else entirely. No thank you very much.

Anyhow, that's the dealio.

I'm assuming, Dear Person Who's Reading This, that you showed up at some point not too long after my exit. (We probably should have partied less loudly so as not to pique your curiosity). Possibly you arrived in a roiling wave of villagers who stormed our castle with torches and rakes and whatever you could get your vengeful little hands on – then went souvenir hunting and found this missive.

Or mayhaps you barrelled in with carloads of cops who cuffed and "subdued" any of Us still in situ, then pillaged our rooms looking for "evidence". Well, here's your evidence – and it sets the record straight.

Whoever you are, and whatever happens from hereon in to whoever you get hold of, just show some mercy, OK? It wasn't Us that started this.

As for me, as soon as I finish this I'm getting the hell out of Dodge; pocket my pen and a pad of paper, grab a hoodie, slip into town on the down low. Maybe that townie chick's working the night shift. I'll whip her up some excellent prose with at least ten good reasons she'd want to drive me to the highway.

Maybe I'll even score a kiss goodbye.

Flight 404
by Bartholomew Cryan

The sky is burning in fast forward, the wind blowing backwards. Formless effervescing plankton expand and dissipate, consuming one another for growth, popping like pixelated fireworks in super-imposed bioluminescence. Their silhouettes scar the conflagrant sky with a silent, salted fear. Eyes roll into darkness, and there is the sound of grinding rocks, cracking hungry bones. The sun splits into fiery jaws, descends onto the shivering earth. Ripped skin is born from flames, shapeless matter whirrs in suspended animation. Hills are formed and defiantly rise. Mountains cough and explode in drowning fire.

Red worms are pulsing in soup. The pan is blackening, the worms ignite. Muted invertebrate screams echo. Worm-broth shudders and splits, and piercing sunlight floods in.

"Sir, will you please close your blind."

My eyes open slowly and I swivel to look at the speaker with incredulity, a blank, humming heat in my eyes.

"Sir? You're blind?"

Gradually, lines are forming in the whiteness. A lady in a blazer. A hat rests, precariously slanted, upon her head, her hair in a tight bun. She is looking at me strangely.

"No, I can see," I say. She squints at me in bewilderment and gestures past me to a window. Beyond the panes, there is the soft lap of blue sky on cloud coast. The rising flare of a new day blushes the billows from beyond the horizon. My view is cut abruptly to alabaster infinity as the woman's hand slams the blind shut.

She rights herself and looks at me with a face of composed confusion. "Please keep your blind down for the duration of the flight, sir."

"Who are you?" I say, kneading my scalp between my fingers and trying to focus my nervous pupils.

She keeps her eyes fixed on me and shifts her weight, taps a silver rectangle name-badge emblazoned in dark print with 'Karen'.

"Karen," she says.

She turns to leave.

Flight 404

There is a pressure in my head that is building with my disorientation. She begins to walk away and I realise with an anxious twist in my guts that I want her to stay.

"Karen, wait!"

She glances back at me, looking tired and bored.

"What?"

"Where are we?"

"Please keep your blind down for the duration of the flight, sir," she says again, emphasising the word 'flight'. "We are on a plane." She makes a frowning face and heads down the aisle.

I look after her, feeling betrayed without knowing why. Passing four rows, she turns, quickly looking back at me, meeting my eyes, then passes out of sight.

Beads of cold sweat emerge from my forehead as my heart begins to pump previously docile blood. My lucidity is returning in unwelcome high-definition. The snores of my fellow passengers are increasingly transmuted to bitter rasps, and the clogged pores of the sleeping woman to my left look like dirty sinkholes.

I fidget in my seat, the anxiety of reality grating on me, filing me to a sharp point, skewering my nerves. I neurotically fiddle with the buttons on my shirt, twisting one off by accident, then decide I should look out the window again.

You've done it before, I think, *but what if it's different this time? You're getting more and more awake now. The pills are wearing off. Try not to panic. What are the odds you die in an airplane crash? Just look out the window and don't panic, never panic. You might make a scene again. It could make everything worse, much worse and then it would really have been better to never have looked at all. You're already biting your nails.* I nip into the quick of my nail by accident and blood blossoms underneath.

I close my eyes and press my forefingers into my temples for a moment.

Peeling the blind up a tiny bit, I glimpse the wing. It jolts up and down under the power of the wind. I recognise the airplane's turbofan engines from Google images, but they look much bigger in real life. The noise they make seems to emit from inside my own head, the sound of dying machines, robot screams. A wintry palm grips my throat at the thought of mechanical failure. *Charred rubble.*

Bartholomew Cryan

I shut the blind quickly and look around. Probing my blazer pockets, I find an amber prescription bottle and shakily unscrew the lid. I summon spittle into my mouth and coax two yellow tablets down my gullet. Leaning over my armrest, I look at the person behind me. Drowsy woman of mid-forties. Her handbag is knitted with bits of fabric and held affectionately to her stomach, her hair clean but frayed. She looks back at me through pinched, tired eyes.

Weighing on the chair in front of me is a corpulent Colonel Sanders lookalike. His furry maw dances to the rhythms of his snore.

The sound of slumbering breaths is constricting the air around me, making it heavy and claustrophobic; the incessant wail of the engines making my eye twitch. *Everyone is asleep. Why can't you be like the others?*

I am jittering in my chair, uncomfortably praying for sleep, when out of the corner of my eye I see movement, a leg changing positions. I lean over to get a look at the person. They are dressed in a grey suit, with a tie-less white shirt and black brogues. He is looking into the desolation of the closed blind. I cough and he turns his head towards me.

My teeth clamp together, pre-empting the surge of quivering bile up my oesophagus.

The man has no face.

Where his face should be there is a void. Like a perpetual cigarette burn on film, as if reality has not processed his face, it is not there.

He seems to look back at me, measuring, waiting.

Are you losing it? You only just swallowed the pills. I dig my nails into the back of my hand, twisting the skin for clarity, willing myself to wake up, my heart to quiet. I cough again, maintaining my stare, and he raises a hand to where his mouth should be, and releases a garbled sound as if imitating my cough. He drums his hands on the tray in front of him, then rises and slips down the aisle.

I unravel a piece of scrunched napkin from my pocket and wipe my forehead, watching him leave. He heads in the direction of the toilets and cockpit. I try to restore order to my timorous breath and begin to viciously chew my thumbnail. *What if he tries to* – I hear the turbofan engine splutter – *crash the plane*. I tear the blind open and look out while starting to intently fold my napkin in half and then in half again and then in hal – *he's going to kill us all* – f and then unfold it again and – *and you'll be too busy* – the plane shudders – *folding a*

Flight 404

napkin – the engine is trailing a light stream of smoke. I tear the napkin into shreds, crushing the detritus between my sodden palms and rising from my chair.

With trepidation writhing in my stomach, I stalk down the aisle in pursuit of the man. I can feel it, a rattle in my bones, a sureness, a palpability of his impending depravity. He is standing outside the toilets and turns to watch my approach. The hollow gaze sets my nerves alight, convulses my insides and strengthens my conviction. The black depths are evil, *you know it*. As I get closer to him, a pungency grasps me, like melted plastic. My lungs are frantically flapping inside my chest.

He turns away from my advance, towards the cockpit door and starts trying the handle. An ebony ooze trickles treacle-like out from his facial-rift and onto the door handle. A tired-looking old man emerges from the toilets in time to watch my clenched hand sailing into nothingness.

I am instantly struck by a consistency under my knuckles, like meat in a plastic bag, imitation flesh. The faceless man jerks under the force of my blow, away from the door handle and I take the opportunity to restrain him under the arms of his suit jacket. Instantly the old man from the toilet raises his voice: "What are you doing, you maniac?!"

He tries to wrestle the faceless one out of my grip but I hold on even tighter.

From the chasm of my captive, a piercing noise begins, like a dial-up modem, like robot screams, like the wail of the engines. The man is shouting: "Help, help! This passenger is being attacked!"

"Can't you see? He's going to *kill us all*! Are you blind?" I shout as the man tries to pry my hands free.

"He's going to *crash the plane*!" I scream in his breathless, sagging face. The man stops and looks intently into the suited murk. "Can't you see him?! Can you not see the void?!" I shriek. He stares into the facelessness with scrutiny, then back at me.

He turns his head down the aisle leading to the cabin and roars, "Help! This man has gone insane!"

You've gone mad.

The thought washes over me like cold water, sucking the wind from my lungs. The grey suit-jacket and its occupant dodge out of my grip. I feel myself sinking to my knees.

The rough hands of the aged man grab my shoulders and I hear his voice, husky and sombre, "... whatever possessed you to do a thing like that..."

I feel like crying. The man with no face is standing nearby and gesticulating at me as static drone pours from him.

I catch a glimpse of the cockpit handle. The ooze has melted through the lock and the door clicks open. The sound draws our attention and for a moment the three of us are still.

Then the faceless man lurches towards the door, pulling a pistol from inside his blazer. The man holding me starts shrieking "Help!" again, as I scramble to my feet. I clatter to the door in time to have it slammed in my face. On the other side, I can hear frenzied machine squeals, interspersed with the shouts of the pilots. I start ramming the door. A tremor in the plane knocks me off my feet. Beyond the door I hear a gunshot, then hissing air.

*

Finally, the intercom crackles. Karen's voice echoes round the cabin: "Ladies and gentlemen, please do not be alarmed if you heard a slight disruption in the cockpit. This was due to a technical fault that has now been dealt with. If all passengers could make their way to their seats, we will be arriving at Glory in 10 minutes."

I breathe out deeply. Passengers have begun to wake up. They peer lazily out of their windows. The adrenaline seems to have made the pills kick in and my head swims dreamily on the pulsing waves of my steadying heartbeat. I linger weightlessly outside the cockpit, waiting for Karen.

The intercom coughs into life again: "All passengers back to their seats"; emphasis on the word 'all'. I rap weakly on the cockpit door with my knuckles, beginning to feel encumbered by my own body, as eyes settle on me from the cabin. She's probably fine. My standing feels scrutinised and wrong, warming embarrassment flickering up my body. *All* passengers back to your seats. I walk quickly and ashamedly down the aisle to the cabin.

A worried but familiar-looking man is sitting in my seat so I look for another, pointedly avoiding the vacant one left by the faceless man. I wander around, row after row of red, newly-woken eyes

Flight 404

studying me from afar, before rising anxiety forces me to duck into the obscene space.

At least you're close to the cockpit. Just in case.

I fidget and try to look out the closed window. Someone coughs behind me and I turn to find the man in my seat staring at me. He looks as if he's seen a ghost. I awkwardly wave to placate him and mouth the word "hi".

He goes white and fingers an amber prescription bottle out of his pocket, shakily coaxing two tablets onto his palm. I drum my fingers on the flight-tray and study a scuffmark on my black brogues to try to forget about the burning stare of the pale man boring into my back.

I get up to escape to the refuge of the toilet. Out of the corner of my eye, I notice the man beginning to fold a napkin over and over in his hands.

The inside of the bathroom is lit like purgatory and purrs with pressure. *Shapeless matter whirrs in suspended animation.* I feel an odd new weight to the inside of my suit pocket and investigate with a shaking hand.

My timorous fingertips close on the cold steel of a pistol.

My eyes widen. I feel sick.

Coughing into my hand, I try to massage my constricting throat which is clogging with a thick mucous. My oesophagus tightens. I notice the palm of my hand. It's stained with black ooze.

I look in the mirror.

Our Tormentor
by Duncan Eastwood

It's surprising how much you can remember.

My brother never stopped fighting right up until they slit his throat. The last time I saw his eyes filled with anything other than terror was seconds before we were captured.

We were play-fighting in the field when the man with the cap grabbed my brother by the neck. I was trapped between the instincts of wanting to run but also wanting to help my sibling, and before I could make a decision it was made for me.

The other man with long hair grabbed me and ushered me gently toward the vehicle. He spoke softly: "Come on, come on", while the capped man's form of coercion involved violently dragging my brother as he kicked and screamed.

The man with the cap giggled, but when my brother's lashing out struck him, the laughter stopped and the blows began. My brother was hit in the back and then in the leg. I could see his eyes dim a little with the sensation, then glow with surprise and fear as the pain began to circulate.

My brother would keep fighting but there would be consequences every time. So my journey was quieter, as I reasoned that if I could just stay away from the pain there might be a chance to escape.

The man with the hat pushed my brother onto the truck. He turned, grabbed my ear and threw me inside. My head crashed into the wooden slats lining the side of the vehicle. I searched for my brother but this wasn't easy as there were so many others in the darkness with us. Their bodies were difficult to make out, blending into one another, but their eyes stood out like darting fireflies in a cave. Filled with the same terror that I could see in my brother's eyes and that was no doubt bursting from mine.

Where were we going? Why had they gathered so many? What was the purpose? There were so many questions, and as some talked to each other I realised no one knew the answers.

The truck doors separated and we stumbled into the light, struggling to keep balance as we tumbled down a ramp into a wooden

Our Tormentor

corridor. Many rushed ahead, into an open cavity up ahead, the only exit from the corridor.

I stayed back until I saw my brother in front and ran toward him. We embraced long enough for me to feel his heart thumping in his chest. We both turned as we heard the clang. At the end of the corridor, the cavity had closed. A metal door had dropped and cut off one of the others.

We could hear him screaming.

The sound of his feet scraping on the concrete floor.

Then another clang.

Silence.

The door rose again. No one was inside. He was gone.

"Next in line!" the man with the cap yelled. The next in line was my brother.

We were both pushed into the corridor. It was so tight we couldn't turn. My brother in front of me tried to swivel his head, his eyes pleading as he pushed back and into me. But I had nowhere to go. We were jammed against the back of the corridor, unable to move anywhere but forwards.

Even though forwards was the only option, my brother refused to take it. The man with the cap leant over the wooden corridor with a large metal shaft and touched it to his behind. The shock sent my brother's legs kicking as he scrambled to get away from the electrified prod. He called out to me as he moved toward the open cavity. I didn't know what to say. My attempts to calm him were futile.

Laughing and angry at the same time, the man with the hat cruelly prodded my screaming brother down the corridor until his legs splayed and he collapsed to the floor.

"Stop playing around and get him in here," yelled the long-haired man. My brother called one last time and I cried out. I tried to run toward him. But the metal door slammed down, separating us for the final time. I stared at the dull, grey reflection and on the other side I could hear him trying to break free. Smashing against the walls. The two men yelled again.

And then that clang.

Silence.

Then I heard my brother kick again.

"Ah, can't you do anything right?" a voice bellowed.

Then another clang.

Silence.

This time it remained so, then... the sound of the men laughing.

I was the only one left in the corridor. No one behind me.

The man with the cap walked along the gangplank. I wanted to run but had seen how pointless that was. He walked toward me with only a metal stick in his hand and indifference in his eyes. He raised the prod and brought it down on my left leg. A jolt surged through my body. My flesh pulsated with the electrical charge. The power forced me forward toward the metal door, which now opened again. My brother wasn't in there. No one was in there. Just shadows.

The man with the cap smashed the prod into my back one last time. The agony was immense. My body smashed against the wall, like my brother before me, the shadows enveloped me and for the first time I was on the other side of the metal door when it slammed down.

I shivered.

Then the long-haired man's large hand grabbed my ears and brought a pistol to meet my forehead.

He pulled the trigger.

The hiss roared in my ears as the bolt ripped through the pistol's chamber and penetrated my skull, driving into my brain. I kicked, like my brother before me, and smashed against the walls.

"Jeez! Two in a row?" the man with the cap laughed. "You're garbage at this!"

"Screw it. He's dead enough." Spat the long-haired man, now with a hook in his hand, and in one movement he brought the sharp end down into my ankle and clean through the other side. The blood was pouring out of my foot as he connected the hook to a conveyor rod attached to the ceiling.

Hanging upside down, the blood raced down my body to my head. The long-haired man now had a large knife in his hand. My pleading had ceased long ago.

"This is the last cow. You skin him after this, okay?" said the long-haired man.

"Sure. You're doing a crap job of everything today anyway," replied the man with the cap.

The knife came to my throat and sliced across it. My blood cascaded onto the floor.

Our Tormentor

The man with the cap brought his own knife and plunged it into my back, cutting across it. I felt the skin being ripped off my body and the cold on my internal organs. The blood continued to pour from my neck.

Before you die, it's surprising how much you can remember.

The Biggest Fear
by Shirley Day

My biggest fear is death. I know – yawn yawn. But see, it's not the point of death: the pain, or the surprise, or predictability of it all. No. It's the possibility of some friggin great big family reunion, that's what does my head in. The fear kicked in when we moved to Norfolk – the Broads. Eels, water and sky, that about sums it up.

Mum bought us these life jackets so's if we fell in the vest would push us face up. The woman next door told her about them. For years I kept trying to remember her face, the woman next door. But even right after it all happened, after I was trying to piece it together, the woman next door never really seemed to have a face.

I do remember her voice though, cigarettes and gravel, that kind of voice. It was her that told us about the lake with the dead kids, and how way-back-when they used to throw stillborns in the broad by our house. Only sometimes it wasn't just the dead ones. Sometimes it was the crippled kids, the ones who had something wrong. Stones in their pockets, hands and legs bound, and in they'd go.

I didn't like the stories. Clarrie, my twin, she was the adventurous one. She was different than me. Not to look at, we were identical. But I think that identical bit's only skin deep. She was more intelligent too. You have to remember we were only nine, so it's difficult to know how it would have all panned out, and I've got a lot more savvy since then. But she could do her times tables any which way she liked. Me, I could only do five and ten, but I had that twiny thing. You know, the *twin sense*. I could get inside her head. So sometimes I'd kind of borrow information.

The disaster happened maybe a week after we moved in. That's death for you. People like to think it gives three knocks, or waddles in and plays chess. People like the idea of getting some kind of warning. But death is like a massive industrial hoover. One minute you're sitting down to breakfast with some woman from next door that no one can quite remember, next minute you're out of the game.

It was the year of the eclipse; seems portentous writing it like that: *the year of the eclipse*. But I don't think there was a direct link with the eclipse and our disaster. Dad made us these things to put over our

The Biggest Fear

eyes, like glasses. We weren't supposed to look at the sun, not even when the moon was over it, unless we were wearing the glasses.

I have to say, it was odd. The birds, well they shut right up, and everything started to go grey. The old lady from next door came out. Dad took a photo of all of us standing there by the water, smiling. It was all *happy holidays*. Then suddenly it starts to go dark. Mum shouts, "Glasses on", and we all obey. It gets darker and darker and darker, till it's done – no more day. Only my glasses, they must have been nicked underneath – they kept pinching my nose.

Now one thing I hate is damaged stuff, so let's just say the glasses, they kind of pissed me off. I had this niggling thought that maybe Dad, he'd known about it, and had given the good ones to Clarrie. Identical twins don't get identical treatment. So I took the glasses off and tried to straighten them up, and as I did I looked around and there's the old woman looking up straight into the sky, no glasses and smiling. So I look up too. No glasses. And in that instance out comes the bloody sun, straight down into my retinas. I can still smell my eyeballs burning.

I didn't need my twin sense to tell me all the doctors thought one eye was fucked. They gave me an eye patch and promised specialists, but in the end it never came to that.

Initially, Mum was over-cautious. But there was stuff that needed doing. We were still unpacking, and the world of the living has a knack of wallpapering over catastrophe. So Clarrie and me, we put our life jackets on and went back down to the broad. Clarrie had this plan. She said how Jesus rose from the dead right after an eclipse, so what about those dead kids? Maybe they'd fancy a little outing.

So she stands there at the water's edge, eyes shut and swaying, chanting some weirdo rubbish like, "Children of the dead, we are your friends, come out to play." And me, I'm supposed to sprinkle rose petals over the surface. So I step forward slowly, because of the eels and the fact that I can't really see the bank below me on account of my dodgy eye – which, remember, I'm really not happy about 'cus I don't like damaged stuff. I lean out over the water and drop the rose petals over the surface. It's all done. No dead kids are rising, and the rose petals have been dispersed. Result, I'm thinking to myself as I straighten up.

I didn't see the little stone step 'cus of my eye, missed my footing and down into the water I went, way down despite the jacket. The whole damn vest thing got caught on some underwater root. So I'm struggling away, and it's cold, and I can see Clarrie on the bank above me, and I'm down there with the dead kids and the mud and the eels and the cold and the one defunct retina, and suddenly it just stops. My little heart, it just gives out. I stop struggling.

Straight off, the life jacket comes unhooked, and my lifeless body goes floating back to the surface through a combination of laws of physics and state-of-the-art life vest technology. Not one ounce of personal volition in the mix. It only took a fraction of a second for me to realize I had no intention of staying down there with the eels, and the dark, and the dead kids. I knew how to get inside Clarrie's head. You remember the times table? Only I must have done it with more force than usual 'cus suddenly her little body falls to the floor. This is a whole different ball game now. I'm not looking for multiplication tables. I'm in her head one hundred per cent, and if you know anything about percentages, you know that's not leaving her any room.

I stayed where I was for a year or so, but to be honest having to look at Clarrie's face in the mirror every morning wasn't a whole heap of laughs. I found a nice counsellor, ever so pretty. I body swapped her for a few months. "Swaps" a bit misleading I guess, because the people you jump, they don't exactly have a say in the matter, and they kind of end up with the bum deal – well they're kind of dead.

Anyway, the counsellor didn't work out. Suddenly I'm a nine-year-old, living in the body of this hyper-efficient young woman. I mean I have all the information, the knowledge about her job and her family. All that crap, it's all in there. But it takes bloody ages to pull it all out. I made some major cock ups before I vacated. I picked age appropriate hosts after that. Usually one a year, though sometimes I'd go for a winter and a summer body. The learning curve's sharp, but I've grown to enjoy the challenge.

The transfer doesn't always work. I'm not a fan of defibrillators. It can be bloody awkward when the vacated body gets brought back to life and you have to crawl back into your old husk, pretending like nothing happened.

Dad died about ten years after we did – me and Clarrie. Because of course once I was in that counsellor's body, me and Clarrie, well, we were history.   Mum struggled on. I didn't keep in touch. She was eight-six when she finally pegged it. She'd been in a hospice for a few

The Biggest Fear

weeks and I did something I've never done before. I took an ugly body, some Moaning Martyr charity worker. My God you should have seen the shoes! Anyway, beggars can't be choosers; no one else was exactly breaking down doors to visit Mum.

I got Mum talking about the Broads, and the lake with the dead children. She found the old photo: me and Clarrie, my dad and mum and the woman next door. Only you couldn't really make out the woman's face. You see, that's what happens when you're half dead. People never remember your face properly. Mum said Mrs Porter, our neighbour, would have understood the tragedy – she had a twin die too. Though no one in the village had been able to remember the twin, or Mrs Porter, or how long she'd been living on the Broad.

When Mum went, I dumped the charity worker without leaving the building. It was a relief to get out of those old tights and bunions. I found a lovely young journalist in the waiting room. She's pretty, with thick blonde hair and a bit of an eBay habit. We all have our faults.

When we got to the Broads, Mrs Porter was still there. She remembered me straight off. It could have all gone differently; me and her, we were the only two of our kind, far as I know. Only, Mrs Porter, she wasn't keen on my style. She said once is an accident, that's excusable, but to use human beings as a life-style wardrobe...

I told her to call in the UN if she felt like it. I told her I never grieved for Clarrie. In a way it had all worked out well because, of course, my eye had been messed up and I don't like a damaged body, never have. I think if she had more energy she would have tried to jump me. But she knew she didn't stand a chance. I'd imagined there was gonna be tea and conversation, the swapping of personal anecdotes, but like I said, she wasn't keen on my style, and I wasn't a fan of her oh-so-superior attitude.

To be honest, I can't even remember how many people I've jumped. I'm good. I've died most ways imaginable – hence my nonchalance about the actual "death event." I tend to avoid drugs; they can cloud your judgment. There's a strong chance you'll pass out before you get to change. Most other methods are fair game. But you see there is always the possibility that death will creep up on me. Some great articulated lorry heading up the backside of my Fiat Panda. Even I wouldn't be able to argue with that. Once I'm out of the game, I'm out. So yes, I fear death because if there is some great big "family" reunion malarkey, I'm not relishing the thought of all that explaining.

When I left that day, I put the old lady out of her misery; put bricks in her pockets and dumped her into the Broad. Like they did years ago. Only this time she'd be staying under. See, she was the only evidence, the only one who knew.

At the moment I'm happy, but no doubt my young journalist host had her mobile bleeping out satellite co-ordinates. They could easily have caught me wheeling old Mrs Porter across the grass in the wheelbarrow, and tipping the old goat feet first down to the bottom. No life vest. So if someone did see me, all I'm saying is… maybe I'll be looking for a place to stay. Maybe I'll come visit. I'm no real trouble. To be honest, you won't even know I'm there.

The Cyclist
by Richie Brown

There is too much sky above the Lincolnshire Fens and the uninterrupted horizon sprawls without end. The dreary flatness of the treeless land is relieved but little by the roads, which run on banks higher than the black fields, sometimes alongside wide, deep drainage ditches, the lumbering clouds chasing their clumsy shadows across the empty distance.

Merle drives her little red car on such a Fenland road that seems to run forever, into nowhere, wishing the featureless miles away and the day gone. She loathes these duty visits to Uncle Stanley, shared out exactly and grudgingly between herself and her sisters. It is madness for him to be living out here alone, at such an age, but he will not move and from a vinegared sense of duty, the three sisters each make their reluctant and separate visits.

"The old bastard," says Merle, but does not hear herself because Merle does not use such language.

When will she get there? The dashboard clock is broken, so Merle looks at her wristwatch, shaking it down her arm a little so she can see it beyond the cuff of her jacket. She still has an hour of driving she reckons, and looks up and there is a cyclist almost in front of her. Merle swerves but even so almost catches him with the passenger side of the car. She drives on, her heart beating furiously, glancing into the rear-view mirror. The cyclist has toppled onto the grass verge but is getting up and retrieving his bicycle.

"Prick," says Merle, but again does not hear, as that word, in that sense, is not in Merle's lexicon. She smiles vindictively; the smile fades: he might have scratched her little red car! Cyclists are so irresponsible, and a complete hazard to responsible and considerate road-users. Such as herself.

In the rear-view mirror, the cyclist is a dwindling patch of neon-yellow, tiny now. Good riddance, thinks Merle.

Merle forgets the incident, content to dwell upon her dull errand, the lack of gratitude the old man will show her, not that she does this for gratitude, and the emptiness of the scenery.

Some miles on, she stops at a level crossing, one of many on the roads of this flat landscape, as the warning lights flash and the barriers drop. A goods train approaches, immensely long, and Merle drums her fingers on the steering wheel as the train crawls towards the crossing and rattles by interminably.

In the rear-view mirror, something snags Merle's eye. Way back, a long way back, a tiny flash of yellow. Merle peers and squints. Is that the same cyclist? No, almost certainly not, as he must be far behind by now. It must be another cyclist, but has she passed another? No, she has not, because Merle is a very observant driver.

It is the same cyclist, she is sure.

Merle fidgets in her seat. Although it had been the cyclist's fault she almost hit him, she doubts he will see it like that – they seldom do – so it is best to avoid any potential unpleasantness. How much longer will the train take to pass? She watches the mirror. The cyclist seems to be moving very fast, but it is so difficult to judge as the flat landscape offers little perspective against which to judge speed or distance.

"Come on," she mutters, unconsciously tapping the accelerator. The train passes by and slowly the barriers raise, and the road is open. Merle pulls away more sharply than she might, pleased to see that the cyclist is still some distance back.

Yet riding very fast, she thinks.

Merle drives on, flicking her eyes to the rear-view mirror more often now. The cyclist does not seem to be gaining on her, but is surely keeping pace. Is that possible? She is travelling at 45 miles per hour, which she deems safe for these Fenland roads. The roads are generally straight but sometimes have bends that take drivers by surprise, and the drainage channels alongside the roads are very deep. Yet, so she might get to dear Uncle Stanley in good time, she puts her foot down, just a little.

Merle concentrates hard upon the road and the driving, edging her speed to 55. She is uncomfortable at such a pace on these roads, leaning forward slightly, gripping the wheel tightly, unwilling to take her eyes from the road to check the rear-view mirror, but at last she does, she has to, and moans a little, for the cyclist is nearer, still a distance off but closer than he was just minutes ago.

The Cyclist

Merle presses the accelerator and the little car picks up speed, rattling and shaking as it increases to 65. She never drives this fast, not even on a motorway, and is frightened at how unsteady the car is, how even the slightest movement of the steering wheel is exaggerated at this speed. She grips the wheel in her thin fingers, not daring to look at what is behind, concentrating upon the road as the little red car races on because it is dangerous to drive at this speed but she must look in the mirror, cannot help it, and he is closer again and before her eyes snap back to the road she sees that his legs are blurs, they move so fast, and how can that even be?

The car hurtles on, to 70, to 75, and Merle is more scared than ever before, than ever before in her life, scared of the speed, of what might happen if she loses control, terrified of the cyclist, because it is not right not fair to ride a bicycle so fast, no-one can do that not over such a distance, and again she checks the rear-view and he is closer again, right behind her, so near that she sees his fluorescent upper-body, those impossibly-fast, pumping legs as vague as smoke, and this is not right either, he has no face beneath his silly little cyclist helmet, just a blur of dark, a smudge, no visible features even on this bright day.

Merle gazes a little too long, then snaps her eyes to the road, thank goodness it is so straight; the noise within the car and the shaking increase, the car racing at 80, the wheel shuddering in her hands, tears trickling unheeded, her whole world now the road, the speed, the noise, the mirror, and she looks again, he is almost upon her, and the shadow where the face is shifts, splits in two, opens like a flower, into massive jaws, scarlet and crimson, lined with fangs, as wide as a dustbin lid, wider, all the time keeping up with her, keeping pace, not missing a beat, not losing an inch, gaining on her and the jaws gape, stretching towards her.

All this in an instant, and Merle breaks, and brakes. The little red car slews wildly, tyres screaming, out of control, and Merle hears and feels the fleshy *thump* as the cyclist smashes into the rear of the car (she is glad, she hopes he dies, she hopes it is dead) and the car hurtles from the road, down the steep bank into the deep, cold water of the dyke.

Merle is uninjured, although her chest aches where she slammed into the seat belt, and the calmness of shock displaces her fear and panic. The water boils around the car as it begins to sink, surprisingly fast, the bonnet slipping in first, bubbling steam and air, but Merle knows what she needs to do, and unbuckles her seat-belt – it comes undone, no damage, she will not drown here like a rat – and kicks off her shoes. If she could she would take off her jacket, but there is no space and no time. Merle knows that if she tries to open the door the water pressure will prevent her, so she must open the window, and squeeze through that, and swim, if she is to live, and Merle intends to live.

Water pours through the imperfect door seals and dashboard vents, rising to the front passenger windows as she winds her window down, and the car lurches forward suddenly, cold water beginning to flood through the open window, making her gasp so she grasps the door, hauls herself through and out, just in time, struggling to hold herself against the force of water, and she is free. Merle does not look back, but swims away from the sinking car, towards the bank, smiling, eyes gleaming with adrenalin.

As Merle reaches the bank and screams in triumph, the water surges behind her, and something erupts from the grey depths, long, slender and black, flashed with neon-yellow, rearing high, and at the top a vast, red maw, bristling with snagged, sharp teeth surrounding a maroon throat, looming over her, dark against the bright sky, then striking at her, so fast, smashing her into the water, and then Merle sees
    nothing, but
    feels much.

Killer Heels
by Sasha Black

Their bodies lie intertwined in the cold moonlight.

Tatiana opens her eyelids and gently rises up on one elbow, gazing down at her naked young lover. In the hard light, the girl's pale skin looks like a porcelain doll. Tatiana leans closer and breathes in her delicious scent.

Her chest heaves as her lips curl open into a snarl. She licks her lover hard, like a starved animal lusting for a long awaited meal.

The girl awakens. Momentarily confused, she pauses at the sight of Tatiana, now straddling her and towering above.

Tatiana does not pause. She lunges, pinning her partner to the bed. They fuck. Hard. Fast. Violently.

*

Water trickles down Tatiana's face. The unforgiving light of the bathroom reveals her full features, a woman of perhaps 40, arresting in her beauty, and strikingly angular. Almost masculine.

She smiles to herself, lost in distant memories, as she showers the lovemaking from her body. Her hands glide across her skin – even the act of showering is one of sensual touch to her.

Her young lover, now towelling off her hair, watches Tatiana. She cannot pull her gaze from the woman who just consumed her. While twenty years her senior, she still appears to be perfect. So slender. So pert. She wonders what memories lie behind that enigmatic smile on her older lover's face. Wistfully, she imagines that maybe Tatiana is remembering their love making? But she senses that Tatiana is not even aware of her, let alone remembering their night together.

The glass door swings open and Tatiana steps onto the cold tiles. She glides toward the girl, who instinctively breathes in deeply, wanting to feel her touch. Wanting again to be consumed utterly by this creature. The draw is magnetic.

Tatiana kisses the girl tenderly but quickly. "Go," she whispers.

Spinning on her heel, Tatiana dries her hands. She holds them out and looks closely. They look strong, like the hands of someone who has worked hard all their life. Her brow furrows. Has the change begun already? Surely not so soon? A sudden twinge of pain in her back confirms her fears.

The girl watches the imposing naked figure of Tatiana from behind. "Will I see you again?" she dares to ask.

Without speaking, Tatiana returns to drying her hands.

The girl watches Tatiana dry herself. She can clearly see the powerful muscles in Tatiana's shoulders and back as they move under her skin. Something else is unusual. The faint outline of a mirror, now long gone, hangs above the sink.

Tatiana pauses, tilting her head to see if the girl is still present. In a deeper than expected and gruff voice, Tatiana growls at her, "Go..."

Sensing sudden and unexpected danger, the girl backs out, grabbing her clothes as she leaves. Tatiana closes her eyes and breathes deeply.

*

The last rays of sunset cut into the room.

Tatiana awakens, her lithe and naked body moving slowly, aroused by the imminent darkness. Eyes still closed, her strong fingers slowly reach down her tummy, her other hand gently massaging her stiffening nipples. Manoeuvring herself and opening her legs so that she can have better access and comfort for this waking ritual, she begins to breathe more deeply.

Her fingers slide inside her panties, down and...

Her eyes snap open. Her pleasure replaced by immediate anxiety.

Yes, the change has definitely begun.

*

Tatiana stands in her black underwear, her hands touching her body. She slips on black nylon stockings, a charcoal grey miniskirt and crimson red jacket.

The cupboard doors swing open to reveal shelf after shelf of shoes. Almost every pair are towering high heels. She knows exactly what

Killer Heels

she is after and reaches for her favourite black Christian Louboutin six inch stilettos. Oh my, how she feels ever inch a woman when wearing these shoes.

She slips her foot into the first, but it's tight. It won't even fit.

"Fuck," she spits out under her breath.

She reaches back into the cupboard to the bottom right corner and pulls out a pair of black patent flats, looking at them in disdain.

*

Tatiana sits in a confessional. She examines the familiar old wooden panels as she draws hard and deep on her cigarette. The door opens and an old priest sits down inside.

Neither speak for a moment.

"No high heels this time, Tatiana? Left it a little late again?" He glances at his watch. "Has the change begun already for you?"

Tatiana breathes in her cigarette deeply before blowing the smoke defiantly from her scarlet lips at the priest. He does not cough or splutter. He just smiles. "Well, to business then, yes?"

The priest produces a contract and passes it to Tatiana. She notices his hands, filthy and ingrained with dirt. He points to the bottom of the papers,

"Sign here and here."

Tatiana pauses.

"Twelve souls for me for twelve months of being Tatiana for you." The priest feigns concern, "Unless you are done with being Tatiana?"

A long pause. "No," she whispers in deep masculine tones.

The priest leans in, and Tatiana can sense the warmth and stench of decay, "You can always default on your end of the deal. And come with me?"

Leaning back as far as she can, Tatiana signs quickly.

The priest cackles as he takes the contract back, "The lengths a girl will go to. Still, you do look divine."

*

Music throbs.

A pulsating sea of bodies move in unison to the music. Women kiss in the shadows, their hands reaching down to tease sweaty ecstasy from their partners. Tatiana stands at the bar. In sharp contrast, she is totally still, her face in shadow as she surveys the throng of nearly all women dancers.

One dancer locks eye contact with Tatiana. Young and sparkly, she smiles knowingly as she is pulled back and forth by the beat of the crowd.

She dances over to Tatiana and pulls her out from the shadows. Tatiana's black hair scraped back over her skull, her makeup heavier than ever, her cheek bones more pronounced. She looks like she is trying too hard tonight.

The girl smiles. Tatiana knows the look. Drunk. High. Ready to fuck. Perfect.

*

Tatiana stands over the sink in her bathroom. A sudden yet familiar pain shoots down her spine, accompanied by the sound of cracking bone. She bites her hand hard to avoid screaming in pain.

In the bedroom, the girl has stripped to her underwear and sits on the bed. Opening the top drawer, she finds a strap-on dildo. She eyes it and grins.

The bathroom door opens and Tatiana steps out.

The girl stands and, carrying the dildo, walks to Tatiana, "Look what I found. Dirty slut." She smiles, "Will you fuck me with it tonight?"

Tatiana snatches the girl and pulls her close, kissing her passionately. The moment escalates rapidly and the girl drops the dildo to the floor, overcome by Tatiana's embrace.

Their crotches grind. The girl pauses and pulls back, her eyes wide, surprised at the sensation.

"Oh, someone is not who she is supposed to be, is she?" the girl whispers

Her fingers fumble up Tatiana's tartan mini skirt. "Chick with a dick?" She smiles wickedly, "Me like."

She drops to her knees and pulls Tatiana's panties to one side to reveal her cock, immediately consuming it, sliding back and forth.

Tatiana feels another crunch down her spine. She looks at her hands, which also crack and snap as they get larger, her forearm muscles getting bigger.

She grasps the doorway, a mixture of agony from her bodily transformation and ecstasy from her blow job. Another wave of agony.

The girl's eyes widen as she takes a breath. "Baby, you just got bigger... you got huge..."

Tatiana pulls her up, and the girl clambers on top of her and couples up, feeling Tatiana deep inside. They fall onto the bed, and Tatiana begins to slide back and forth. The sensation is familiar yet strange at the same time.

The rhythm gets faster. More cracks as Tatiana grows stronger, her face subtly changing to more masculine features. The pace increases, the two writhing.

Faster. Faster. Faster still they fuck.

Feeling herself climaxing, Tatiana locks eyes with the girl, who is lost in the sexual fever. Tatiana whispers "I'm sorry" as she produces a six inch silver blade and in one single motion cuts the girl's throat.

Tatiana climaxes and wails as she is drenched in a fountain of hot sticky blood.

The girl, her eyes imploring, can only look on as Tatiana falls back down and pins her to the bed. As the blood squirts, she continues to thrust every single orgasmic moment from herself and into the girl.

Tatiana is once more wracked by agony as her body begins to transform.

Her angular features rounding, her broad shoulders shrinking, her hips widening.

Silence save for heavy breathing.

Tatiana pushes the body from the bed; it lands with a wet thump on the tiled floor. Looking at the ceiling, she stabilises her emotions.

She has the body and demeanour of a seventeen year old, her lips filled and reddened, her cheeks full and rosy. And her eyes. They pierce the soul with the promise of unspeakable pleasures.

She isn't just beautiful. She is impossibly feminine. She breaks down and weeps uncontrollably. She looks down to her side to see just the ankle and foot of the lifeless body.

Her breathing slows as she gets a grip on her emotions.

Calmness.

Lying in her crimson bed of blood, Tatiana runs her fingers down her bloodied body. She moves over her engorged nipples and breasts, her taught tummy, down to her warm, wet and waiting lips. She enters herself with her fingers and begins to rub back and forth. She brings herself to climax.

Her breathing slows, and she smiles. "The lengths a girl will go to," she muses.

What's Yours Is Mine
by Nick Yates

He opened his eyes to nothing. The darkness was complete, no shadows or shades of grey, just black.

Where am I? Where's Dad?

"Dad, Dad," he shouted, an edge of panic and fear in his voice.

"It's ok, Son, I'm here."

Relief washed over him; his Dad was here too, somewhere in that darkness.

He tried to stand, tried to go to him, but he couldn't. Something around his chest restrained him, pinned his back to a cold, wet stone wall. He felt at a leather strap with his fingers, it was tight, immovable. He struggled, tried to wriggle under the strap, but there was one more at his waist.

"Dad, I'm stuck. Where are we?"

"It's okay, Son, I'm here," he sounded confused.

"Don't worry, Dad. Try to stay calm."

He forced himself to stop struggling and took deep breaths, trying to clear his mind, like his Dad had taught him... before he'd lost...

He had woken up to this darkness with no memory of how he'd got here, just a buzzy headache and a cotton wool mouth. When he thought back, it felt like days, but in truth it could have been hours. He just didn't know.

He'd driven his old man back from the hospital and had sat with him in his front room. The doctor had confirmed it, what they had been fearing for some time now. Their conversation had been difficult, his Dad had been upset and angry, struggling to cope with the reality of what was happening. He could understand that, of course: who would enjoy being told they were slowly losing their mind; told that very soon those little episodes of forgetfulness would get worse? How was anyone supposed to cope with the prospect of forgetting their own children's names, forgetting they even had any children? It must be terrifying, particularly for a man like him.

He instinctively reached out, but the straps held him fast. "Dad, hold on, okay. I'll think of something."

"Okay, Son."

He thought carefully, then checked his pockets for his phone. It was still there, but the battery was dead.
How long have I been here?
Perhaps not long, the battery had been low already.
"Dad, do you have your phone?"
No answer.
"Can I have your phone? Could you slide it to me?"
He heard a shuffling in the darkness. He was glad his Dad wasn't panicking. After everything that had happened recently, this must be hell.

He thought back again to the conversation they'd had, emotional and fraught, made worse by his Dad's wife, Rita, hanging around in the background, listening in.

He'd never liked the woman, never trusted her; she was a real bitch, a gold digger, in his view. His sister, Sally, had pure hate for Rita though, couldn't even look at her. She called her the painted whore and had said it to her face the first and only time they had met.

He pictured Rita's Botox face in his mind, mascara-heavy eyes wide with shock at the news, rage appearing when she realised what it meant.

There was a scraping sound and something hit his foot; the phone. He reached down and pressed the screen. It lit up. No service, one bar of battery left. He swore under his breath and tried to stay calm.

The screen pushed back the darkness slightly, a nimbus of light spreading out. It wasn't enough to see his Dad, but enough to see what was immediately around him.

A basement of some kind, judging from the pile of old boxes to his left. He looked at the screen – still one bar, still no service. He thought about turning it off, saving the battery, just in case. But he needed to know where they were.

He reached across, straining against the straps, fingers brushing rotten cardboard that fell apart as he touched it. Something fell out, an exercise book of some sort, old and dusty with familiar handwriting. It was his handwriting, or had been twenty years ago.

We're in Dad's basement. The thought shook him.

He looked at the phone again, still one bar of battery, but now one bar of signal. A spike of adrenalin shot up his spine, scattering his thoughts. *Who has done this? How? Why? Make a call before the phone dies, who should I call? 999?*

What's Yours Is Mine

The phone started to ring, vibrating in his hand. His sister's name appeared on the screen.
Please, God, don't let it die on me.
He pressed answer, and her voice came immediately, urgent. "Dad, where the hell are you? Why did you hang up when I called? What happened at the hospital?"
"Sally, listen. You have to come and help us, we're trapped in Dad's basement."
"David?" The phone went dead. The nimbus of light disappearing, plunging him back into black.
"Dad, did you hear? That was Sally, don't worry, she's coming to help."
"Okay, Son."
Did she hear? Will she come?
He hoped so, but he hadn't had time to explain properly.
Who could have done this, in Dad's own basement?
He thought back to earlier, sitting in the front room. He thought about Rita's face again, the reel of emotions he had seen playing out in her features, and... something else...
Her? How?
He ran over the events in his mind. She'd been the dutiful wife while they talked through the consequences of what the doctor had said, listening in silence then disappearing to the kitchen, coming back with a pot of tea and a plate of biscuits. Rita didn't do biscuits; she was a health freak, a body obsessive. The word 'sugar' wasn't in her vocabulary.
He sat upright, eyes wild. *The bitch, the fucking bitch.*
His Dad was wealthy in anyone's book; oil executives tended to be. He guessed he was probably worth a few million at least. The woman knew that, he was sure it was why she had married him. She'd get it all if... he realised what he'd done. The phone call.
Sally will be on her way now.
"Dad, we've got to get out of here."
No response.
"Dad?"
"Okay, Son."
"Dad, is that all you can say? We need to find a way out, we're in danger."

Why isn't he more concerned?
"I love you, Son, always remember that."
He froze. His Dad was an old school type, brought up not to show his emotions. He'd spent his entire childhood craving affection and attention from the man, but had never got it. Until now.
Yesterday, was it yesterday?
Between cups of tea, his Dad had told him he loved him, the first time he had ever done that as far as he could remember. He'd cried when he heard it, all those emotions held in check for so long flooding out, bursting the dam he had so painstakingly constructed.
It must be the illness.
He had read about it, how it could change personalities, turn sufferers into different people. He almost smiled then, the irony of what it had taken to hear those words after so long.
Come to think of it, his Dad had just said the exact same thing, word for word.
Strange.
"I love you Son, always remember that."
Again?
He knew his Dad was worried he might soon forget he even had a son to love. Perhaps that was why he had repeated himself.
"I love you too Dad, I don't need to remember it, I'll always know it. Don't worry, we're going to get out of here. I promise."
He struggled against the straps, desperately trying to find a way out. Then he froze. The darkness had changed, was somehow less substantial. He could see shapes, outlines appearing in the gloom. He looked up at the ceiling, a single light bulb glowed thinly, little more than an orange filament.
He saw his Dad's silhouette, standing, hands by his side.
"Dad, Dad. Did you switch on the light? Are you free? Can you untie me?"
The figure didn't move.
"Dad?"
No response.
"Dad, what are you doing? Help me."
"I love you, Son, always remember that."
"I know, Dad, why do you keep saying that?"
He was panicking now; something was wrong.

What's Yours Is Mine

The light grew brighter. The figure still hadn't moved.
Who is doing this?
He strained his eyes as the room slowly materialised around him. He could see the pinstripe suit worn specifically for the doctor's appointment, rumpled now.
What has happened to his tie?
The face was still in shadow, except the mouth.
He looked harder. *What is that in his mouth? Has he been gagged?*
"I love you, Son, always remember that."
How is he speaking through that gag?
Slowly the light intensified, until the bulb in the ceiling blazed, illuminating his Dad's face fully... a corpse's face.
How? What?
He dangled from the ceiling by his tie, eyes bulging out of a purple, swollen face. It took a moment to sink in, his senses overwhelmed, refusing to believe. He looked again, studied that face, realising with horror that his Dad must have been dead for hours.
How? Who slid the phone across?
Rita stepped out from behind a pillar, held up a voice recorder and pressed play.
The corpse spoke. "I love you, Son, always remember that." It wasn't a gag. The voice came from a speaker strapped into its mouth, forced in tight between the teeth.
His Dad had told him he loved him for the last time.
The woman stared hard at him, plastic face set in a permanently startled expression. She smiled as she smashed a hammer into his face.
"Hello, David. Make yourself comfortable, Sally will be along shortly."

201

Second Chance
by Maggie Innes

There is no easy way to tell a woman you've just met that her dead husband's heart is thumping in your ribcage.

Ba-boom. Ba-boom. Ba-boom.

So George took it slow.

He sipped the strong, dark coffee that Alison had given him – her hands trembling, however hard she tried to hide it. He summoned up the remnants of his counselling training from way back when, and created a Safe Space. Kept his distance, feeling his cashmere trousers slip-sliding off the brown leather armchair. While Alison perched stiffly opposite, looking confused and in pain – like she'd been impaled on the pristine brocade sofa. George took a moment. Harnessed all his self-help public-speaking books and 'owned the room'.

Broke his story down into manageable steps.

First, the long, slow decline. The breathlessness that inexorably enfolded his chest in a suffocating death embrace, the grotesque swollen limbs, the crushing, constant fatigue. Silent, un-tuned guitars propped up against the wall in his bachelor bedsit; well-thumbed cookbooks unopened on the shelf; the social work resignation letter; muggy days gawping at moon-like faces on daytime TV while gasping for air like a beached fish. Just one toothbrush left in the bathroom mug. A circular heat mark on the bedside table where Zoe had always placed her herb tea when she stayed over. Zoe, who liked hill-walking, spontaneous picnics, festivals and hot, long, gymnastic sex. He didn't blame Zoe for leaving him – or his walking sticks, his blue lips, his puffy ankles. His hopelessness. All his life people had left him; why should she be any different?

George gave a self-effacing shrug. He could see Alison was gripped by his story. She gazed at him, her eyes an unusual and vivid shade of blue-green. Turquoise. Like warm sunlit Mediterranean pools. They really were quite something. Impossible to look away from. So compelling and new, yet somehow so… familiar. It was all George could do to carry on.

Second Chance

But still, he gave the phone call from the transplant co-ordinator the dramatic delivery it deserved.

A heart was available! On paper it had the potential to be a perfect match. Could he come in? On the taxi ride to the hospital, George stared at his fingers, pale and waxy and numb, and felt so keenly that his body, his future, was being rubbed out in front of his eyes. He hardly dared hope that this time, this heart, could give him a second chance...

George's voice faded. Raising his hand in wonder, he wiggled pink, plump fingers pulsing with life. Some kind of miracle! Alison slowly reached out, appearing equally awestruck, and took his hand in hers. A jolt convulsed George's body. He felt a powerful urge to get up and enfold Alison in his arms.

Steady. Don't scare her.

Instead, George smiled shyly. Alison smiled back.

Gladys, the transplant nurse, was the first face he saw afterwards, milky eyes behind statement red glasses. George could smell lunch on her breath – cheese and pickle on spongy white bread. He knew Gladys well; it was difficult not to, amount she had to say. Now she smiled with genuine delight. Everything had gone even better than expected. His new heart was strong and healthy.

Ba-boom. Ba-boom. Ba-boom.

George paused for effect. Alison still held his hand in hers. She leaned slightly towards him and he felt a powerful sense...of what? Recognition. Relief? This too was going even better than expected.

He rattled through his post-transplant recovery, so quick and complete it surprised even the most experienced doctors on the unit. His return to work, only to realize he was wasted on social work, and his complete reinvention of himself as...

"...a currency trader?" Alison asked.

This time, George's smile was generous.

Got it in one.

This time, Alison didn't smile back.

George's story had a momentum of its own, racing away from him. He described drinking Japanese whisky where once he was a Guinness guy, driving fast, playing tennis, pumping iron, becoming socially confident. Charming even.

Alison was staring now, those turquoise eyes wide and questioning, as though meeting someone in the street and desperately trying to place them. She let his hand fall. George, too late, realised maybe he had said too much. Gone too fast.

Stupid.

He quickly cut the rest. The dreams he'd had pretty much from day one, disjointed snapshots of a former self, a former life – and there, still and serene at the centre, with the physical impact of thirst and hunger and pain and ecstasy all rolled into one – this woman's face. Those eyes. An obsession that bit into his every waking moment, and when he was asleep, just grew even more urgent. Until timid good guy George was obliterated, and left inside his shell was a raging beast, driven on by an inexorable inner drumbeat. The heart that was pounding even now, faster and faster, insistent and triumphant.

Ba-boomBa-boomBa-boomBa-boomBa-boom

Alison was fast – up off the sofa and heading for the door. But George was faster. Her arm felt impossibly flimsy in his pulsating grip. Touching her again fired another thunderbolt through his body and he almost gasped with the rightness, the inevitability of it.

Don't go. Please.

Alison was whimpering a little now. George stroked his thumb down the pale inside of her forearm, lacy with veins. He felt her tremble, try to pull away.

Don't. It's a lot to take in. Ssh.

George guided Alison back to the sofa. The bond he could feel between himself and this woman was like nothing he'd ever experienced. He wanted her. Not just with his heart, but with every cell of his body. He had to have her. He would have her.

They both knew it.

"How… how did you find me?" Alison's voice was small, but remarkably calm, considering.

George hesitated. Should he tell her how the hospital's confidentiality policy had thwarted him, and endless newspaper advertisements and social media posts had also drawn a blank? Meanwhile the dreams and desires were eating him alive, torturing him day and night.

One day it came to him. Gladys! Who turned out not to be nearly as talkative when it really mattered. Trust her. He could still hear the crunch of those ridiculous red glasses as he drove his fist into her face.

When she finally dribbled out Alison's name, his heart leapt in his chest. Elated to be so much nearer his goal, his destiny.

Second Chance

Ba-BOOM. Ba-BOOM. Ba-BOOM.

No. Better not tell Alison that bit – especially not what happened after. Poor Gladys. George remembered he had liked her. Once. But it felt such a long time ago now. A different life.

"George?" He realized Alison was saying his name. "George! Don't let him do this! A good and kind person is in there somewhere. Don't let him – "

"Shut up!"

George looked at his hand, shocked. Alison lay crumpled on the floor, clutching her cheek. The mark was already showing – red, and hot. George rushed to help her up, but even as he apologized the contempt was rising like vomit in his throat.

She deserved that. She doesn't have any respect. Never has, never will. George shook his head, as though to scatter the thoughts.

Bitch. Bitch. BITCH.

Alison was babbling on. How they assured her the heart recipient was a good man, a kind man, someone who deserved a second chance at life. Someone who would give back, make the most of this sacred gift.

They were wrong, George replied. He was an empty shell, a husk. Now he's tasted lust and pain and violence he doesn't ever want to go back. He can't.

He crushed his lips into Alison's. Felt her gasp and go limp, as though surrendering completely to him. The sense of absolute power was exquisite. Every colour was more vivid, every emotion more intense.

Then the strength in his arms was waning, and Alison's body felt slippery as silk, impossible to hold. George grabbed for empty air. Dropped to his knees, dazed. Breath was hard to find, even harder to keep. He really had to concentrate.

Luckily, Alison broke her story down into manageable steps.

First, the beatings, the humiliation, the imprisonment. The constant fear. Then, her final fight back. She gave it the dramatic delivery it deserved. As she spoke, George could feel the heartbeat in his ribcage starting to slow…

Ba-boom.

Alison laughed – it was such a cliché really. Sleeping pills and whisky. No seatbelt. Black BMW driven at speed off the road. She played the wounded, grieving widow to perfection, sobbing as she agreed to donate her husband's organs to help others.

Ba... Boom...

As soon as George called, she had sensed it. That the heart, the evil, was stronger than him. Would have to be stopped. Still, she wanted to hear him out. Just in case.

Alison stroked George's cheek. Her eyes, those clear turquoise pools, were now implacable chalky puddles. He struggled to speak, to beg, to say he was sorry. Ssh, she murmured. It's a lot to take in.

Sleeping pills in the coffee. Again.

But this time, no second chances.

Ba......

George felt himself being dragged, his head bumping off furniture, over carpet then smooth flooring. Alison was still talking – her voice sticky like treacle in his ears. Occasional words filtered through.

Rented house. False name. Leaving tonight.

A sharp push and he was tumbling down concrete steps, his wrist giving a sickening crack as it snapped. Far, far away, a door slammed. A bolt shot.

Silence.

Sour smoke and the first tentative pinch of flames licking his skin.

Boom......

Sum of My Memories
by Elizabeth J Hughes

I remember.

We were standing on the roof of the old mill down by the canal. Taking turns for a drag on the joint Jono had brought along. Swigging down the cider we had swiped from the offy round the corner. We were just hanging out, 'cos that's what you do when you're 17, feel immortal and have a burning rage deep inside, driving you to rebel against something only you can understand.

I don't know who first came up with the idea of walking the beam. It was probably Billy 'cos that was the kind of idiot thing he was always coming up with. The beam lay across one of the gaping holes in the roof. Below it was nothingness which stretched out right until the point that the concrete floor filled it. But I am getting ahead of myself.

Once someone had suggested walking the beam, well, then it seemed the only thing to do. Billy went first; he wobbled quite a lot and somewhere about the middle suddenly found God – of course we all laughed at him but eventually he had edged his way to the other side.

Once one had made it across, it meant the rest of us had to; no matter how lame we thought it might be. Jono went next, skipping across like a mountain goat, even pausing mid-walk to jump up and down a bit. The jumping caused a creaking sound, which had him skittering across the remaining gap.

Then there was just me. Of course, somewhere deep inside was a voice telling me not to. But when do we ever listen to those inside voices? Besides, I was high, drunk and, well, the others had done it.

I stepped onto the beam and shuffled forward. The hole seemed a whole lot wider from this angle; for a brief moment I thought about stepping back. Oh, how I wish I had.

I must have been about the middle of the hole when the cracking sound began. Suddenly my mates weren't shouting and whooping anymore.

I took another step but there was no beam to step onto.

I was falling. Looking up, I could see the pale, terrified faces of my friends, Billy's mouth a perfect dark O.

I seemed to fall for ages. I suppose I was also screaming. I don't remember, I just remember the rushing sound in my ears.

I heard my dad's voice saying, "It isn't the fall as will kill you, it's the landing" and you know what, it was. I smashed into that concrete floor. Pain shot through me like a red hot poker that just kept giving. My broken lungs fought to suck in air as I lay there. Before the blessed darkness came, I looked up, I saw my friend's faces looking down in horror. I heard their trainers squeaking as they ran.

Now I don't know what you were told about death, but I distinctly remember being told that when you die you go on to something else. In my case I was expecting to wake up in heaven. I admit, I was a bit hazy on the actual details, but I was fairly sure that there would be some angels sat around on clouds strumming their harps. What actually happened was I woke up back into the existence I had passed out in.

I opened my eyes – well, actually, no I didn't, they were already open – and saw the hole I had crashed through.

The first thing I noticed was the pain. If I weren't already dead, I would have been fairly sure I was dying. I lay there and I screamed. Only I didn't, I lay there; screaming is a thing living people do.

I tried to float above myself. That's a thing right? The out of body thing? Yeah, right! Take it from me, mate, it isn't.

It was sometime after I had given up screaming and was wondering where my so-called mates had gone that I noticed the fly. It buzzed around my head for a while before coming in to land on my goddamn eyeball. It walked all over it, even gave it an experimental lick. Its tiny feet trampling all over my sodding eye. Man, I wanted to blink, to knock it off. But I had nothing, I was just existing.

It left my eye and began to investigate my nostril. I felt it push itself inside, travelling up towards my brain. I didn't realise what it was doing in there. I was too busy screaming in my head at the fact I could feel its nasty little hairy feet stomping around inside.

After the first fly, the others soon followed, each one searching for a way in. Pushing inside, clambering around on my eyes, in my ears, up my nose, feasting on the blood which had pooled around me.

Sum of My Memories

A couple of days later, I felt the first stirring of life within me. Tiny maggot mouths rasping off my flesh from the inside. Slurping from the soup of decay I was becoming.

Thankfully the ability to feel didn't continue for long after the maggots hatched. Although I was left with the memory of how it felt, which was almost worse.

The circle of life continued within me. Flies laid their eggs, maggots emerged and fed until they were fat and gelatinous, turning in time to flies who mated and then started the whole thing off again.

I am pretty sure other bugs and creepy things joined them at the buffet. But it was the buzzing of the flies, day and night, that filled my head.

As time wore on, my body swelled up around me, the gases let out by my decaying organs and feeding inhabitants filling the cavity.

Eventually, like an over-filled balloon, my skin split and disgorged the squirming maggot soup I had become, which seeped away through the cracks in the concrete beneath me.

I am not sure when the memories started. Time had ceased to have meaning soon after I fell. At first they ran through my skull like an unstoppable, jumbled train. Snapshots of a life I had lived.

Soon, though, the jumbled train slowed and became ordered, flowing like a movie in the darkness. I saw the person I had been and watched as baby grew to laughing boy and from boy to man.

I saw a child on a golden beach, giggling as rippling waves pulled at his toes. My father picked me up and swung me high into the air. My shrieks and squeals echoed. I remembered the joy, love and light. I walked between my parents on a golden beach.

I saw an older boy on a golden beach, his hood pulled up. Sulking. My parents walking ahead, a gap where I could have been. Shoulders bent.

I saw a young man sat on a golden beach, a can in one hand, a phone in the other. Shoulders hunched against the world. My parents walked alone along the beach as I updated my Facebook status: *Wish I was somewhere else.*

I saw the world as it had been, my family, my friends.

I saw the love which had been given and I had grown to reject.

I heard the words I had spoken and felt the pain I had caused.

I saw my mother's tears and my father's bewilderment.

I wondered if they looked for me, imagined them on the nightly news begging me to return. Did they question Billy and Jono, or listen to their lies? Did they assume it had been my choice to go? Did they believe I was out there somewhere, living life as I wanted, hoping one day I would walk back in? I wondered: did they miss me, or was it a quiet relief?

At last I understood. I had turned my back on everything that I had been. I listened to a rage that had no meaning. I chose rage over those who loved me. But the rage had left me cold and alone.

Finally, my memories having run their course, I saw that last day. Saw mum asking me to clear the table and me, like a spoilt brat, storming from the room, grabbing my coat, slamming out of the house. I saw their faces, sad and tired. So very tired.

It was a while before I noticed the fog. It curled itself along the walls, sending questing tendrils towards me.

My memories have reached the last hours now: climbing over the railing, scrambling up the rusty staircases, standing in the early autumn sunlight on the roof. Looking out over the city; the yellow and grey trams trundling past. Ferrying the slaves of corporations and society. Not for us, that fate – no, we were free, slaves to nothing... Just the rage inside.

The rooftop lies in the golden light. I take the joint from Jono. Billy stands on the beam; we laugh as he starts to pray.

I hold out my hand, wanting to stop the inevitable.

Jono is over now, they are both looking at me. I take that step and...

The fog is covering me. The memories have ended. There is nothing now. Just silence.

Fingers
by J.M Hewitt

What's your worst nightmare? That haunting one you share with your friends in the playground? *Imagine sliding naked down a giant razor blade and landing in a pool of alcohol. Imagine being tied up and having your fingers chopped off, one by one...*

That one with the fingers. That's me, right now, as a thirty-year-old woman. I'm strapped to a bed, having my digits removed with a cigar cutter, one by one.

This basement, this prison is truly the stuff of nightmares. It's dank, cold and I can hear water dripping. There's a window up high with frosted glass and bars. I can see people's legs as they walk past, going about their daily business. The first time I woke and noticed the window, I screamed for help. That's how I lost my second finger. I had already lost the first.

I am now four fingers and one thumb short.

I don't scream anymore.

My name is Lucy and five days ago I was one of those people up there. My only concerns were what takeaway to have for dinner; red wine or white, or vodka? Now, a week later, I couldn't even hold a bottle of wine or a glass of vodka.

The man who snatched me off the street and brought me here knows what he is doing. I'm hooked up to a drip. He ties a cord around my fingers to drain them of blood before taking them off and then he affixes a tourniquet.

A shuffling noise joins in with the dripping water. I stiffen, close my eyes. It's him, and if he thinks I'm sleeping maybe he'll pass me by. I almost laugh; how's that for a childish dream? If I can't see him he can't see me.

"Lucy.

His voice is low and gravelly, almost pleasant, and I don't even want to know how he knows my name. I'm sure I didn't tell him.

I open my eyes and level my gaze at him. I realise, for the first time, he is not alone.

There's a woman with him. She's no more than a shapeless, hunched-over lump sitting in a wheelchair. She has a blanket covering almost all of her body.

"Theresa," the man says, softly, and bends over, leaning his chin on her shoulder, a horrid gesture of familiarity. "This is Lucy, the lady who is helping you."

I flick my confused gaze between the two of them. How am I helping this woman?

Theresa raises her eyes to meet mine; she smiles shyly.

"Theresa, show Lucy how she's helped you," he says and straightens up, moving away to leave Theresa in the spotlight.

She shrugs the blanket off her shoulders, moving them in an almost sultry manner until the discarded garment falls to the floor.

She's wearing a vest top and, despite my own state, I feel a wave of sympathy as I notice that both of her arms end just below her shoulders. Still smiling coyly, she lifts her left arm, waving it and a small giggle escapes from her.

There is something there, a skin tag, or a bit of saggy skin. I lift my head, caught up in the curiosity and then I blanch as I realise what it is and, subsequently, why I'm here.

Attached to her arm, crudely sewn on to her shoulder stump, is my thumb.

Dizziness strikes, the ceiling spirals around as I fall backwards. Mercifully, I faint.

When I wake up I'm minus another finger. All I have now is three fingers and a thumb on my right hand. My left hand looks like Theresa's shoulder, nothing more than a rounded post with five tiny, bloodied stumps.

At this point I begin to wonder if I actually want to survive, or at what stage of the ongoing amputations I will want to die. What about when he runs out of fingers and thumbs, what happens then? And how long can a human body survive having pieces of it taken away? Will I still want to live as just a head and torso? I don't think so, but I guess I won't know until I get there.

I struggle against my binds and it's a useless task. I thrash a bit more, if I can only loosen these straps, but they hold fast. They are buckled, like the ones used in a mental asylum or a prison hospital. They will never weaken or break.

Nor will I!

Fingers

In a moment of fury and stark desperation, my survival instinct kicks in and I hump my body up and down and from side to side. I writhe so hard that the bed moves across the floor. I stop, breathing hard before going at it again. I'm whooping and tossing and concentrating so hard I don't even hear him come back in. I don't know that he's standing there, with Theresa, until he brings his hand down and thwacks the top of my bed.

I freeze, motionless at his sudden appearance.

He is angry, and by the dried tears on Theresa's face I don't think his anger is just because of the commotion I was making.

He waits until he is sure he has my full attention and then he spins around, whips the blanket off Theresa and with a long, white, hairy finger he props up her left shoulder stump.

The thumb, *my* thumb that is attached to her, has turned rotten. A yellow discharge weeps from between the black, stubbly stitches and the thumb itself has turned a nasty green-grey colour. I can smell it from here.

"W-what about the other fingers?" I cry. "They might work."

As soon as the words leave my dry, chapped lips, I can't believe I've said them. I'm encouraging this maniac to sew my fingers onto this girl. So fierce is his rage that right now, I'd chop my own remaining digits off if it would buy me some more time in this life.

And it strikes me, the question that I was pondering earlier; when will I give up? Not quite yet, obviously. The realisation is cheering but only fleetingly.

My head is soon plunged back into the darkest, depths of horror as he wraps his hand around the rotten thumb and yanks it off her arm.

Theresa screams.

I join her.

I pass out again.

I'm almost happy in the underworld of dreams. If death is like this, then maybe I would welcome it, after all. But I wake, again, eventually. I don't know how long I've been asleep but I can tell immediately that something has changed. I look down, count; three fingers and a thumb. My relief is short lived as I locate the source of strangeness. I'm missing both my feet. The left one looks like it has healed a little better, which suggests he took that one first.

Funny, how he works from left to right. And the fact that I have this thought tells me I'm closer to madness than when I arrived here.

I'm not alone. Theresa is here; calm, shy Theresa who gives off a vibe of wanting to be friends. I have to use her. I have to try.

"Will you help me, Theresa?" I ask quietly. "If you help me, I can help you. I work for a plastic surgeon; he's one of the best in England. He can get you new arms that are even better than the ones you had." It is a lie; I work in a pharmacy.

"I've never had any arms," she replies, wide-eyed. "I was born this way."

So she's lived decades like this, why, why, WHY does he need to change her now? And what is she to him? Wife, daughter? My time is too short to find out so I rush ahead.

"Unbuckle me, Theresa," I plead. "I'll take you with me, I'll help you, we can help each other."

"Can't come with you," she says flatly.

She hunches over so her head is almost touching her knees. I wonder what's wrong now, then she moves, and I realise with her disability this is the only way she can possibly wheel her chair.

Then she is beside me, leaning over, baring pointed, yellow teeth near my neck and I inhale sharply, then I let the air out, a whoosh of relief as she attempts to unbuckle the straps using her teeth. They are her only tools.

It takes a long time and my eyes are always on the door, wondering where he is; could he arrive at any moment? My heart thuds in my chest and I feel lightheaded. I focus on the wound on her shoulder where he ripped my thumb off. It is red and livid, with an aroma of rotten vegetables.

She moves back, breathing heavily, and I am free. I sit up, leaning on my right hand.

She pats her lap and holds her stumps open, as if for a hug. I realise that the only way I can get from my bed to the door is by using her as transport.

I let myself topple and then I'm on her, and she leans to the left, hunched right over, and I use my right hand, and together we wheel ourselves to the door. She talks as she wheels.

"He tried arms, before, but they never work. Too much blood loss, or something," she whispers. "He thinks if I had digits I'd be able to do more, you know, around the house. And then he gets so angry when it doesn't work."

"And my feet?" I ask, matching her quiet tone.

Fingers

She shrugs. "He gets mad."

So my feet are useless to them, but he took them anyway, out of anger.

I grasp the door handle, open it and peer out.

It's a hallway, as dark and dank as the basement and Theresa nods.

"The only way out." Her tone is grave, serious, and I look upwards.

It's a kind of well with a steel ladder attached to the side. At the top is a metal lid. I don't know if I'd be able to remove it, even if I made it to the top of the ladder.

"That's the only way?" I hiss.

She nods sagely. "I have to leave you here."

Then I'm falling forward, landing painfully on the concrete floor at the bottom of the ladder.

"Jesus, no, come with me, please!" I cry. I don't understand, surely she wants to escape this torture chamber as much as me? "What about when he finds out you helped me? He'll kill you!"

She smiles, still sweetly, but something has changed. As she is backlit by the open door, she looks very different; older, weaker, tired.

"He already has," she says. "He's given up on me. He can't change me or make me normal, so I'm useless now. Maybe he'll find a new project." She looks at me and there are tears in her eyes. "He told me he put methanol in my drink last night."

I know methanol, I know that if ingested it can take around twelve hours for the deathly symptoms to appear. Any time now Theresa will be vomiting, her blood pressure will fall and she will go blind before her body starts to shut down.

Theresa retreats, wheeling awkwardly back into the basement, closes the door softly behind her and waits to die.

I lie on the floor, looking up at the edge of the sky that shows through the ill-fitting lid.

I put my foot stumps on the bottom rusty rung of the ladder and bite my lip at the flare of pain. I hear an animalistic noise from the next room. It could be Theresa dying. Or it could be him, coming to look for me.

I grab the second rung with my right hand and heave myself up.

I begin the impossible journey towards the light.

Jessica Brown

Gooseberry Pie
by Jessica Brown

Edna crouched lower, reaching for the gooseberries that she knew were hiding in the midst of their parentage. She felt a tightening in her back, her aging body hindering her needs, but she continued to gather the fuzzy fruits with a nostalgic glow.

Cooking and baking were her passions. They were a constant throughout her life, something to lean on, to distract and give her confidence, when the inevitable obstacles of life arose. People came and went, her children had left and emigrated with her grandchildren, but the lure of homemade shepherd's pie and cherry cake always brought them back to visit her. She loved that she could make her family instantly feel at home with just a mouthful of ingredients, despite their new lives a thousand miles away.

Nobody loved her cooking as much as her husband, Charles, and Edna prided herself on it. The look on his face when he entered their quaint kitchen as she slid a golden crusted pie from the steaming oven, the corners of his mouth moistening, his Adam's apple protruding as he swallowed with compulsive want. It was intimate. He wanted something that only she could provide to his exact tastes. Nothing could satisfy him quite like her baking, not even that bitch who had offered her body to him like she was a raw piece of meat.

She had found her husband, pants down, hulking over the kitchen worktop, humping what appeared to be her best hand-carved chopping board, until she saw the red nails and pale legs wrapped around him. Yet Edna looked upon the event – an event that would test the sanity of any wife – with sentiment. It had been their making. Edna had known he wouldn't leave her for that rake of a woman – she probably couldn't even cook! He loved his food and Edna could sate him just so. They were more devoted to each other than ever before, and her baking was improving each day in line with their relationship.

Gooseberry pie. The 'Marmite' of baking was Edna's favourite recipe, and she was certain that no-one could outwit her composite of sugar, fruit and spices. Anyone who had politely stated their preference for apple, or plum, had humbly requested a second slice

Gooseberry Pie

after tasting. She'd always borne affection for the underdog and felt a certain affinity for those phlegm-coloured, sour, vascular berries.

Edna carefully straightened her posture, smiling fondly at the family of fruit trees before her. She stroked a leaf maternally, before turning and pottering back up the patio path to the French windows that were seeping with the scent of sweet baked pastry. It was ready! Edna quickened as much as her age would allow.

Charles was already sitting at the head of the table in wait. She donned her oven gloves and swooped to the oven door, peering inside. Perfection.

Placing the pie on the cooling mat by the window sill, Edna took a deep breath. "What do you think, Charles?"

Charles shifted his eyes to hers pleadingly. She did love the power that she had over him, no matter what age they were.

"We must wait for it to cool. You will burn your mouth!" she teased.

She began to wash the gooseberries she had picked in the garden. Her neighbour used to comment that she should make a large batch of filling and freeze what they didn't need, but she found the idea ludicrous. It was the process that she loved; why would she not want to repeat and perfect it as often as she could? As one pie came out, another could go in. It never had to end; Charles always had room for more.

As the syrupy fruit simmered over the hob, Edna gently hovered her hand over the freshly-baked pie.

"This will be lovely with some cream, Charles."

She shuffled over to the fridge, removing a pot of cream, before opening a kitchen drawer to grasp a large funnel. Laying it on the table, she plugged in the blender, opened the lid and plopped in the whole pie. It splatted into several chunks as it hit the bottom. She poured the entire pot of cream on top of the steaming boulders, fixed the lid, and pressed the button to turn the pie and cream to mush.

Charles watched, the whites of his eyes bulging. He didn't know how much more of this he could take.

Edna silenced the blender. Picking up the funnel, she carried the heavy contents over to Charles.

"Here we go."

Charles started to squirm as Edna ripped off the duct tape over his mouth.

"No, no", he muffled lethargically.

Edna tilted her obese husband's bloated, vomit-covered head back. Clutching his nose until he gasped, she rammed the tube down his throat. He gagged as she expertly slid it down to his stomach and taped it into place around his lips.

Grabbing a spatula, she gradually scraped the contents of the blender into the funnel, milking the creamy sludge down the pipe. Charles half-heartedly strained at his restraints, his bare feet paddling over the stagnant piss-stained floor, his trousers squelching with excrement.

GULP. GULP. GULP. He swallowed involuntarily.

"I think this one's my best yet, Charles. Don't you?"

Helper
by Steven Quantick

"I want to help you. Please let me help you."

How have we survived so long as a species when we refuse help so readily?

I mean, the human race can't move forwards unless we help each other.

I saw a woman pushing twins in a pram. She was carrying her shopping for that week and somehow trying to manoeuvre herself into a lift.

She was nice, she was polite, but when I asked if I could help she said, "No, thank you" and continued to struggle.

If I pushed that pram and its precious occupants down a staircase she wouldn't have any trouble asking for help, would she?

I suppose it was this that led me to assisting the dead with their problems

But I'm getting ahead of myself.

I've always been very intuitive about what people need.

The dead are attracted to how... alive we seem. Some of them don't know they're dead and when they look at us, they see something that doesn't quite add up. Some poltergeists are the equivalent of poking us with a stick to see if we're real. To see why we're different from them. They're trying to figure out if they're alive. Sometimes when they find out they're dead, they dissipate, to be at peace. Then there are the other times.

I'm a health and safety inspector for the company I work for, so I spend a lot of time in condemned buildings. I was in a bell tower when I first sensed someone standing behind me who was not there.

At first, I dismissed the feeling. Like when you're alone at home, you walk into a room and start as you see out of the corner of your eye that someone is sitting there, waiting for you. And then you look properly and it's a pile of clothes

But a pile of clothes doesn't breathe down your neck.

A pile of clothes doesn't fill your head with screaming.

And in that bell tower, everything I thought I knew about the universe changed. The tangible and the intangible, the spiritual and the physical. And I clutched at my head in pain as the screaming rose in volume, and I realised whatever this was, it didn't care if I believed in ghosts.

And by sheer instinct I cried out, "Stop!"

And it did.

And I took a breath. I let myself rest for a moment, tried to calm myself in spite of the frantic twitching of my heart.

And I tried to consider what I would do if someone intruded in my home

I'd scream. I'd make a fuss. And if I was the intruder and I didn't mean any harm, I'd assert myself as non-threatening.

So I told it: "You want to know why I'm here. I'm here to condemn this building as unsafe." And I don't know why I said it, but I added, "And I'm here to help you."

I could feel how angry it was. It swung the bell wildly back and forth until it cracked against the wall and fell hundreds of feet onto the floor of the church. I tried to stay calm, and in my mind I frantically cycled through everything I'd ever read or seen about ghosts.

And I remembered something about unfinished business. I think I got that one from Casper. And I thought that it was worth a try.

So when everything finally went quiet, I told it, as gently and kindly as I could, that it was dead. And I gave it permission to move on.

Everything went quiet, and I heard a beautiful sound, like someone exhaling, like someone so relieved to finally be in bed after a long day. The longest possible day

I knew I needed to do this again. So whenever I was somewhere old I listened. And I started to learn how to hear them speak. This is how I know about the poltergeists.

"There's something not right about you..." one of them said. I couldn't just bluntly tell him I was alive and he wasn't, so we talked for a while, and he figured out what he wanted for himself. A sigh of relaxation and he was gone. At peace.

I had a friend in the council, Timothy, and even outside of work hours I'd go to him and he'd search his files and look for condemned properties for me to carry out my good work. We'd wile away our evenings imagining the possibilities. Imagining emptying the world of

Helper

restless spirits. Travelling to the ends of the Earth to meet their needs and resolve their lack of meaning.

"Who else gets the opportunity to have every chapter of their life close in satisfaction?" he'd say, "And who would imagine that we could even find that in death?"

And as the months and years went by, giving the living what they wanted seemed far less satisfying.

It didn't mean I stopped trying to do good for my fellow man, but I must admit the dead began to prove themselves more worthy of my attention. At least they didn't have any issues with asking for help.

Then there was that basement. Timothy gave me the address, citing some old news stories reporting intruders, scraping noises, screaming.

As I descended the stairs, there was a heavy atmosphere, an unrelenting sense of need that had gone unfulfilled for a very long time.

The presence I found there slid into my subconscious, and in a frantic, rattling whisper told me that the woman he loved had been taken away from him. In this case I knew that explaining to the poor unfortunate soul that he was dead would do little good.

"I know I'm dead", he said, "but I can't stop."

This happened from time to time; they needed closure with someone they cared about.

I remember a number of occasions where their relatives were still living. So I'd arm myself with information only their dead relative would know, and I would persuade them to come and meet with their dearly departed. And when the dead had spoken their piece and the living had shed their tears, they gave a sigh of relaxation and they were gone.

So I knew I needed to find this girl.

He told me he'd died ten years ago, that this girl had only been a young girl of about fourteen when she was taken from him. I assumed it was because she was deemed too young for him. So I followed my usual course of action. I returned to Timothy and he looked over the archives.

Aside from the news articles he'd cited in sending me there, there was nothing about the basement. Literally nothing. Any additional records had been misplaced or removed and not returned. Or destroyed. Which happens more often than you'd think, to be honest.

My friend was able to turn up one tiny scrap of information: a home address. And sure enough, when I knocked on the door, there she was.

I found the girl to be extremely open-minded, considering the circumstances, and within a week I was leading her into the basement. She took in her surroundings, and then she seemed to recognise them. Her eyes widened. Her breathing shallowed. She tried to keep her voice calm as she turned and spoke to me.

"What are we doing in this place?"

Sometimes the living become very unsettled when they sense the raw, untamed presence of the dead, so I explained to her the presence I had felt, and that it had asked me to bring her here.

She began to cry. But it didn't seem to be out of gratitude. A cold feeling crept into my stomach.

"What are you going to do to me?"

And before I could answer, the voice echoed through my skull, its previous warmth replaced with malice and poison. "Kill her. Give her to me. She is mine."

Helping the dead was one thing, but this was a step too far.

But as I turned to face the door, Timothy was standing there. His face looked different. He was smiling the most unusual smile. A satisfied grin with that same malice, that same poison. A smile shouldn't make you feel like you want to crawl away into the corner. Something was wrong.

Before I could say a word, he reached into the room and pulled the door shut. And with some finality I heard a bolt slide across, sealing me inside the room with the hysterical young lady and whatever foul thing Timothy was apparently in league with.

The poor girl hurled herself against the door, drawing blood from her clenched fists as she pounded on it, begging to be released, but it was no good, and I remembered that Timothy had only *told* me the records were gone. He'd brought me this girl's address. The only bit of evidence needed to lead us both here.

This was a trap.

I could barely understand her above her wails of despair, but it seemed that whoever this presence was had taken her to this very basement when she was a little girl. And it was in the process of her rescue that the presence had been killed.

"You said you would help me."

Helper

He was right. I promised. And I had to keep my word. Because if I didn't, we'd both die here. If I didn't, I'd never be able to help the dead move on again. If I didn't... I would die.

And I didn't want to die. Not like this

There were loose bricks scattered around the room. The girl was so busy trying to open the door, she didn't notice that I had taken one in my hand. I pictured all of those that I had helped to find rest, all of those that I would help to find rest in the future, and I let the thought of all the good I would do push me into action.

I tried to push back my revulsion, I tried not to think about what I was doing as I raised my arm, and allowed the momentum of the brick to carry it into the back of her head.

She screamed again, her delicate blonde hair quickly cascading into blood red. And I told her I was sorry.

Another strike. This time the trauma to her skull took away her sight, and she feebly flailed at me, unable to find me.

Another blow to her forehead. This time there was a crunch, like standing on a packet of crisps. And I told her that this was for the greater good. That I was special. That I needed to live on.

But she couldn't hear me.

Her twitching leg was the only sign that she had once been alive.

The brick was covered in shards of skull and brain tissue. I thought I was going to be sick. Or scream. Or both. I felt suddenly warm and I realised I'd pissed myself. Then a sigh of relaxation, and I expected the spirit to be gone.

But he wasn't gone.

"I can't stop," he said. "I need another."

Timothy opened the door and, with the rationality with which one would explain that we need to pop to the shops for milk, explained that this was our chance to make a difference. He had come to idolise the dead. And I was their slave. He showed me where to dispose of the body, a place doubtlessly selected by our mutual friend in the basement. And as she slipped out of sight into the abyss, I was certain that I saw a hundred lifeless pairs of eyes staring up at us.

Six months later I came to recognise his type, and he didn't have to tell me where to find the girls anymore. Blonde. Blue eyes. Innocent smile. They reminded him of the daughter he lost. I didn't want to ask how he lost her. I was just trying to help.

Steven Quantick

And with every body that I hid, I hoped it would be enough; that he would finally pass on. But he couldn't stop. Not ever. And I promised I'd help. No. More than that. I wanted to live.

The Left is Sinister
by Thomas Cranham

I would ask a favour of you, dear reader. It's a simple task, one that anyone can accomplish, be they young or old, man or woman, of any religion or race. I want you to cast your mind back, though not far, only to the beginning of the day, when you yawned so wide you could have swallowed a whale and stretched your arms to the stars, to the first thoughts when sleep abandoned you and consciousness returned. I want, no, I need you to tell me which side you were lying on when you first awoke.

See, I'm a good man; this isn't some dreadful school examination. It is but one simple question with four simple answers. You were either lying on your back, front, right side or... or the left. Simple, isn't it, not a difficult task at all. Some might say as hard as taking a breath, picking a flower or as hard as driving a knife along your thigh so that blood runs as thick as a river... just so you can still feel. Not difficult at all. Child's play, if you will.

The thing is, I'm worried, scared, terrified. So I've done my research; looked high and low for months and days, days and months. I investigated the academic world and internet, in dusty libraries, leafing through fiction, non-fiction and even children's picture books. And the conclusions worry and scare me; they have put me on the edge of a blade where I can either fall to salvation or destruction.

Putting the conclusions down on paper feels wrong. It could give them life, even make them final. But I must, for they are the truth, no two ways about it. Others, with more intelligent minds than I, have also found that knowing which side you're lying when you awake decides who you are. Whether you're a person of conscience or otherwise, a good fellow who would assist an old dear across the road or someone who would push her in front of an oncoming car, it's all decided for you. That's the truth. The evidence is everywhere and I can't deny it.

It starts with innocent infants, new to the world, full of possibilities, who often sleep on their backs, wake and play, run around, crap and eat and crap and then sleep on their front. They aren't consistent. You might think it's because they're young, or are attempting to get comfortable. Wrong. Wrong, wrong, wrong! There's an internal war between good and evil raging inside their tiny minds, one that will rage on for the rest of their lives with both sides winning short-lived advantages.

You're laughing at me, I know you are. Think of the nights you spent as an adult, unable to sleep, counting sheep for hours until sleep finally took you. And then, lo and behold, you wake up on a different side to normal. That's the war intensifying, missiles flying; men, women and children of good and evil being blown to pieces, and the conflict will continue until a balance is found.

Questions. Yes, you will have questions as I did. I asked myself, can good or evil take total control? Well, dear reader, we're all different, all good and evil to varying degrees. Yes, you who think you'd never hurt a fly, that you're good to the bone. You couldn't be more wrong. Evil and its thoughts are there, biding their time, waiting for the right moment to strike and urge you to lie to your closest friend, cheat on your girlfriend, slice and dice your dear, dear mother and cook her for tea even if she tastes like gone-off chicken. Even if it's weak, evil is there; trust me, it's there, ready to play some games, have a little fun.

How can you tell who's winning the war? I'll answer your question with another. What does the Latin word 'sinister' translate to? The left. Always the left. If you wake on the left it's bad news, terrible, not good, not good. Evil has thrown good to the floor, bloodied and broken. Evidence: Attila the Hun, Genghis Khan, Hitler and countless others. Stalin, Himmler, Idi Amin and Pol Pot. The list is endless. And they all had two things in common. All evil to the core, and all awoke on their left side. Coincidence you say. Rubbish.

Coincidence is a word used by those who do not wish to believe the truth; the truth that waking up lying on your left means evil has the reins for a while and will hurt, maim, strangle, or murder as it sees fit.

I've been told I'm waking on my left. I can't remember whether or not I have. My memories are hazy. They're the sun momentarily glimpsed behind the clouds, but recalling them is as easy as catching rain in a sieve. They'll forever be out of my reach.

Last night I had a bottle or two of gin to calm my nerves which had been shredded by Chloe's words. Who's Chloe? She's a nobody, who unlike me is so very confused. One minute so supportive of my conundrum, the next doing everything possible to hinder my research.

The Left is Sinister

A clever, beautiful young girl I met last week in a local bar, who I'd been pursuing for what seemed aeons. I spied her from my dark corner, where I sat with only a glass of whisky for company. The whore was hardly dressed, her skirt no more than a belt, her top meant for a child. She showed copious amounts of smooth, pure skin that hit me like a gram of cocaine: she was an angel incarnate.

I made my move, gliding past the scum of society as blood rushed to my loins, feeling so high my toes barely touched the dark floor. I bought her a drink, we chatted, she smiled and I suggested we find somewhere more private. Faces turned to watch us, the perfect couple, as we left the bar. A smile, the most beautiful smile, filled her face and her eyes sparkled with mischief. We went into an alley and in the darkness I took her.

Chloe's parents are searching for her; I saw them on TV, faces covered in tears and snot. But if only they knew, she has no intention of leaving. Girl's doing good, assisting me, loving me. And sometimes I only wish to be free of her; there I am, pulling my hair out, cutting my arms and legs, eternally worried that evil will take hold, and she's chained herself to the bed, naked, screaming at me, setting my head off rumbling like a volcano ready to blow its top and destroy everything in its shadow. It's always the same; I end up hitting out to release the pressure, so my brain doesn't explode. I don't understand why Chloe brings it on herself – the games with fists and knives and blood and screams.

My head's everywhere. All I can think of is waking on my left, of evil winning the internal war. But then I contemplate, it can't be, I'm moral, I feed my dog and take her for walks and love her every day. But just in case the worst happens, that I start waking up on my left side, I have my sweet, sweet compatriot Chloe to watch over me every morning. So it doesn't really matter that I can't remember. Through bloodied lips Chloe tells me I'm a saint, I'm safe and that I woke up lying on my back. She never lies: I look into her big black eyes and recognise the truth. Though, each day, I still ask her, only to be sure. I wish never to succumb to evil. Never, ever, ever.

Dear reader, the question though is, do you know which side you woke up on this morning? Can you be sure one-hundred percent? I hope so. I truly do.

Bloated
by Penegrin Shaw

She'd sucked three cocks and it wasn't even lunchtime.

Though the last was the biggest, the first had been her favourite. It had a freckle two-thirds of the way up the shaft, which she liked; a Marilyn Monroe cock, or a Betty Page burlesque bayonet! It didn't talk much, that cock. It didn't try to take her away from it all, or ask her to call it Daddy. The quiet cocks were the best cocks. The cocks that took "no" for an answer. Well-mannered cocks. Soap-scented *please and thank you* cocks. The first cock was all of the above and it paid in perfectly crisp notes straight from the cash machine.

Three cocks before lunch was good going in a recession. Everyone on the planet was struggling and she had to eat, didn't she? She wasn't like the other girls. Sheila had class. She'd eaten Japanese food in a posh Mayfair restaurant once; raw fish, not too *un-cock-like*. Delicious. That had been a *three-cocks-before-lunch* week, but that seemed ages ago.

A gust of wind whooshed her hair momentarily as she walked to her next appointment. She never visited her clients, but this one was different. Ray was fat. Really, really fat. More than a big bastard, Ray couldn't leave his own home. In human terms, Ray was a giant, easily the size of an American fridge and confined to his bed for the last half year.

She picked up his lunch (an expense she included in her fee) and negotiated the daytime cobbles of Saxon Central in her night-time heels.

Cocks. That's what zero qualifications and a cute arse does for you. No place of her own, no car, a dated wardrobe (not much casual attire) and no husband – *not that she wanted one of those* – but she'd not tried too hard at the interviews. She needed her Jobseeker's Allowance. No, she was good at impaling the penis. She enjoyed that.

Sheila smiled to herself. *Three in a row on a Tuesday morning would take some stress out of the week...*

Her heels wobbled the fuck out of her as she reached his door. Someone had covered it with flyers for comedy clubs and unsigned band nights. She ripped them off and dropped the litter onto the street

Bloated

in the *I'm-not-fucking-recycling* bin, because she was proper East End and everyone knows that you'll never get a Cockney to recycle. Ever.

There was no need to buzz. She'd got a key cut months ago and expensed him for it. He was a darling, Ray. He just signed the receipts off when she waved them in front of his chops. This was all part of it, of course. The sweet, long game. Her *apertif.*

Sheila had always had a favourite. A muse. Her last; a seasoned, miserable old boy who'd become something of a hoarder. Living in absolute squalor on a half-decent street, he too had been overweight but was no Colossus. His end had shaped her and given her new purpose. After some months and a whole fanny-load of patience, she had rewarded herself. *Delicious.*

As she climbed the stairs to Ray's studio apartment, she could smell him. Cheesy sweat, wet dog, musky armpit and arse all rolled into one *sickfuck* cologne. He would have heard the door and would be listening to her footsteps now...

Sheila looked forward to seeing Ray. It wasn't just the power. She liked him and somehow, it excited her. *If only he knew.*

She checked herself in the mirror in the hall outside his room. Adjusted her hair and blouse. Increased the cleavage on show with a push of tit, to sway the tit/blouse ratio in the favour of tit.

Inside the room, the giant in the bed lay as if his legs were apart, but all flesh met and touched the rest of him and he was a mountain of it; a one-man orgy.

Ray didn't look well at all, but he smiled. He had a kind face, a child's smile, a blue-eyed boy now an overweight man. The bed was a king, but Ray was so big it looked like a toddler's bed.

The sheets were yellow and stained from sweat. No one loved this baby. No one visited Ray, apart from a lady from the council who was paid to, but she only turned up to check if he was still alive, tick a box in her day, sometimes bring a friend to see the man in the flesh and humiliate him. That woman hadn't been doing her job. The place had been in a state for weeks and Sheila had a mind to report her. *Not that it mattered now.*

"I've got your lunch, Ray," she said, taking off her shoes. "They're doing salads in there now. Told them where to go." She unzipped her jeans and rolled them down her legs. Ray was peering over his own stomach to view the show, straining his neck in eagerness. It looked like an over-sized jellyfish had come in through the window for a nap, crushing a man beneath it.

"I told them to do one, because you're a real man and you need a real man's food." Sheila peeled her knickers down her legs, revealing a tuft of sculptured pubic hair; more *urban fro* than *military bearskin*. She kicked the knickers off in an area of carpet where cans of cola, fly-spray and value deodorant had formed a Stonehenge for the cockroaches to gather and worship, which they did, praying for something amazing to brighten their mundane insect existences.

She took the first burger from the brown paper bag she had brought with her. The grease seeping through it, creating a dark stain; the bag mirrored the bed sheets, mocking the fat man, teasing him.

Ray looked excited now, craning his neck to look at the paid-for-pussy or the burger, or both. It looked like he was trying to do a sit-up.

She climbed on top of him, causing pain in his legs from the sores. The veins on his swollen frame gave his skin the appearance of an eye-ball. It didn't repulse her. This was her job. She was a carer, of sorts.

She lowered herself onto his stomach, feeling the heat of his body on her, between her legs.

Ray was excited, but she couldn't tell just then. His cock was lost in himself

"I've been waiting for it all day, Sheila," Ray panted, not nearly enough air in his lungs. The sweat was dripping from his brow and his eyes were bulging at the food as she pushed the first burger into his face.

"I know you have, you filthy, fat, bastard," Sheila said, writhing on top of his stomach, causing him more pain and discomfort than ecstasy, forcing the food into his mouth and reaching once more into the brown bag.

Ray could barely breathe as he ate the food being shoved into his mouth, excited by it all, this perfect moment, perfect union between woman, man and food. Burger sauce dripped down his face, onto his chest. Onto her chest. A piece of lettuce, covered in grease and melted cheese, fell onto the floor and the cockroaches went for it, accepting the offering whole-heartedly

Somewhere beneath him, Ray felt the pressure build and the first sensations of ejaculation.

Bloated

Sheila took off her blouse and rubbed the third burger onto her breasts, before forcing them into the fat man's face as he gorged on the processed meat upon her.

"That's it, you fucking pig. Eat it. Eat my tits!"

Ray moaned as he erupted into the folds of himself, nothing escaping; a hot, wet mess trapped in the tight folds of Ray.

The power made Sheila wet. *It was nearly time to end Ray.*

She knew Ray had come, but she carried on riding his bulging belly, rubbing herself upon him, enjoying it. She slapped him hard and it sent ripples across the bed as if she'd dived into a pool with a wave machine.

Sheila had spent months feeding Ray to get him to this weight. To get him to this perfect size, so he could no longer leave the apartment and no longer escape her. She'd seen the record breakers on television. She'd seen them hoisted out of buildings when they needed to get to the hospital. She'd got Ray to the point of no return. He was a true, wonderful, heavyweight, who could no longer live a normal existence. He'd had all independence finally taken from him. Sheila had done well, again.

She once ate at a Japanese restaurant, but what she had beneath her right now, the mountain she had conquered, this had become her Japan; her very own sumo.

Many a cock told Sheila what to do, but this one was hers and it did exactly as it was told. It was today, on this perfect *three-cocks-before-lunch* day that she was going to end Ray's miserable fat life. After his final meal, this last supper, she would try him. *Raw.* Ray was prime tender steak. None would intervene. None would care. There was probably a list as long as his shopping list of people wanting his flat.

What could he do? Helpless, this mass of stretched skin and meat within.

As she writhed, she hadn't noticed the change in Ray. His expression. Was that a smirk on the childish face? Something behind those blue eyes?

She wondered if he'd sensed something, yet he displayed not fear, but something else. Ray closed his eyes and his smirk became an expression of agony. Sheila was confused.

Ray's chest seemed to tighten and convulse, then contract. A rumble from within him, the bed shaking, then waves becoming more than just a ripple, Sheila was brought to orgasm from the movement as she tried to understand what was happening.

Never had she felt anything like this, no cock, nor fingers or vibrator had ever taken her on this journey, but she was frightened. Something was wrong. Something was wrong with Ray. No longer a child's face, this was something terrible in its place. A demon of Ray, a monster of him.

The thing that was Ray was laughing at her plight and confusion, a deep laugh in tune with the low rumble from within him, then its face contorted in pain once more as its stomach ripped apart, and from it spurted a jet of lava, hot bile and gases, flesh and food and blood, spraying inside Sheila and around her, as the mountain became a mighty volcano.

Now it was Sheila's turn to feel pain, as the lava filled her insides, up her anus and vagina, burning through the walls of her stomach, upwards into her ribcage, cooking the flesh of her breasts from the inside. No words escaped her. She'd had no time to really scream as it was so quick and final. Sheila sizzled as her eyes popped like someone biting down on a couple of lychees. The windows were open, but the whole of London didn't give a shit, as usual.

The lava inside Ray was gone. The volcano was mountain once more, then it became a sloping hill, as Sheila subsided into the mound that was Ray, slipped within him like a sinking ship, the *Sheila Armada*; an animal disappearing beneath the mud, consumed in a pit of Ray.

Torn skin moved back as one. A soft-top roof.

On the floor, the prayers of the cockroaches had been answered and they were converted. Ray turned his head and smiled at them, knowing they would worship here anew and pick at the morsels of Sheila that had splattered the walls and dank carpet.

Sheila was gone. The apartment was quiet. The sheets were ruined. A waft of mixed grill met the street outside, making the passers-by hungry.

The beast that was Ray was, once again, bloated.

Can YOU write a Twisted Story?

If you think you can, or if you just want to help new writers by offering feedback, join the growing creative community at www.Create50.com

Twisted50 is the first book to arise from the Create50 community and initiative. Can you write a short story? If you can, join our growing community of supportive writers at Create50. It's free to join at www.Create50.com

Join the writing community www.Create50.com

Check out the book series website www.Twisted50.com

Follow Create50 on Twitter @MyCreate50

Join the Facebook page for updates
https://www.facebook.com/MyCreate50